MY BROTHER'S DESTROYER

Low Profanity Edition

CLAYTON LINDEMUTH

MY BROTHER'S DESTROYER Low Profanity Edition/Clayton Lindemuth

ISBN-13 : 979-8557177375

FOR DONALD LINDEMUTH,
THE MOST VIRTUOUS FATHER
AND ROLE MODEL
A SON COULD WANT.

I moved the lantern close to Fred's head. His eyes was broke open and red. I stood there looking at him. Wondered if I was man enough to put him down, if I had to.

Fred said, How 'bout you murder the evil cowards threw me in that ring instead?

—Baer Creighton

CHAPTER ONE

Dogfighters ahead, fractured by dark and trees. Twenty, at least. Their voices led me this far. I touch the Smith and Wesson on my hip. There's a nip in the air, with the harvest near over. The longer I'm still, the colder I get.

One of these devils stole Fred.

Problems for him.

I'm crouched behind an elm, pressed against smooth bark.

It's dark enough I could stand and wiggle my pecker, and they wouldn't see. They're occupied around a pit. The place swims in orange kerosene light with so many moths the glow flickers. Hoots and hollers like they're looking at strippers. Can't see in the circle from here, but two sorry brutes inside are gutting and gouging each other. Two dogs bred for it, or stole from some kid, or some fool like me.

All my life I got out of the way so the liars and cheats could go on lying and cheating one another. I can spot a liar like nobody. But these men are well past deceit.

One will suffer.

Fifty yards, me to them. I stand, touch my Smith & Wesson one more time. Step from the tree. A twig snaps. I freeze. Crunch on dry leaves to the next tree, and the next. Ten yards. If someone takes a gander he'll see me—but these boys have their minds on blood sport.

Sport.

I test old muscles and old bones on a maple. Standing in a hip-high crotch, I reach the lowest limb and shinny for the elevation. I see men's faces on the other side of the ring—and if I don't see dogs killing each other, that'll be fine.

I know some of these men—George from the lumber yard, and the Mexican who runs his forklift. There's Big Ted; his restaurant connects him to other big men from Chicago and New York. Ted's always ready to do a favor, and tell you he did it, and send a monthly statement so you know your debt. Kind of on the outskirts, I spot Mick Fleming. And beside him is Jenkins. Didn't expect to see the pastor here.

"Lookit that! Kill 'im, Achilles! Kill 'im!"

Why looky looky.

That's Cory Smylie, the police chief's son, shouting loudest. Cory—piece of cow pie stuffed in a rusted can. Buried in a septic field under a black cherry tree, where birds perch and crap berry juice all day.

I make the profile of Lucky Jim Graves, a card player with nothing but red in his ledger.

The branch is bouncy now, saggy. If a stiff breeze comes along, I'll be picking myself off the ground.

That looks like Lou Buzzard. The branch rides up my crack like a two-inch saddle and each time I move, leaves rustle. But I want to know if that's Lou because he's a ten-year customer. It would be helpful if these devils were already drinking my liquor. A little farther out, and I'll see.

Snapped limb pops like a rifle. I'm on the ground and the noise of the fight wanes, except the dogs. Hands move toward holsters and silver tubes sparkle like moonlight on a brook. These men came prepared to defend the sport, and have more dexterity than I could muster on two sobers.

"You there!"

The voice belongs to a fellow I know by reputation, Joe Stipe. We've howdied but we ain't shook. A man with a finger on every sort of business you can imagine, including mine. He owns a truck company, the dog fights, and making book. A few years ago, he sent thugs to muscle me out of my stilling operation. We aren't exactly friendly.

Men gather at Stipe's flanks as he tromps my way. "Grab a lantern there, George. We got company."

I sit like a crab. The light gets in my face.

"Why, that's Baer Creighton," a man says.

"Baer Creighton, huh? Lemme see." Stipe thrusts the lantern closer.

"That's right."

"Don't tell Larry," another says.

"He ain't here tonight," Stipe says. "What you doing, Baer? Might have gotten yourself shot."

"I was hanging in the tree because you's a bunch a no-count assholes and I'd rather talk to a bag of beaver scat."

They are quiet, waiting for something let them understand which way things will break.

Not tonight, boys. But I'll sure as mighty hell let you know.

The hair on my arms floats up and static buzzes through me. I look for the man with a red hue to his eyes. Isn't hard to see at night—it's always easier at night—and it's the one that said, "Don't tell Larry."

I don't try to see the red, or feel the electric. Gift or curse, I subdue it with the moonshine.

"It's Baer," Stipe says.

The men disperse back to the fight circle, where a pair of dogs still tries to kill each other. Stipe lingers, and when it's him and me, he braces hands on knees so his face is two feet from mine. I smell the liquor on him.

My liquor.

"Come watch the fight with us assholes." Stipe looks straight in my eyes. "And later... you breathe a word of this place, I'll burn you down."

"I didn't come so I could write a story in the paper."

I crawl back a couple steps and work to my feet. My back and hips feel like a grease monkey worked them with a tire tool, but I won't show it. We're face to face and Stipe's a big somebody; beats my width by a rain barrel. The man who gave me the electric stares from the fight circle, that circle of piss and blood and clay.

Expected to see Larry here. After thirty years of meditation, I don't know whether to blame myself for stealing Ruth... or him for stealing her back.

"I didn't mistake you for a newsman, Baer," Stipe says. "So what brought you to my woods?"

I meet his eye for a second or two and take note of his bony brow. "Nothing to say on that." I turn and after a step he drops his hand on my shoulder. Spins me. I get the juice like I stuck my tongue on a nine-volt. His eyes pertineer shoot fireworks. He's so full of deceit and trickery, he's liable to shoot me straight.

I lurch free.

"You remember what I said. I'm going to burn you down. I'll find every sore spot you got and smack it with a twenty-pound sledge. You'll pull your head from a hole in the ground, Baer, to see that awful sledge coming down one last time. You best get savvy real quick. Don't mess with a man's livelihood."

Heard rumors on Stipe going way back. His truck company made lots of money after his competition died. Stuck under a broken hydraulic lift. Curious, is all. He has those lugnuts by his side when you see him in town, like he's a president with his own private secret service. Always some jailhound on the work release with a mug like a fight dog after a three-hour bruiser.

"There's no such thing as impunity, Stipe."

His look says he doesn't ken my meaning, and that's fine. You'll smack me down and every time I look up, I'll see Fred. I'll shove that impunity down your throat and you won't know you're filling up on poison. That's what I'm thinking, but words aren't worth a bucket of spit. I back away. His eyes are plain-spoke menace.

I'm so torqued I have to look for my voice. "Not quite time to call it war. But I'll let you know."

I tramp into the woods and every square inch of my back crawls. I get far enough that the static doesn't bother me—but bullets do. If I was twenty years younger I'd run in spite of low-hanging limbs. But I'm fifty. My hipbone feels dipped in dirt, so I stomp along. Deep into the woods, I turn.

Stipe still looks my way, but him and his boys are all shadows, demons.

Farther out, when the fight circle is a slight glow through distant trees, I rest a minute on a log. They know I live and work at home. Wasn't thinking I'd tip my hand, but part of the curse of seeing lies is not being good at telling them. And knowing the devil who stole Fred was in that crowd works against my better judgment. It's hard to hold your tongue while the plan sorts itself out. You want to let the man know something god-awful brutal is coming his way.

I stand, work my joints loose. I come to Mill Crick and follow south a mile. Pause at my homestead, a tarp strung tree to ground, a row of fifty-five gallon drums, a boiler and copper tube.

Fred growls.

"It's me, you brute."

Fred's in shadows under the tarp. His tail taps the diesel turbine ship-

4

ping crate he sleeps in. I hammered over the nails and reinforced the corners with small blocks. It's been home to four generations. If I picked hairs from the boards, they'd be white like Fred, red like George, brown like Loretta, and brindle like Phil. All relations of his, though I couldn't name the begats.

His voice turns quiet.

He has words and I have words. We know each other well enough to talk without losing hardly anything to translation. He knew it was me tramping into camp when I was a half mile out, most likely. He only growled to show disapproval, and now that he's voiced his concern, he can go back to sleep.

Dog needs it.

Fred's one of those pit bulls they like to fight so much.

It was October third, the night that cleaved summer and fall. I gathered apples at the Brown place across the road in an orchard strangled in grapevine. Hauled buckets back and forth to my still. Farmer Brown died a dozen years back and no one claimed the property. I was thinking on Fred, how uncommon he is, how he'd yammer for hours on any manner of subjects. He'd been missing three days.

Neighbor farmers tilled the fields. I'd scrounged inside the house a dozen times, stripped some plumbing and re-coppered my still. Helped myself to a few shingles—the loose ones at the edges. I stole Brown's cast-iron bathtub and hauled it on his wheelbarrow to the brook below my camp. Then I carted enough lumber to build a platform above the mud, and strike a post for a small mirror from Brown's wall. Every night before I turn in, I scoop crick water into the tub. Haul a leather satchel of stones from the fire pit to take away the chill.

I stole all that, but me and Brown were tight. Plus he's dead.

There was a full moon that October third night but the clouds kept it smothered. I came around the house hauling two buckets of apples. Headlamps flashed from the forest a half mile off, bright like God Almighty made them on the spot. They turned on the dirt road headed my way.

I know those woods. Nothing there save a logger's doubletrack. It curves around a side hill where Joe Weintraub cut the hemlock to let the hardwood grow in. Seven years ago. Lost money on it, he said.

The headlights came closer. Truck had a regular gasoline engine, not diesel. Swung onto the driveway.

5

I dropped my buckets and dove. Headlights passed above. I crawled a dozen feet and scanned over the grass. The vehicle reversed, swung onto the yard, lurched forward and stopped. I couldn't scope the make, but the truck was full-size, white or silver. The left side of the tailgate glowed like someone cleaned a layer of dirt off half.

A man jumped from the driver's side. He dropped the tailgate and pitched a white ghost that looked like a burlap sack of grain to the weeds. The door slammed, the engine roared and the rear wheels spat dirt.

I waited.

Taillights disappeared around the bend toward town. I dusted my sleeves and knees, grabbed a couple spilled apples. I looked at the white clump beside the driveway, then back at the house, then to the hill where the truck came from. Then back to the white clump.

Couldn't pull my eyes from the ghost. It took the shape of a small body, hips, shoulder.

I hurried, then stood with buckets straining my forearms and shoulders. Blood slicked Fred's chest and head, and a gash opened across his chest. Caked blood blackened his eye and his neck was splotchy. The blood smell cut the whiskey numbness in my mouth, and I could almost taste Fred's bleeding. Could almost taste my dead dog.

I dropped to my knees. Fred growled—he said, I'm alive but you got to do something 'cause I'm pretty well whupped.

I looked at the moon, shifted my shadow off Fred and catalogued the wounds. None looked fatal but he was almost dead. Those slashes were moist, but the bleeding had stopped—most sopped in his coat. He'd likely ran out of air. Temporary suffocation. Did they call the fight out of boredom?

I looked to the road where the truck come out. Headlights glowed single file in the forest. Stipe and his boys. I vowed right then every one of them would meet a cruel end.

I carried Fred in my arms with his feet straight up and his head against my shoulder. Now and again I dropped a kiss on his muzzle. It irritated him but that was okay. Give him a reason to stay alive.

"You're some kind of ugly," I said, and Fred said, There's no cure for stupid either.

My house is across the road from Brown's. I don't go there but to store my liquor in the basement. I put Fred on the kitchen table. Struck a match, lit a kerosene lantern that cast a wicked shadow on the wall. It was the first time I was in the house and didn't ponder what Ruth touched last. Where she last stood. What she thought while she was standing there. Almost thirty years ago.

I moved the lantern close to Fred's head, saw his broken eyes.

I stood there looking at him. Wondered if I was man enough to put him down, if I had to.

Fred said, How 'bout you murder the evil cowards who threw me in that ring instead?

"You're going to mend," I said. "But I got work to do."

I carried the lantern back down the hall to the medicine closet. Filled my arms with cleaners, antiseptics, bandages. Set them on the table by Fred. In the big bedroom I dug up a pink tackle box sewing kit.

My hands shook. I found a jug of corn whiskey and gulped. Spent three minutes putting thread in the needle. I cupped my hand and poured a shot of shine, then shifted to Fred's side and held my hand over the big slash across his chest. Dripped whiskey on it.

Fred growled.

I emptied my hand into the cut and touched the ragged edge. "You hang in there a little while and I'll patch you up right. Yessir."

I touched my wet fingers to the clots, and clumps of dirt stuck to his coat near the wound. Gash put me in mind of a cut of meat from the butcher. I grabbed a clean cloth from a drawer, a bucket from under the sink. Went to the well out front and worked it until cool water splashed, then washed my hands and filled the bucket.

Inside, I held a soaked rag to the gaping cut. Fred's throat rumbled but he understood if only one creature on the planet cared for him, it was me.

I worked the cloth across ratty knots and clumps of blood. Soaked the rag in the bucket again and dripped water into the slash. Crust adhered to the edges like scorched meat to the bottom of a skillet, but the water worked it loose.

"I'm going to find who stole you," I said.

Fred said, Uh-huh.

"And there's going to be an eye for an eye come out of it."

Fred's a survivor. He's spent the last two weeks growing stronger. I step under the tarp and hunker beside him. "You doing good tonight?"

Fred sleeps with his head on the left and his body curled to the right. I scratch between his ears, careful of his scabs. I want to look over his cuts and slashes, his smashed-in eyes—but it's night and I settle for feeling his busted body. Lot of heat from the slash across his chest.

I pop the cork from a jug, cup my hand, pour a little. Work the wound. Fred growls—that hurts you ignorant prick—and I say, "Easy, Fred. You know I love you."

I work shine into every wound except his smashed eyes. I shake when I look at them. Black jelly starting to scab. He sleeps with that mess against the blankets, risking infection. But he almost took off my hand the last time I daubed liquor on his eye sockets. I'll check again in the morning.

I have to see about the mash before I wash off the day's stink.

Anything with sugar will make moonshine. Fermented grain or fruit—apples, plums, strawberries—keeps the air stinky sweet. I lift the plywood lid from the first fifty-five gallon drum. Smell washes over me so thick it almost sticks to my clothes. The mash is apples and pears from dead Farmer Brown's orchard. These big yellow apples have so much sugar, you don't have to add any to the mash. Give it a cake of yeast, and in almost no time you have to distill the mash or you'll have thirty gallons of vinegar.

Men don't pay near as much for vinegar.

I lift the lid on each barrel. Three are corn. Corn takes longer. Different mechanics. The sugars are bound up tight. Have to cook the mash and stir it, keep it agitated. If something goes wrong, you'll have to add a five-pound bag of Pillsbury cane—but no more than one. Two bags and you're in sugarpop territory. The men who drink sugarpop'll come for you, once they get over the evilest headaches they ever had.

The final fifty-fiver sits a dozen yards from the rest. It's empty, but I have an idea for it.

There's no sound but whispers from trees and water rolling over rocks at the brook a few yards into the dark. I gather smooth oval crick stones from the fire—anything but sandstone. They're still warm, but not hot. Tonight's bath won't be a slow soak. I roll them into a leather sack and tote them to the tub. Rest them easy on the bottom. I skim crick water into a five-gallon bucket.

I have something in mind for that barrel, which is why it's away from the rest. Something Stipe and his boys won't like.

Stipe and his boys sure appreciate shine, though.

Natural
Pet Food

We only recommend natural foods that are free from artificial flavours, preservatives, and added salt or sugar.

A little help
for our
Friends

We donate more than 4% of our net profit to charities that help both animals and people, and last year we gave over 5 tons of unsold or damaged food to local animal charities.

Click
& Collect

time by buying online and you can

PetsCorner

Dobbies Garden Centre, Dooley Lane,
Otterspool, Cheshire, SK67HE
Tel: 01614 275063
Email: marple@petscorner.co.uk
VAT No: 256 4322 10

----- [REPRINT] -----

-----Sale-----

1	GS Blos Pnk Mesh Har Toy	10.99
Total:		10.99
VISA		10.99

User: Sophie B 5497
05/03/21 14:39   808-72831

Family run since 1968, we sell
different, superior quality food and
accessories by staff properly trained
promoting ethical policies
- it's the Pets Corner Difference

CHAPTER TWO

Joe Stipe sucked in the sweet smells of battle. The last match had taken forty-five minutes. Even the victorious dog teetered, ready to fall over. Stipe tucked his thumbs under his waistband. The deepest scent was the earth. The ground was black with centuries of accumulated humus, matter once alive and now dead. The scent of trees hung above that. Then sweet engine exhaust as revelers fired their trucks and motored off.

Stipe stepped to the pit and leaned against an oak shipping pallet standing on end. It formed part of the ring's perimeter. Employees broke down the fight circle. They lifted pallets over the steel pickets that held them erect. They'd leave the pickets. This circle had many fights left before the dogs wouldn't enter. Stipe's men guffawed as they retold moments from the night's spectacle.

How Achilles had turned and placed his stunning career in jeopardy. The men had gasped. He'd never been a coward. But his turn became a feint. Achilles had whirled around his opponent in a flash of teeth and fury. He'd snapped his jaws to the other's neck and the move proved the winning gambit. For the next twenty-five minutes he never released. The men watched in silent awe until his opponent finally wheezed, trembled, and died.

Achilles was far from a coward. He had demonstrated his bravery matched his cunning. He would someday be a grand champion. It was worth reliving a dozen times, from every conceivable viewpoint.

Stipe listened to his men and smiled.

He studied the ground where Achilles's opponent had bled. The dog's bladder and sphincter had released. The odors were still there, trampled into the black dirt. Stipe's nostrils flared. He thought he detected the very evidence of Achilles's inspirational performance. He released his breath and leaned closer, inhaled deeper, savoring the stink.

That was the last scent. Death.

Stipe was alone with his three closest workers and two hangers-on. Lou Royal, Stan Lucas, and Mitch Freeman disassembled the fight ring. In minutes they'd stack pallets four high on the beds of three trucks, low, below the bed walls. Police chief Horace Smylie attended, but Stipe insisted his operation remain clandestine. Wusses—and there were a lot of them around Asheville—would raise a stink.

They'd never stood beside the ring... They'd never felt adrenaline gallop through their veins. They couldn't understand what Stipe provided.

A fourth man, Ernie Gadwal, loitered at the edge of the lantern light. He was half Stipe's height and looked like a weasel. Always lurking, always spying. He wanted a piece of the action but had nothing to offer.

A fifth man, Burly Worley, stood with his hands crossed at his groin. Stipe knew Worley, going back years and years.

"You staying out late," Stipe said.

"Wanted to bend your ear."

"Have at it."

"I got myself unemployed. Didn't know if you could use any help at the garage. Driving even?"

Stipe shook his head. "That's rough. But I'm full up on help."

"And the other sort of help?"

"I don't think you play as rough as these boys." Stipe noticed Stan had stopped lifting a pallet long enough to grin.

"Thanks." Burly turned.

"Hold up, now."

"Yeah?"

"Hold up, is all I'm saying. I'm thinking."

Burly Worley had a wife and a son. You could bet real money Burly would raise him right. Burly was the kind of man who wasn't happy unless he went to bed tired and broken from a hard day's labor. No smart organization turned its back on help like that. Burly had the ethic. In the modern age of pussified men, it made sense to hire him on principle and build a job underneath him.

"I don't have anything," Stipe said. "But I want to think on this. How long you been without work?"

"Two months."

"Sign up for the unemployment, did you?"

Burly scowled.

Stipe extracted a fifty from his pocket. "For now, help Stan and the boys red up. Come see me at the garage tomorrow. I'll think of something."

Burly looked at Stipe's hand almost as if to reject the money. A battle played out on his face. Pride fought duty, and his wife and son won. Burly grabbed the bill, nodded to Stipe, and spun to the other men.

Stipe watched him for a moment. Burly was an example of an honest, principled American getting screwed by the system. He was tough, ornery, and prideful. A good Christian, he said meaningful prayers every night. Stipe would bet on it. He wasn't like these others Stipe saw around town, the wusses.

Even in Gleason, city ways had crept in. Being a gentleman aroused more dirty looks than thank-you's. It demeaned a gal; as if she couldn't open the door herself. And correcting a woman was plain obtuse—what right did any man have to correct a woman? Whether they'd read the Good Book or not, right and wrong were right and wrong. These she-men were failing their divine charge.

Children weren't tolerated, so much as coddled. Self esteem was more important than competence. Rights were more important than achieve-ments. You couldn't watch a Sunday football game and not see enviro-whackos selling cars. Sitcoms featuring dull men and dominant women. Smart-mouthed kids. Nowhere in society except Stipe's fight ring could men find a gritty thrill. Nothing else filled men's nostrils with the rich odor of blood. Nothing fulfilled their innate lust for carnage. Stipe alone was willing to battle for the old ways.

Stipe noticed Burly Worley staring toward the remaining trucks. Stipe turned.

Cory Smylie sat on a tailgate, hands on his knees, head low like a calculating dog. Cory had a wrestler's build, thick shoulders atop a wiry frame. His smooth face and greasy hair combed to a duck's ass in the back. All he needed was a t-shirt and a deck of Marlboros folded into his shoulder. You'd never know he was a half-century removed from his decade of choice.

His father was Horace Smylie, Gleason police chief. His mother was a modern woman. Nether had the inclination or gumption to keep him on a short leash, set some boundaries, by God. Cory had enjoyed every toy, pursued every whim. His parents had taught him the world owed him his dreams. Stipe could tell to look at him.

Cory was a perfect example of modern flawed thinking.

Since taking an interest in him, Stipe had learned Cory's history from his father. And learned his present circumstances from other men in their mutual orbit. Stipe knew things Chief Smylie didn't.

Cory had rejected higher education. When economic realities slammed him to the dirt, he'd chosen the easiest path. He used connections forged as the child of a well-traveled mother. Began a small-time hook and crook operation. He stole. He sold drugs. He lived for intoxication. And then he lived in jail.

His father knew most of what had landed him in the slammer. Chief Smylie was a Christian who believed in second chances. He waged a personal campaign to get Cory accepted at UNC Asheville. But Chief Smylie didn't know his son only set foot on the university grounds to deliver drugs.

Cory Smylie was irredeemable. But given the vastness of Stipe's enterprise, odd jobs presented that were uniquely suited to irredeemable men.

Unlike Burly Worley, Stipe didn't care if Cory Smylie ended up dead, in jail, or disappeared. However, Cory had performed his recent assignments. If Stipe could turn him into a man, he'd be striking a blow for mankind.

Thinking of his problem with Baer, Stipe lifted his arm and stepped toward Smylie as if to take him under wing.

"Tell me. You got an eye for the rifle?"

CHAPTER THREE

"What did you say?" Baer stepped into the group—they were all in Larry's grade, a year ahead. They were the boys Larry jawed about getting in with. They were cool.

Burly Worley said, "You heard me—"

Baer swung left and right. Connected with skull and jaw, and as he reared for a third swift blow one of the other boys grabbed his arm. Another joined with a knee to his groin. Baer doubled over and a fourth boy drove him to the floor with an elbow to his shoulder.

They were beside the lockers, twenty feet from the principal's office.

Boys shouted and cursed. Girls screamed and wilted. Inched closer. That blonde Larry was all crazy about leaned against a wall locker. Shifted sideways for an unobstructed view.

Baer absorbed kicks at the bottom of the pile. Burly Worley sat on Baer's legs and pummeled his kidneys. Baer spat blood, struggled to breathe. At last only Burly hit him, in the same section of his back, over and over. His stomach turned. Kids shouted. The blows ceased and the crowd parted. Baer rolled to his side and stared at patent leather shoes and cuffed trousers. Principal Doolittle had lifted Burly by his lapels and slammed him into a locker.

The girl was there, the blonde. Ruth Jackson, the snotty daughter of the Asheville judge.

"What did you get yourself into?" Larry said, kneeling at his back. "Come on, get up."

"You heard what Burly said," Baer said.

"My office, Creighton." Principal Doolittle pointed the way, as if Baer hadn't had a dozen visits in the last month. "This is the last time."

"You're out permanent?" Larry said. "Permanent?"

They walked home. Baer dragged his feet, kicked loose rocks.

"'Expelled', Doolittle said."

"Why you always starting trouble?"

"You heard what Burly said about Ma. Why wasn't you in there with me?"

"Because she *is* a whore."

Both boys were skeletons with skin stretched by growth spurts into knots of knees and elbows. Larry was bigger, but Baer had more moxie.

Larry had been acting aware of their poverty. Every disdainful smirk on another kid's face aroused shame on his. His pants ended before reaching his ankles. His wrists extended beyond his sleeves and he'd taken the habit of rolling them, even in winter. He talked of wealth. Mused that his penchant for mathematics might carry him beyond his beginnings.

Their father worked in Asheville, but lived with another woman and took his earnings to her. Their mother sewed, cleaned, catered.

And performed other services to put food on the table.

"She ain't a whore! She's your mother!"

Baer swung. His fist glanced Larry's head. Baer connected shoulder to shoulder and drove Larry to the field. On the ground, he landed a punch to Larry's gut before his brother wrestled sideways. Larry jumped to his feet with a pocketknife in his hand. Baer led with a left before Larry could open the blade. Caught Larry in the nose.

He stood dazed. Baer brought another. Larry fell, but not without grasping Baer's shirt and dragging him along.

On the ground Larry used his weight advantage to straddle Baer. Pinned, Baer brought his knee up hard.

Larry toppled to the side, hands cupped over his groin. His mouth was open like he wanted to speak or breathe and could do neither.

"You heard him say it, and you know she ain't," Baer said. "And even if she was you got to stand up for her. Jerk."

· · ·

14

Mother didn't understand why her boys were always at sixes and sevens. Baer made sure she didn't know why they'd fought this time. They'd entered the house sullen, bruised and bleeding. Mother trotted from the kitchen and cuffed each.

"What happened?"

Neither brother responded. Larry, leaning forward and breathing shallow, eased into a seat at a desk closest the door. Baer dropped Larry's books in front of him.

"Fine. You got homework? Sit and do your homework."

"Ain't got any," Baer said.

"Sit at that desk and read something," Mother said. "Here, read this."

"The Constitution? Again?"

She pointed.

Baer turned on a lamp with a green dome and a brass base, the only item in the house that suggested money. He opened the pamphlet to "We the People."

Larry remained hunched with his hands at his groin, showing immense concentration.

The brothers sat at opposite sides of the room with a glass-topped coffee table between. A painting of no particular ocean hung on the wall above Baer. Mother returned to the kitchen and trussed a chicken.

Baer read until his eyes flitted ahead, skipping lines. His hands joined the revolt and flipped two pages at a time. Three. Behind, Larry mumbled and growled. Whimpered. Baer closed the pamphlet. Mother appeared.

"Where you think you're going?"

"Take a piss."

She grimaced.

"What?"

"You come right back."

He entered the bathroom and stood above the bowl. At the bottom of the water, colored the same yellow as the stained porcelain, lay a rubber. He flushed the toilet and urinated into clean water. Rinsed his hands and splashed water into his eyes. Came out wiping his hands on his pants—

The lamp was off.

Larry watched, mouth flat, eyes hollow. Baer returned his glazed look and lifted the cord from the floor below the outlet.

"You're supposed to be the grown-up," Baer said.

He shoved the plug into the socket—thinking as he did that the cord felt shaved to bare copper.

15

Electric flashed through him. He crashed backward on the coffee table. The thick glass held but the legs collapsed. He quivered on the floor, eyes open, unseeing. His lungs shook and his heart rippled. He was aware, detached.

A dormant cluster of cells awoke deep within a corner of his mind.

Mother beat his chest with paired fists.

Baer batted her arms. "Ma! You're going to kill me!"

She rocked back and sat on her legs, skirt crumpled above her knees. He saw rug burns.

"Oh baby," Mother said. She took his hand.

Electricity trickled through him as if from the room, like he was an antenna.

She got to her feet and stalked to the lamp. Lifted the unplugged cord at the base, hand over hand like a rope. She studied the burned plug where it met the cord.

"Who whittled this down?"

Baer watched her eyes fall on him, then shift to Larry.

Baer felt the shock again, strong.

"I didn't do it," Larry said. His eyes pulsed red. He collapsed. "My balls are like lemons."

Mother drove her sons to the hospital. They watched Baer a few hours and released him.

First time I saw the red light in a man's eyes was after Larry tried to electrocute me.

The glow wasn't particularly strong, but my sense of it was. Whether I get the electric first or the red depends on if I'm standing next to the liar, or can't see his eyes.

That's all I know about my curse, except it started when I beat Larry and he tried to murder me for it. After that, it was hard to trust folks when I could see they were lying all the time.

Suppose I'm like a rat. Every time I try to cross the cage they shock me.

The curse wanes with age and drink. Sometimes I go blank. Nothing. Then someone shows up for liquor and I know I still have it.

Everybody lies, and I see every one.

CHAPTER FOUR

Cory Smylie slugged a can of Coors. Tossed the empty behind the seat of his F-150. He'd had speed for breakfast and was deep into the rush. It was time to moderate things.

He lifted a .30-06 from the window rack. He'd followed an old logging trail a quarter mile off the road. Parked in an overgrown thicket of blackberry brambles. He locked the truck. A gym bag below the seat stored items he didn't want found.

Stipe had given him this task. Though Cory hadn't been looking for work, it aggravated a part of him that he knew he needed aggravated. The thought appealed like the sting of pulling off a scab. Stipe had intimated that this next assignment would do far more than elevate him in Stipe's esteem.

It would make him feel like a man.

Cory placed his hand in his pocket and felt the folded piece of paper Stipe had given him. "Get his attention, and make sure he finds it."

Stipe had said his dogs weren't natural-born killers. They only developed into brutes through the patient application of training, conditioning. Nurturing. A man was no different. You take this task and help me solve a problem, your nuts'll swell into cannonballs. You'll walk with an honest swagger, not this pimp-punk-bitch thing you got now.

Cory had hunted these woods years ago. His father had bought him a rifle and four-wheeler at the age of fourteen. He'd been up and down these trails and knew where he was going.

At fourteen it was difficult to score alcohol, especially as the son of the police chief. Cory had heard of a man who lived in the woods and distilled hooch. He'd stalked the man with binoculars and ingratiated himself with the man's niece. He'd even approached his camp while the surly jerk was absent—only to meet a bristling brindle pit bull.

That was years ago, but Cory Smylie hadn't forgotten.

He used the rifle barrel to forge a path through a ten-foot barrier of leafless briars, then set off at a brisk pace. The woods had changed in the intervening years; trees had grown, some had died. A giant stump with the center rotted out was now a jagged pillar on one side, with the rest crumbled. Cory arrived at a flat rock that sloped downward and came to a steep drop-off.

He could take a prone shooting position at the edge. But if he engaged from the top of the rock, Creighton would never find Stipe's note.

Cory stopped and thought. If Creighton was a thorn in Stipe's side, how much more appreciative would he be if Cory took matters into his own hands? He had seen Stipe's altercation with Creighton. He'd heard the threat.

Hadn't Stipe almost implied that Cory would be that awful sledgehammer?

Cory slung his rifle and urinated over the edge of the rock.

Yeah. He'd do it.

It would be a military operation, like a video game. The crag below him offered a cave-like recess. He'd observed Creighton from there years before, awaiting opportunity to steal moonshine. When he'd crept to Creighton's still and heard the dog, he'd chanced a look back. It was an open firing lane, and even at high noon shadows masked the cave. It was a perfect blind.

Cory circled to the back of the rock and followed the terrain around the face. A well-worn trail cut below the rock and led up a steep incline to the dark cavern. Cory grabbed a rope hanging from the ledge and pulled himself up. He hesitated at the opening. The cave was only ten feet deep, but who knew what strange animals hid in the shadows? A bobcat? A bear? He unslung his rifle and pointed into the depths while his eyes adjusted. In a moment he saw ancient fissures. Bones from a small animal. A crumpled Schlitz can—a relic of the famous Schlitz Indians.

He sat on a rock positioned behind two boulders that blocked most of the cave's opening. The place felt contrived, as if nature couldn't have deposited these rocks so convenient. Had Creighton done all this so he could hunt deer without walking very far?

It would be funny if he ended up getting shot from his own blind. There was a word for that. I—yeah, it'd be funny.

Cory leaned against the boulder. He placed the rifle barrel in the V-shaped slot formed where the two rocks met, and sighted through the scope. He saw half of Creighton's camp, two hundred yards away. Creighton sat on a log beside a fire. No way he'd expect an attack so soon. It was only morning. Seven o'clock.

He was going to kill a man. He'd thought about it—who doesn't think about killing men? Right? You see the dogs go at it and you have to wonder what it'd be like to cross the line. To do it. Because there's no looking back—if you kill someone you can't smile an apology. You have to know beforehand that every angle's covered. No mistakes. You can't get caught because you can't flash your dimples at a judge.

His heart thudded. He realized he was pulling the trigger already, without aiming. Without taking the safety off. Was it loaded? Yeah. This was the real deal. Cool down.

Smoke another joint. It helps your reflexes.

Yeah.

He fished a baggie and a book of cigarette papers from his front pocket. Leaned rifle on rock. He pinched marijuana into the paper and rolled it.

He was going to kill a man.

Yeah.

He could shoot. Lord, how he could shoot. When he was fourteen his father took him to the range and couldn't believe the targets he was hitting. From fifty yards there wasn't a ten-inch bulls-eye he couldn't nail every time. Then his senior year he'd returned to the range with his buddies and refined his skill. He was a sniper.

Cory lit the joint. Sucked in the smoke and held it in his lungs until the burn felt good. In a moment, normalcy. He was cool.

Creighton was a man. He could kill a man.

～

Joe Stipe was not happy seeing me; those fights are invitation-only. Lou Buzzard had a couple of my jugs with him, and Stipe was drinking. But I get the feeling Stipe won't let my challenge go unanswered.

I have a fire burning, and coffee percolating. Me and Fred split a few eggs. He's timid crawling out of bed, and when he does, he's slow poking his way about. Both of his eyes are scabs.

I keep him up to date but he's reluctant to talk and his speech has an edge. He sniffs around the crate, crawls back inside and licks his jowls. Finally he cocks his head, and while I look at his eyes he says, What are you doing about it?

I'd like to say something stronger than "My wheels are turning."

Fred perks up, jabs his nose high in the air.

"What you smell?"

Don't know.

"Well, I'm a little on edge. You holler if you whiff something funny."

My still sits in a little hemlock cathedral, the lowest limbs are thirty feet high. A couple of black cherry trees nose through, but nothing else has the gumption. Hemlock keeps the air fresh. When a breeze wipes away the mash barrel stink, there isn't a place on the planet that smells cleaner. Trees sway with the wind and it isn't uncommon for a bad storm to blow one down. Six years ago, I sat under the tarp thrilling in the belly of a tornado's baby brother. Wind boomed like thunder. Thunder sounded like God. A hundred yards away, a hemlock let out a yell. Roots popped out of the ground and the whole thing pitched over. But hemlock patches are thick and other trees caught it. To this day it grows at a sixty-degree slant, its limbs tangled in the arms of five other.

I climbed to the canopy and it was another world. Birds you never see up close. I looked down and those green pine needles looked soft as pillows. A breeze had everything swaying, felt ready to come down. Jumping seemed credible, over riding a sixty-foot hemlock to the ground. Spooky place.

More so drunk.

I'd like it if none of this evil with Fred ever happened. I don't want to be a five-year-old pointing my finger saying, "He started it." If there's a fight, let's not stand around jawing.

But what's the Good Book say about being slow to anger? Isn't that a virtue?

Most times I sit on a stump next to the fire. Water gurgles over rocks at the brook; wind rustles leaves. One time when the humidity was thick as week-old cream, I sat so long I saw a mushroom grow. It's best when all the woods works to keep me occupied. A red squirrel chatters. The wind blows. A pinecone drops. A sparrow darts limb to limb. A moth lands on a stump and his wings don't match—that'll take a good ten minutes to marvel...

A leaf pops up off the ground.

I no more than wrinkle my brow when I hear a rifle report, must be two hundred yards away. I spin on my log and peer between trunks.

Some fool hunter wandered in on my posted land—though I have a sign up every ten feet the whole way around. That, or Stipe's boys are making war. Either way I'll set somebody straight.

The ground lays wavy. There isn't but a single place a hunter could sit two hundred yards off and reach me through all the trees.

There's a rock overhang with a pair of boulders in front that make it look like a Hun machine gun nest. From the still site it's a narrow aperture—some freak phenomenon lined the trees right—I can see it when I stand so.

I don't see anybody up there, but I wouldn't. It's a natural blind. I set off to my left, make a wide circle up there and

Crack!

I dive to the dirt. I look back at the tarp, confirm there's hemlock between Fred and the Hun blind. Fred's safe.

"You stay where you're at, Fred. I'll sort this out."

Fred says, This about last night?

"That's a fine question."

I'm only saying, Fred says. That sounds like a sniper to me.

I crawl to tree cover and then run. One more shot rings out and the bullet sings like it bounced off a rock. I'm moving fast as old legs and hips can carry me. I slow when I wheeze. Pull out Smith and rotate the cylinder. Keep it pointed ahead.

I'm not playing games—I'm going straight in.

At fifty yards from the Hun blind, I'm exposed. There must be a hundred firing lanes. I hunker behind a tree and catch my breath. Rethink. I'm royal torqued, getting sniped at in my own woods. But if I get myself killed on account of being angry, old Fred will starve to death.

I breathe slow until my anger settles.

When I can't make out the rocks of the Hun blind between the trees, I continue the circle I started on. Seventy or eighty yards farther, I'm partly behind him. But it's been minutes and minutes since he last fired. He saw me take off through the woods—only a fool would get pinned in a blind. He most likely slipped to another perch and has me in his rifle scope right now.

I squat and look out between the tree trunks as far as I can see, and scan leftward from the Hun blind. He's behind one of those trees. He's got a rifle barrel pointed and enough of his head sticking out to line his eye behind the sights. If I could only see him. I cover the whole swath and back again until my eyes stop at the blind.

No electric. No red. He lit out.

Or not.

Was it coincidence? A hunter popping off shots at a running squirrel— and me running behind thinking I'm getting shot at. That would make sense—except for the stupidity of it.

I slip from tree to tree, closer and closer to the Hun blind. Twenty feet out, I peek from behind the rough bark of an oak. My heart thuds, and neck sweat chills me.

The overhang sits upslope and the last ten feet are steep. I have a rope tied off to a tree trunk on top; it hangs down to the trail. The blind consists of two rocks, with a fissure between that makes a perfect place to poke a rifle. The overhang casts everything in a deep ugly shadow. The still air holds your scent from any animal that wanders by. If I try to shoot inside the blind, I'll have to hit a one-inch gap. Or ricochet lead from the rock ceiling and hope it keeps him low while I charge.

"Come on out! Before I come in and get you!"

Silence.

I point my Smith & Wesson in the air. Fire.

Look out through the forest again and wonder if he's already gone. I get to the rocks, it'd be easy to shoot me in the back.

I aim at the overhang.

Fire.

And run. I'm low. Boots thudding. Smith firing. I shoot the ceiling once, twice. Each discharge sparks and smokes and zings like a Yosemite Sam gunshow. I point at the crack between the rocks and fire again. Got one shot left. I charge up the final slope. Don't even grab the rope—I scramble my winded self forward. At the last second I dodge left to right. Swing my gun arm inside. I follow, ready to plant my last bullet in some sniper or die from his.

Smells like dope up here.

Cavern's empty save a piece of paper on a log seat and three shell casings. I pick them up. Thirty-aught-six. That ain't a hello gun.

I swipe the paper. Sit on the log and observe a clean line to my still site. This has to be where the shooter drew his bead. I catch my breath. Retrieve a flask that's been flapping in my pocket, and take a long, steadying pull. Feel the paper in my fingers but my eyes point out there... Am I the sitting duck, now?

I unfold the paper.

It's easy to kill a man who lives in the woods.

Of course he didn't sign it.

I stew a minute.

Sure, you sit this far from my camp and you have the patience, you can take me out. But it won't be as easy up close. Fred'll catch your scent, or I'll see you, day or night.

No. You want to visit me again, you come right back here to the Hun blind.

I'll have something for you.

I stand outside the blind, looking in. Looking above. Slope of the rock gives me an idea. The nearby trees—a four-inch birch not thirty feet off— gives me another.

I'm back after twenty-five minutes. I have a hundred feet of barbed wire from the fenced-off plot behind Farmer Brown's. I have my ax, thirty feet of rope, and a twenty-pound burlap sack full of hopping mad.

Somebody wants to send me a message?

Come on back for my answer.

I climb around the crag to the top where I have the rope. It's a steep angle and slippy. I find a boulder the size of a carving pumpkin. Cradle it between my knees and scoot across the top. Leave it where the rock is flat.

Next I gather smaller rocks—about fifty. Scavenge all over and finally pull most of them out of the crick. I want them round and smooth. I make the bottom of my shirt a bucket and fill it. Five trips. Finally, I use the axe to hack an eight-inch piece of maple, keeping each end at a harsh cant.

Years ago I hung a rope over the ledge to help me get up the trail. It's tied to a tree on top. I scout a faint bowl in the downslope surface and set my pumpkin rock there, and prop it in place with the eight-inch maple. Wary, I stand back a pace. That'll work. Carry the smaller rocks by twos and stack them against the upslope side of the pumpkin. Soon it's the only thing holding back an avalanche. I cut the rope hanging over the ledge, weave it under the maple strut and tie it off. Careful not to trigger the trap, I lower the rope back over the ledge.

It's easy to kill a man who lives in the woods.

Next, the barbed wire. I study my resources. Birch tree. Rope. Wire. Plenty of sticks and rocks. A hemlock close to the trail.

I head back to the homestead, pass the house and stop at the shed. Grab an auger with a one-inch bit.

At the Hun blind I drill three holes into the side of the hemlock closest to the crag. Chop a six-foot branch from a distant hemlock, and whittle three pegs so they'll stick four inches proud of the tree. One, that'll act like a trigger, another for a stake.

With the back of my axe head I drive the stake into the ground about twenty feet from the birch tree. Loop the rope over it and jam the other end between my belt and britches. I climb the birch hand over hand until the tree bends, then kick out my feet and let my weight bow the tree to the ground. I tie off the rope.

The tree fixed, I loop one end of the barbed wire around the top and arm the trigger, pulling taut as I can. The hemlock branch goes across the trail, so anybody who wants access to the Hun blind has to push it aside. That'll pop the trigger and release the bowed birch. I string the rest of the wire across the trail.

Anyone who pushes that branch aside will get castrated with rusted barbed wire. Then he'll pull the rope for support and get buried in rocks.

It's easy to kill a man who lives in the woods.

One visiting, too.

CHAPTER FIVE

When Ruth flirts at the edges of my thoughts, there are only two things that will drive her off. Write her a letter, or drown her in shine.

After seeing Larry last night and getting shot at today, my distrust of mankind is all but confirmed. I need to mope on Ruth. Can't sit in the woods and hope a conspiracy of squirrels and butterflies will hold disgust at bay.

I keep a notepad in a plastic box under the tarp, and a pen adjacent.

Ruth—

I don't call you Dear no more. But we been over that, so I don't got to say it again. I thought I hadn't told you in a long time why I write, so I oughta refresh you. That way you'll get out my head for a little while.

Fred is better than he was at least. Still don't like to move around, but he eats and shits and that's two-thirds what a dog is for.

You know I can tell a liar. Well, I remember sitting with you and thinking you was the only person in the world who told the truth. Even after a little likker!

Aw hell. This don't work so good—knowing you won't ever say anything back. You know where I live. You come here, honk the horn.

Baer

. . .

I tear the love note from the pad, fold it, tuck it in my pocket. I need to swing by the house later anyway, so I may as well stick it with the rest until I mail them. Only thing I go in there for is storing letters, liquor, and patching up Fred. The house has a history.

I said in the letter that she told the truth. I never called her out on the giant lie she told, that set me on this path, and her on hers, and Larry his. It's ridiculous how we pretend, can't get along honest because little things pop up. Pride. Shame.

Ruth and me scrogged enough to make a jackrabbit blush. We were young. By the time she told me her lie, I'd been set thinking she was the only one in the world who'd never flash red or give me sparks. And so these last thirty years have been about disbelief. If I register the truth about her, there will be no way to avoid the absolute fact that everybody—everybody—is a liar.

I'd rather stoke an imaginary love affair.

I stow the pen and look through the trees, and back at Fred. He's no more interested in what's going on than I am, and I spend a minute shaking Ruth loose from my head. There's one thing that works even better than writing letters.

Looking at Fred.

He'll never be right again. His eyes are black crust. Flies land on them, until he starts twitching and grinding his head on the ground. The rip across his chest—I sewed it shut that first night at the house. I keep it pretty well disinfected with moonshine. He breathes better now, but his windpipe is still half-crushed. He'll wheeze after no more effort than licking his sack.

Fred's like that ornery hound the old-timers were looking at. They watch the dog lick his nuts and one says, "Boy I wish I could do that," and the other says, "I bet he bites you."

Fair to say I look at Fred and I don't think on Ruth.

Three blasts from a car horn filter through the trees and arrive at the still without a note of urgency. Someone's waiting on some shine, up at the house. Sounds like Pete.

I check the Smith on my hip and gander off through the woods before getting off my stump. I sit real quiet. If there's a sniper out there, getting ready to move, I want to see him.

I should have fixed a whistle to that birch tree, or a string-pull fire-cracker.

Come on the house from behind, enter through the basement. Up the stairs, out through the front door like I was inside napping. A Ford with half the front fender rusted off sits in the drive. The bed's intact. Pete Bleau. He'll be after a dozen jugs, so I carry four on the first trip. He sits in a cloud of stogie smoke and rolls down his window. He's so fat, if he was an inch taller he'd be round. I hold up the jugs. He nods. I rest them in the straw lining the truck bed. Nestle them down separate, like they're nitro bound for the gold mine.

"Usual," he says.

I bring four at a time, and snug them in. Finally I stand beside his window. He shells a handful of bills from a wallet that looks like he pulled it from a shipwrecked corpse.

Bleau's quiet. His eyes glow red. "Henderson says you been cutting your shine. I know he's wrong, but his shot house moves half this. He's put the pressure on my price. Told him I'd ask if we could come down a notch."

"You tell him if he's cutting my shine he better not sell it with my name. Any more talk on the subject, I'll raise the price. He can go to hell. You tell him that. And you go to hell, too."

I snatch the bills from Pete's hand and static pops through me. I tuck the money in my pocket, and studying the red hue in his eyes, think to pull the green out and count it.

"All there," he says. "Don't trust me no more?"

I hope there's a dollar or two missing because that would account for the red and the juice. I hate to know there's deceit and not dig it up. But the count comes out. So it's something funny about him and Henderson. Or who knows what. That's the point I hate, not knowing.

"Henderson says I cut my squeezins?"

"Uh-huh."

"Henderson says?"

"He kind of danced around it."

The hair on my arm stands. "He said me or you, one, cut it? That it?"

"What are you saying, exactly?"

"I always trusted you because thieving's work and you're lazy. But I was wrong. Shaving a little off the top of each jug gives you, what? An extra gallon? Two?"

"Hold on 'fore you say something you'll regret. If you ain't already."

"More'n that, huh? Three? That it?"

"Come on. Easy now."

"So you screw him out of hundred-sixty proof, and got the gall to come barter me down on account of lying to him. I've never seen such optimism. But it doesn't make sense, for you and me to keep working together, Pete."

"Hell, Baer. Don't be so uptight. This is a misunderstanding is all."

"Don't think so."

Pete drags on his cigar and the cherry burns hot. He exhales. Smiles. "Yeah, I cut it."

"Now you're saying you cut it."

"Yeah I cut it, but I won't no more. You got me. You got some wiles, is what. I dunno. But there's no reason we can't have a new understanding."

"Like before we had this conversation, we both understood you'd cut my shine and kick my name in the dirt?"

"That's awful strong. I got the wife to feed."

"I've seen your wife. Do her justice to miss a meal." I step to the truck. Drop my hand at the open window, a few inches shy of Pete. Stare into his eyes. "You saying you won't ever cut my shine?"

"Scout's honor."

I wait. Pete sweats, but his eyes aren't red no more. "Guess I'll see you end of the week."

Pete sighs. Nods. "You're a good man, Baer. And we understand each other now."

If I didn't work with liars and cheats, I wouldn't work. I slap the Ford's roof and back away.

It's four miles to Gleason—or two flasks.

On the road to Gleason, some places are more eye pleasing than others. The bridge over the crick—the spill tube shoots water fast and heavy. The current has opened a hole where trout grow the size of pond bass. They hang back in the shadows and watch. Wily, far as fish go. Rest of the road is a place for cars to cut across a field or forest. On the left, most of the way, is corn or wheat.

Starts with Brown's land. Craddock tills it, then goes on and tills his own land too. Mile and a half later is Werner's land, then Sinkey's. On the right there's woods all the way, except a quarter-mile stretch of cow pasture that belongs to Sidell.

I'm in the post office. Slap six singles on the counter. Harry takes the letters I saved for Ruth. Seems dishonest to put more than one to an envelope. Plus I speculate she keeps them separate, each with its own postmark, so she can find the one she's looking for, easy. I write the date by the return address, in case it helps her.

Harry holds the stack edgewise, raps them on the counter, tosses them in a bin.

"How long 'til they get there?"

He grins. Says the same words as the last hundred times. "Couple day. Only going Mars Hill."

"Right." I push my stack of singles to him. He rings me out and drops the change in the jar for the three-year-old angel named Susan Wilkes, got the leukemia.

I nod.

"See you in a couple," Harry says.

The Second National Bank sits across the street and down Main a few blocks. I watch the sidewalk and brood on those letters, and how there are as many as four or five I'd write different, now. In all these years I must have spent two thousand dollars on stamps. It's no different than being in the woods and saying "hello" to yourself, and saying "why, hello, how are you" right back. There's no one in the woods, and the trees don't care. The squirrels bark no matter what you say or do. Sending letters to Ruth is like that. I write things I wouldn't, if I knew she'd write back.

Wonder if I'm writing letters to someone else—

I step into a man who doesn't move.

Joe Stipe.

"Stipe—"

"Didn't see you, Baer."

"Had my eyes on my feet."

"Glad I run into you. Wanted to talk about our misunderstanding last night. It's providential good luck you're here, and I run into you."

"Yeah. Something I'll ask you, too."

He lands his hand on my shoulder. Stipe's the size of three mules' asses and about as slow. His arm weighs like a bucket of lard and he leans as he talks. I keep my eyes on his free hand.

"Let's sit a minute," Stipe says. "What are you looking at?"

"That awful sledgehammer you promised, I guess."

Stipe pulls me to a bench. The three lugnuts he was jawing with step away, and turn their backs like Stipe said to make it private. I'm thinking Stipe is the devil behind the bullets and the note, but I have to play it cool.

"You come on us kind of sudden, in the woods," Stipe says.

"Well—"

"We're an exclusive group, you know, with the dogs... "

"Picked up on that when you said you'd burn me down. Something change?"

"No, that promise is good as gold."

I twist the cap on my second flask and his eyes follow. I offer the shine and he pours it down his gullet; stops the flow with his tongue. He hands the flask back and I gurgle some.

"Lou Buzzard buys from you," Stipe says.

I watch his face. There's no juice running through me—he hasn't said anything but fact.

"I talked to Lou," Stipe says, "and he vouched for you. You got to come spend some time with your brothers-at-arms. Gimme another hit of that." He takes the flask from my hand. "You got to come out with the boys, else I won't be comfortable the way things sit."

"Your comfort's real important to me."

"I want you there, and you oughta fetch a jug o' that shine."

He gulps a half-hour drunk from my flask, takes the cap from my hand and screws it.

I nod, but I don't feel it. "Next time Lou stops by, he can let me know when y'all are getting together."

"No need. Every week, same night. You know the place."

"I—uh."

I'm not good at untruth. Ever since I first got the shocks, I'd kife a cookie and sense I was sending electric all over the place. Had red flames shooting out my eyes. Everyone would know I was telling lies. So I was the fool who confessed every crush to every girl. I was the one who told Deputy White we all knew he was gay as a jaybird. I was the one who told my first boss his son was robbing him blind. It never settled in my head that no one else in the whole world sees red. No one feels electric like me, and most folks are happy with untruth, both telling and hearing.

"What's on your mind, Creighton?"

"I don't know about me going to them fights."

"That ain't what I wanted to hear."

"I didn't want to say it."

"Sunday next. Bring one o' them jugs. Bring two." Stipe braces his hands on his knees and rocks forward, wobbles. "Them's good sqeezin's. Gimme another slug o' that."

I hand him the flask. He empties it.

"You know, Stipe, I got a dog named Fred. White pit bull."

"Bring him." He passes the flask to me.

I glance back at his friends.

"Someone already brung him. Telling the truth right now, I'm liable to bust your party, if I come."

Stipe smiles like he's got his grandbaby in his arms. The prick's got secondary dimples, his cheeks are so fat. But his eyes flicker like he's a boy sticking firecrackers up a bullfrog's ass.

"Next I run into you, it won't be friendly like the middle of town." His cheek twitches but his smile holds. "I'm giving you a chance, but looks like if there's a pile of manure in a field, you'll walk a country mile to step in it."

"Which one your boys fought my dog?"

"White pit? Star on his chest?" He winks. "I never seen that dog."

CHAPTER SIX

I thought I could have kept myself sloshed, but Stipe stole my slosh. Now I'm exercising in the sun without liquor protection.

Stipe's one of a handful of organizers on this half of North Carolina. He arranges dog fights, makes book, and guards the sport. Dogmen take it serious. Talk about dead dogs soldiering on in Valhalla.

I heard about him years back—rumors and lies. Said he kept his fight business on the other side of town, hidden in a swampy draw. Nobody would ever wander back there without a gun to his head. Seeing the truck that came out of the woods to unload Fred, that cued me to his new location. From the sight of it, new isn't the word.

Running fights every week is only part of Stipe's living. He has his hands on every form of commerce in the county, but the bulk of his dough comes from the trucking company. His fleet hauls from here to every city or crossroad-and-church in three states. He doesn't get the big warehouse business, as they keep their own fleets. But Stipe connects every small company that needs connected to the world. One of his drivers runs to Cincinnati and stays fresh on my shine, so I know a little about Stipe.

It's six, eight miles from my operation to Stipe's complex. Truck company sits cattycorner to his house on a fifty-acre plot. The quarters sit back, and way off to the side is a barn-turned-mechanic's garage. They work on his semi-trucks, and keep more parked in rows on a cement pad. All that, surrounded by wood and hills.

Stipe keeps a few lugnuts at his side most of the time. They're wandering around here, somewhere. Could be that one of them was shooting at me from the Hun blind.

Stipe's white GMC pickup sits beside the trailer he uses for an office.

A man might sit in one of these trees and plink bullets on that complex. The men coming after him wouldn't have a lick of cover. A man who knew how to shoot a rifle could cause all sorts of mischief. But this thing burning in me isn't about getting wicked on men guilty of other crimes. May as well find an old lady and slap her silly, the moral's the same. Got to keep retribution correlated with the evil that deserves it. There has to be accountability, but more on the part of the man setting things right. I have a rifle with a scope, and an eye that can drill a piece of lead through a man's ear at a hundred yards, when I'm sober. But I don't want to wind up in hell over it, and sober isn't likely. So I brought Smith and a pair of binoculars.

I'm here to reconnoiter. Last thing I want is more trouble before I'm ready for it.

Don't know what I thought I'd see. I watch through the field glasses and not a lot goes on. Stipe's truck is white and looks brand new. The day after I found Fred, I went back to Brown's place looking for clues. Found oil had brushed off the truck's undercarriage. Stipe's trucks aren't likely to leak oil—not when the man has mechanics on the payroll.

I'm amenable to Stipe being the one who stole Fred because I like him about the same as ass rot. But that isn't the truck I saw. So how much evil I can park on this man's porch, if I'm to stay honorable about it? Sure he's evil, but unless he gave the order to steal Fred he's a secondary target.

A man crosses the lot from the trailer office and drives a rig to the barn. Nothing happens for a while, and I dwell on other things.

Stipe said he'd burn me down.

I'll burn him down. Those are his kennels, off to the side of his house, way in back. Lined up two-high, he keeps his animals in wire cages where they walk in their own droppings. Must be ten brutes in there licking wounds, commiserating. Waiting for somebody to do the right thing.

Cut them some slack.

A man comes out of the garage and looks this way. Pull your thumb out your yin-yang and get to work. Stipe don't pay his boys to think. I adjust the binoculars and zoom in close. He hasn't shaved. Big mole on his chin. If I had a mole like that, I'd saw it off. He turns and looks left, then right, across the field. Waves at somebody.

I gander rightward and spot a man on the run, carrying a rifle. He vectors toward the wood's edge. I zip back to the left, way, way over. Another man's running with another gun.

Crack!

Wood bark stings my cheek. I drop the binoculars. Mechanic's on one knee, taking aim for another shot. I duck and his rifle flashes again. I let go of the tree and my shoulder's stings like a nest of hornets picked one spot and dive-bombed it. Bounce off limbs and hit the ground. Knee smashes into my binoculars. I stretch along the ground sideways, extend my leg. Something pops. Doesn't make sense, those men starting a skirmish right after I ran into Stipe.

Unless he left instructions to kill me on sight, and didn't have the brass to do it himself in town.

Noise in the brush off both flanks. Mechanic pops off another shot, and another. Walking bullets down the tree. Pin me down.

Dry leaves sound like thunder. I wriggle. There's brush cover. These boys won't see me until they're on me. But they aren't stupid. They hunt buck, put on drives, sweep the woods and funnel animals so they have to run a gauntlet.

I'm the game.

The crunching closes in on both sides.

There are fifteen feet of brush and trees between my position and the field that leads to the mechanic. Big old rhododendron thickets. I crawl as best I can, not dragging leaves or making trail. Don't let my shoulder leave a blood mark.

C'mon, you ragged knee! They're coming quick.

Rhododendron grows tight and low. I lead with my left shoulder. Bust through. Trunk's only four-inches thick. I hide like a kid behind a flagpole.

Pull Smith and wait.

Sounds on the left side stop. On the right they come closer. That's right. You boys shoot each other, and I won't have to.

"He split!"

"Bull. I'd have heard him."

"Well, he ain't here."

"Go in and see."

Rifle clicks. I hunker down. A gunshot cuts leaves above my head.

"Wait! Don't he carry a piece?"

They keep jawing. Don't sound like Stipe's lugnuts at all. They must still be in town. These boys are near comical. Come dark I'll bust out of here with six-inch flames out the Smith tube. They want to dance, we'll shake it up.

Another shot from the mechanic's barn.

"Hey, Norm? Norm! What you doing?"

"Well, you go in if you want. I'm loyal, but I'm a truck driver. I ain't about getting shot."

They are quiet. Whispers. I get electric all through me.

"I guess we'll go on home, now. Nothing left to do here."

"Yeah, he sure got away real good."

Footsteps on leaves, first one, then the other.

They make sounds with their boots—hell, I can see one by his pant legs. He's tramping up and down, quieter each time. Kind of grabs my cool by the balls. I brace Smith against the rhododendron trunk and sight on the edge of his pants. The shot will cut a groove, but won't cripple him. The man on the right stands still, waiting on me to come out I guess. I'll test his conviction.

I squeeze. Slow. Don't pull the trigger—with a pistol you can't even think about breathing, or the shot'll—

Crack!

Smith jumps in my hand.

"Shoot him! He shot me! Shoot him!"

I hit the ground and crawl. Bullets smack branches and leaves. Splinters in my back. I spy a depression about six-inches deep and half as big as me—I slide in the good parts and leave my legs up and out.

Now there are two guns firing. Dirt kicks in my face. One stops, then the other. A lever-action rifle clicks twice.

I come out of the brush. Gun steady on the shot man's face.

"Howdy."

He holds his rifle sideways, lever open. Empty breech thirsty for one bullet. I gander at the man on my left, with his rifle trained on me. Eyes have a tinge but I want some electric.

He says, "I got one left."

"If you did, I'd say you better make it count. But you're telling lies." I swing Smith. "Let's trade off and see who's left standing."

He drags his front foot back an inch. I pull the hammer.

He pulls his hammer.

Got electric up and down my arms. Nape of my neck.

"He shot me! Shoot him, Reed!"

"Nah—Reed? That it? Reed? Like blows in the wind, this way and that? Like a pussy willow—that kind of reed? Pull that trigger for me, Reed."

"I will, you keep running your mouth."

"I don't think so. Take Hopalong with you back to the garage. When your master gets home, you tell him Baer Creighton was along, and brought his bullets."

He glances sideways. Shot man has his hands wrapped around his leg, and blood soaks his pants. Reed lowers his rifle.

Awkward. When you have a pistol on a man, it's hard to put it down.

"I didn't come to shoot you." I wave Reed over to the other. "I was sitting in that tree minding Stipe's business, and you boys come out raising hell. More I ponder, more it torques my ass. Move out 'fore things get ugly."

Reed takes the other man's shoulder, and keeping an eye on me, they forge through undergrowth.

Wonder the location of the man who was at the garage.

Well, he isn't behind me—there hasn't been any noise. The other two men bust through the brush, and with them in the field, everything is quiet. I could sit here by the tree trunk and wait until they come back, but I have an itchy idea about the dogs in Stipe's crates.

Sun floats on the horizon like it won't ever dip under, but that's my pulse, my nerves.

I trek back the way I came. I need to get out of this neck of woods, where it would only take six men to flush me out for a turkey shoot. Headed east the forest opens up big, woods and hills, on and on. After putting a half-mile between me and Stipe, my heart settles and I have a comfortable sweat on my neck. I find a beech on a side hill with a view of the garage, way off, and drop my haggard self to the dirt. Lean back and probe the slice on the top of my shoulder from the mechanic's bullet.

I didn't lose much in that scrape.

Birds flutter and red squirrels bark orders at somebody. Not me. A hawk circles way over the trees, floating down on a dying thermal. Getting shot doesn't feel too awful good, but the liquor helps.

I reckon I won that skirmish. Yessir.

CHAPTER SEVEN

I wake with a chill rippling through my back. It's dark all around. There are lights down the hill—Stipe's operation. They have the purple glow of security lamps. Men work in the garage, guns handy.

I suspect a guard roams the premises. If it was my operation there would be, after a shootout. I'll keep my eyes open. But either way there are dogs in that compound waiting on freedom.

From way off comes the sound of truck motors, that low rumble that lopes through the trees like a cold wind. Engine shuts off and the noise doesn't end so much as steal into the shadows and black.

I have to shiver, but not until I listen to the woods.

It's like with those booby traps at the Hun nest. When the enemy sends a sniper to harangue you in your own house, you strike back. Once you have an advantage, you press him back on his heels.

If I cut those dogs loose, Stipe's cash flow takes the hit. He has to be fighting some of his own animals every week. When he wants new dogs, they cost money. If I make him shut down his fight circle, the cowards who bet money on his animals will look for other ways to satisfy their habits.

Fight chickens. They don't have souls—not like dogs.

I get up a little giddy. My brain's like a razor. I'll slip down the hill, circle in back of Stipe's joint, ease up on those sad, sad dogs. They have to be itching for liberty. If they want to come home with me, I'll feed them.

39

Let Stipe wonder where they're at, whether they're dead or wandering the hills with a chewed-off foot.

Creep along as if people are nearby, though I'd see their deceitful eyes in the dark.

I find the field a few hundred yards off, where we had the showdown, and then I head to the back of Stipe's complex.

The dogs are quiet. I come up slow. The wind picks up at my back and the dogs grumble. The pen is set off thirty yards from Stipe's house. Inside the window a chandelier is on. I bet Stipe's at the garage or the headquarters trailer between. I drink a slosh out of the flask to settle the stomach flutters.

"Hey puppydogs. You take it easy, now."

One snarls and another joins. Now the whole batch is snooting mad. Noses bang the chain link and teeth flash white in the purple glow. I glance back to the garage—sound of wrenches on concrete. No alarm.

Up close to the pen, I try to reason with a brute. "Hey you. Your name Killer, something? Easy now. I'm cutting you some slack, you hear?"

I put my hand flat on the mesh. He gnashes at it. I've seen buck-toothed women who could eat corn on the cob through a fence like this, but Killer can't pull it off. He gets to sniffing—whiffs Fred—and his tongue wets my hand. The other dogs growl. I poke a finger through the mesh and he licks it. All right. We're at peace.

I pull the latch.

Killer pops out like he was sitting on a coiled spring. He lands six feet away, and spins. His back bristles like a wire brush. A snarl pulls his lips back so his face is all teeth and eyes. His voice is low like that truck in the bay.

Well...

"Don't you go back on your word."

Other dogs bark. Killer steps closer. His head is low, shoulders like a bull dozer blade ready to plow me flat. I pull Smith, though I don't want to shoot.

Killer doesn't know what a gun will do—he doesn't even blink. He takes another step and his voice pitches higher.

"Hey! That's a six-time champ, you dumb son—"

It's someone from the garage, standing with a tire tool in his hand. I skirt sideways along the kennel. Dogs bang the wire. Killer pivots. I get past him and turn. Killer launches. Knocks me against the wire. His mouth feels like a vise with nails. He shakes me to the bones even as he falls back to earth.

Don't go down, Baer. That's death for one of us. But Killer is heavy and I'm sporting a buzz. I drop to my knees and he rears hard. I topple to my back.

I'm dead and I know it.

"I thought we was cool!"

We struggle.

From the corner of my eye I see that mechanic coming at me with a tool in the air. Killer has let go of my arm and he's at my neck. I can't breathe, and his teeth feel like knives.

He snarls. Eases a tiny bit and snaps a better hold on my throat. I get a breath and his mouth smells like mud and rotted cowhide. He's clamped tight again—if I don't get air quick, I'm Alpo. He shakes like to snap my neck. Lowers me and jerks back, and every bone in my spine pops. I open my mouth and can't speak. I have terror in my blood, shooting fast through me. Can't breathe!

I'm sorry Killer, I'm sorry—

I shove Smith against his head and pull the trigger.

Now I have blood all over, and a dog letting out his last air. I roll him off and wiggle to the side, get my feet under me. Feel my neck all slippy with dog drool and blood. The man with the wrench stands off twenty yards, stopped cold by the pistol shot. I cough.

I bet that's Norm, who tried to shoot me in the tree. I point Smith. Step back. Another.

He drops the tire tool and lifts his hands head-high. I step back again.

Stipe's at the edge of his trailer, holding his hand at his brow under a security light. The glow doesn't reach me, this far out.

"Lou," Stipe says. "What's going on?"

"That's your boy Creighton out there. And that's Achilles by the crates. Shot."

"Creighton shot Achilles?"

"He's right there!"

Stipe raises his arm and orange explodes from his hand. He can't see me but he comes close for guessing. He fires again, and again. He points one way, then another, random. Bullets smack the kennel. He's shooting his own dogs.

That pistol sounds like a forty-five. Big heavy bullets that come by so slow you could almost run alongside and have a conversation.

"I'm going to hunt you down, Creighton! I'm going to crush you!" He walks toward me, into the darkness. Fires again. Again. He pauses and I figure he's out of bullets, but in ten seconds he's letting more fly.

I back away at a full stomp. "There you go, Stipe. That's an eye for an eye."

I don't go three more steps before I see I opened up a whole new war. I killed Stipe's champ.

Wonder what kind of retribution I have coming now.

CHAPTER EIGHT

I'm in no mood. Bank teller is a kid with lawn mowed hair and Mount Rainier zits. He studies the scarf I wrapped over the bites on my neck. Collects his thoughts and prepares his pitch. He's one step removed from cashiering at McDonald's. Thinks he knows all about the central bank and the history of money.

A year ago I was foolish enough to explain gold to a bank man. Now every one of them smiles at me. But when it's all done, I know my money's safe. Whether they lock me up the rest of my life or not, nobody will get their claws on my dough.

"It's good to see you again, Mister Creighton. We have a new checking account you might—"

"Promise I'm not." And why don't you pop that cussed thing on your forehead?

"Why is that, Mister Creighton? Regular money not good enough for you? You know the price of gold went down? You keep pulling funds away from us, but how much are you losing by avoiding paper?"

"Maybe if you folks sold gold, you wouldn't be so afraid of it."

"We're not in the commodities business."

"Since Nixon dropped the gold standard, you're not in the money business either."

I take all my cash but a few dollars—a hair shy of seventeen hundred. Combined with the fiat paper in my pocket I have eighteen hundred and forty-eight dollars. I head down the street nervous and suspicious, but nobody minds me. A couple turns and a couple blocks later, I'm at Millany's Coin Collectory.

The shop feels academic and conspiratorial at the same time. Millany has numismatic gems—coins pulled from a dozen shipwrecks. Bullion from Africa and Canada, silver from all over. He has collector guns, and memorabilia from every army that ever lost a war. He papered his walls in Confederate bills. And the equally debauched Union Greenback.

"Thought you was due," he says. "What'd you do to your neck?"

"I was sucking face with a rattlesnake and I goosed her. I need out of some paper cash."

"I can help."

His's been the only place in town to buy gold since 1974.

"I got seventeen hundred." I take the stack of fiat paper from my pocket and rest it on the counter.

"Two maple leafs will put you at sixteen fifty."

"Two it is."

"Surprised you ain't a seller these days."

"Why's that? Trend's down."

"You been buying since, what? Buck ninety-five, thereabouts?"

"Gold's going to twenty thousand. People will trade corn and wheat before they give up food for a stack of government paper. Mark my words."

"Not this genetically modified stuff. They'll use cod in Boston and tobacco here."

He exits to a back room and closes the door. He's gone a few minutes, like he has to find his way down a few flights of stairs to a vault deep in the ground. That, or he sits behind the door a long time so no one knows the real money is one wall away.

He comes back and I have a bayonet in my hands that was sitting on a cardboard box.

"Austrian," he says. "See the OEWG on the ricasso? Fits an 1895 Mannlicher. In the market?"

"Got all the edge tools I need."

He passes the coins. They gleam through plastic. He counts the stack of bills on the counter. Stops at sixteen fifty, and passes the rest back.

"Pull a seat," he says. "How goes the country commerce?"

I stay standing. "I got a long walk."

"Suit yourself."

"Generally do."

I nod and he grins and that ends it.

Mae's house sits on the low side of town. I cut across the field by the pond and pick up the road. She lives in a weathered tinderbox with a door that has a hole wide enough you could pitch a horseshoe through.

I knock. She doesn't answer right off. The kids inside yell like animals. I rap the door again and hold back so I don't bust it. Then I push it open.

Bree stares at me. Her hair is like straw with winter frost; she smiles and rushes to me on feet unaccustomed to taking orders. Her sister Morgan comes from the other room and hollers, "Uncle Baaaaaaaar!" Joseph wails.

"Baer?"

"Yeah, honey?"

"Uncle Baer, that you?"

I lift Morgan in one arm and Bree in the other. Shoulder aches. I have to steady myself before turning the corner. Mae looks so much like Ruth I can hardly stand to see her. She has the same eyes and nose—there's a dimple on her nose you could almost fall into—and her cheeks are high.

I used to tease Ruth she was part Cherokee, and Ruth always hushed me on account of her father. Wouldn't do for a man of standing to confess Injun blood.

Mae looks like her mother except her mouth, and the streak of hair she's dyed black so she looks like an inside-out skunk. Her mouth is all Creighton.

"What are you doing? Come in. Sit down." She lifts Joseph and smooches him until he giggles. "Is it so cold outside, you have to wear a scarf?"

"Started shaving sober and almost cut off my head. So I quit."

"Quit drinking?"

"Shaving."

I carry Morgan and Bree. Drop into a sofa built for people who like to believe their furniture has emotions or something. Sink so low my eyes are level with my knees. The girls wriggle from my arms and start climbing me.

"So how's Fred?"

"He eats and craps, and that's two-thirds what a dog's for."

"What's the other third?"

I study her. "Conversation."

She smirks.

"Anyway, I was in town."

"Buying more coins?"

Her face is all smile without a hint of red, and the only thing uncomfortable is the kids clawing my hair. And the couch that kind of mopes.

"I come in town for a little business is all."

"Stay for supper?" She mutes the television with a remote.

"Got supper in my back pocket."

I take her in without letting my eyes wander up and down. She's wearing pink sweatpants with a hole in one knee, and a baseball jersey that doesn't hide her mams worth a damns. Flip-flop shoes and painted toenails. A crucifix on a choker.

Morgan has a fistful of my hair. She pulls until I look at her, and she meets my look with wide eyes and a wider grin. The baby powder smell—and baby skin—is too much. She points. "Whiskers." I crane my neck and scratch her with my cheek. She giggles and Mae watches.

"I wanted to give you something."

"Oh, Uncle Baer, you don't—"

"I know it, and that's half why I do it." I pull an arm free from Bree and dredge fifty dollars from my pocket. I put it on the end table. "I don't need it."

Mae unfolds her legs, and with Joseph in one arm comes to me on the sofa and stoops. She wraps her other arm around my neck. Smells like watermelon candy. With her arm around my neck, her rack presses my shoulder. Her hair is up in my face. I don't feel as easy and comfortable as I might in the woods staring at a campfire.

She pulls back and there's water in her eyes. She smiles like they're good tears.

"Where's Cory?"

Her eyes roll. "We aren't together."

"He know, this time?"

"I told him not ten minutes ago. He just now left, all mad and yelling."

"Did it take? Or you want me to tell him?"

"No. I'll handle Cory."

I try another direction. "So who's buying the food?"

She glances at the fifty dollars and back to me. "Food stamps."

"Where's your grandpap? Rich old Preston Forsyth Jackass?"

"You know all about that."

She sits on the couch.

"None of my business," I say.

"I don't even see him. It's been two years since I tried to visit the Baptist home. You know how he is."

I know how he is. Preston Forsyth Jackson, three names so blue he has to use all of them.

"I don't care," she says. "I'll make my fortune on my own. You have to let me tell you about my MBA program. The Jacksons can keep their money."

Bree snuggles against my chest and makes a tiny fist around a fold in my shirt. She pulls buttons.

"Cupboards full? You getting by?"

She frowns. Shrugs.

I look at the wall behind the television. See a photo of my brother Larry, and Ruth with baby Mae in her arms. The side of the paper is yellow from too much sun. That photo dates to a few months after I came home for my mother's funeral. My girl Ruth met me at the door holding baby Mae. By then Ruth's daddy—the honorable Preston Forsyth Jackson—had booted her out. He ran an ad in the paper saying the whore known as Ruth Jackson wasn't his daughter.

His wife made him pay for another ad the next day retracting the statement but how do you tell a town you didn't mean that?

Everyone knew it was on account of her holing up with me. But before she holed up with me she did it with Larry. So Mae sits here with a rip in her knee and three hungry kids. Her eighty-four-year-old grandpa Preston yells at the wall at the Baptist home. Waits for it to say something back. And all his money sits in a vault at the Second National bank, instead of buying a couple hamburgers or a can of Similac. Because neither Larry nor me backed off Ruth when her daddy laid down the law.

"I don't know what I'm going to do," Mae says.

I fight free of two kids and a needy couch.

The kitchen table looks like a linoleum floor with aluminum on the sides. The oven is clean but a burner is missing. I open a cabinet and it's flat empty. So is the next, except a bag of flour and another of rice.

In the other room, Mae is silent. Bree and Morgan sit on the sofa watching me with eyes that were happy a minute ago.

I slip a hand in my pocket and feel two plastic-sheathed coins.

CHAPTER NINE

There ought to be a law against mothers living in decrepitude.

Millany stands at the door of the Coin Collectory, looking out. Has a stogie in his mouth. He steps back and I come through.

"Changed my mind on one of these coins."

"Flaw? What? Let me see—"

"Nah. Changed my mind."

He hesitates. A tinge of red escapes his eyes but there's no juice with it.

"Keep your commission. I don't care. I need more paper than I thought."

The red goes away.

"Ah," he waves his hand. "Give me the coin."

I flip him the maple leaf and he pulls cash from a box.

"Everything all right?"

"Fine." I stop. Think back to October third. "Who owns a white truck? Silver truck?"

"That fella wearing flannel and a John Deer cap."

"Prick."

Walking back to Mae's, I pick up a thought I dropped earlier. All those letters I've been sending to Ruth, without ever getting one in return. I'm no better than her old man in the Baptist home, cussing at the wall and expecting it to talk back.

Coming up on Mae's house I stop dead. There's an F-150 in the drive. Mae drives a Tercel.

The truck is white.

I glance at the house. Circle for an eyeful of the tailgate, white as the rest of the truck, and shiny. He's washed it—no dust in the rims. I suppose every kid washes his truck; it isn't always to get rid of evidence.

I go to my knees, brace on my hands. The oil pan is dry. Not even a bulb saving up for a drop.

But the truck is white, and Cory Smylie was at the dog fight.

I hesitate on the porch while feet stomp and move inside—heavy feet, boot heels. I have my hand ready to rap but I wait. She said she'd handle Cory Smylie. But if I hear anything wild, I'll tear this door down.

Whispers. A shout. Stomping gets louder. I step aside and the door flies open.

He's three feet across the porch with his leg swung over the steps before he turns. Has Mae's money in his fist.

"Why hello, Cory."

He misses the step and skids. I get a bolt of the juice. He stomps toward his truck.

Mae's at the door.

"That the money I left you?"

Red face. Tears streaming. She nods.

I tramp after Cory. He's already spinning tires. I swoop down for a rock the size of my fist and chuck it. Sandstone clangs on metal and the tires lock. Truck skids. Door flies open. He charges close. I smell his breath. The hair on my forearms stands so hard it tickles.

Trickery.

I step back as his knee comes up. Kick out his other leg and he's on the ground.

"Gimme back Mae's money. Fifty bucks. Then get out of here."

I'm ready to stomp my heel two inches through his nose. I've knocked the red out him. He scowls but his hand shakes. Nothing but a playground bully with a truck. He pulls the green out of his pocket and throws it at me. I let it fall.

"Get out of here."

He crabs away, wobbles to his feet. Limps from the kick I gave him.

"You know, it's supposed to work the other way. You're supposed to bring the money to her and your kids."

Ten feet away, Cory finds the courage to meet my look. He climbs into his truck. "Yeah, well the word's out about you, Creighton. You're sixteen kinds of dead. Stipe's liable to bend you over one of your own mash barrels." He slams the door, floats me the bird at a forty-five degree angle —I guess that's hip nowadays—and guns the engine.

"Stay away from Mae."

He fishtails off, waving his middle finger out the window. He can't keep the angle right, and the effect isn't near so cosmopolitan as a minute ago.

Mae's on the porch. Her cheek is swollen.

"He hit you?"

She won't nod. "He said he needed the money."

"More than his kids need food?" I hit the wall and wood cracks. Lucky I don't put another hole in it.

"Uncle Baer!"

I walk back to town. Was going to give her cash, but now I'll give her food. Let the lazy cockroach steal it from her. What this town needs is one good cop. A sheriff unafraid to string a hoodlum by his toenails until he understands the rules. But our law would rather watch dogs slaughter each other. Whole miserable country gone crazy. You hear the radios from two hundred yards. Feel the music through your feet before you hear it in your ears. No one cares. They're good kids, expressing themselves. And someday they knock their women around like their daddies did. Whole world needs its britches tore down and its ass spanked raw.

I'm at the grocery. "You do a delivery for me?"

Merle looks up. "What's wrong with your neck?"

"Ran afoul a gang of lady vampires, south of Sutton, by the bridge. You do a delivery?"

"Where to?"

"Up the road. Mae. You know, she rents Smotherman's place. It'll be a lot of grub."

"Fit in the bed of my truck?"

"If that's the limit."

Merle's an affable son of a gun and that sits good. I grab a cart and fill it. Six jars of peanut butter, six of jam. About forty pounds of pork, chicken, and hamburger. Rice, noodles, potatoes. Fruit. Milk. Eggs. Cheese—six kinds. Can't have too much cheese. Pretzels. Kool-Aid. Canned veggies, fruit, soups. Spices. Frying pan. Two.

There's a woman with a basket comparing two cans of fruit. Her name is Emmy; she works at the bank where they don't know what money is.

Her gaze drifts past her hands and she takes in my feet, then all the way up. Easy on the eyes, herself.

She says, "Which of these would you pick?"

I take one out of her hand and put it in my cart. "You keep that one."

She bats eyes.

I fill one cart and bring it to Merle at the counter. "You want to tally this while I grab another cart?"

"Sure."

He empties items and I start again. Pass through the same aisles as last time, seeking nuggets I missed. Creamed corn. How can a woman raise babies without creamed corn? Tomato soup? Bah! Nobody likes it. But she'll have bread and cheese for grilled sammiches... two cans of tomato soup. Formula. Diapers. Soap. Toothpaste. I don't know about the rest of the stuff in this aisle. Lady products—she's on her own.

"You throwing a party?" Emmy says. Her voice is a hair from self-inviting. I recall a time at the bank she looked at me from behind the counter and was thumping eyelids like she had dust in them.

"No party, Emmy. This is a bunch of food."

Her face floats in that cloudy water look that says she doesn't know what to do next. She's pretty, but a liar lurks somewhere inside. There always is.

Finally, last, I stop in the aisle with the antacid and Tylenol. I call to Merle, "What you got that'll put a man to sleep?"

"Melatonin in that aisle." He points. Smiles. "Bullets behind the counter. What kind of sleep, Baer?"

"Mela... "

"It's the bottle with the sleeping woman on the picture, see?"

"Yeah. This work?"

"Guaranteed. Problems sleeping?"

"Sorta precaution."

Back at the register, Merle works up a grin the size of a small motor home. "You're already at two hundred and fourteen," he says.

"That all?"

I unload and he scans. I pack bags and stick them in the cart. Let him ring the melatonin, and slip it in my pocket.

"Three hundred fifty-eight and thirty-two cents," he says.

I hand over eight hundred dollars. He looks at me funny.

"Put the rest in credit for Mae Creighton. She can't have cash. She can't have cigarettes or liquor. She can't spend a penny if Cory Smylie's with her."

"Let's see. No liquor, no smokes, no Cory Smylie."

"That's right."

"You know we don't do this sort of thing. Ordinarily."

"I can't be coming back and buying her groceries every week."

"I'll handle it myself. Difference is four forty-one, sixty-eight."

"Appreciate it."

He writes the number on a slip of paper and initials it.

I say, "You send word when the money runs out. Those kids need to eat."

"Gimme an excuse to get some of that hooch you make." His eyes twinkle red. He doesn't drink.

"Running apple tonight." I stop at the door. "And you don't need no excuse."

CHAPTER TEN

I wake from a nap in the middle of the woods, waiting on dark. My shoulder seeps. Blood and lymph trickle down my arm. Teeth punctures in my neck are hot like to start a fire.

If it isn't the holes I already have that worry me, it's the ones I'll get if somebody sneaks close with a rifle and goes to work. It doesn't feel good, thinking the only reason I'm alive is no one yet got serious about killing me. Not when I have so many folks flirting with it.

Even feeling like I had a set of eyeballs watching me, I slept a couple winks. Dreaming of Mae is a wistful thing. Not some pervert thing—she put me in the mind of Ruth so strong it's like losing thirty years.

Sun's about done for.

I lean on an oak, have the thirty-thirty rifle across my arm and Smith on my hip. Looking ahead through undergrowth, I'm close to the edge of a clearing by a pond that dates back a hundred years. The farmhouse is long gone, leaving nothing but toppled foundation stones on the ground, arranged in a twenty-foot square. I have my back to the tree and it feels dicey every time I come.

I watch the woods until I'm sure no one's out there, but how do you ever really know? Not that anybody but Millany would have a clue it was time. I recall that red glint in his eyes, and the tingle of juice.

The woods are more shadow than light.

I listen.

Chipmunks dash across leaves. Eventually a buck wanders through the meadow and grazes at the edge, not far. I'm downwind. He keeps his eyes my way. Trigger finger is itchy but my apple mash is ready, and you don't get much of a window on perfection.

The buck lives another day.

The wind turns. The buck swings around his head and looks straight through me, like I'm a hundred yards deeper in the woods. Deer eyes don't work too well—it's my smell he's after. Even if we don't communicate, eye to eye with a buck is a majestic thing. He bounds off, and like that, it's dark. I wait until the thrill's gone. Shift to the side of the tree; reach inside a two-foot rot hole; feel along the left wall.

I check the darkness behind me. No one. But I think a spooky thought —what if that buck was looking at some man staking me out, watching where I keep the metal?

I wait. There's no sound.

Inside the rotted hollow I find a nylon cord hanging from a row of fifty-penny nails. I lean my rifle against the tree partway around, and lift the cord, one hand after the next.

It's a strain.

Inside the tree, a bucket hangs ten inches down. I never had the nerve to check in the daylight to see if a man can get the angle to see sparkles in the shadows. I grab the wire handle and hold the bucket, keeping everything inside the tree. Give it a quick shake.

Drop the coin inside.

There are thirty-some years' of gold in that tree.

CHAPTER ELEVEN

Ernie Gadwal didn't bother to crouch. The forest was almost dark and Ernie stood four foot three. Though prone to mousy twitches and scurrying movements, he forced himself to be calm. Through the trees he watched Joe Stipe's nemesis.

He'd been spying since learning Stipe had launched an offensive against Creighton, weeks before. Ernie had seen Baer Creighton find his massacred dog. Ernie had been in the shadows across the dirt road, braiding three strands of dried grass. He'd looked in through a window as Creighton drank shine and stitched his dog back together. Ernie was eating a hot dog across the street at George's when Creighton stopped at Millany's Coin Collectory. And he'd watched from his Subaru Outback while Baer bought groceries for his niece.

Ernie Gadwal was a clinger in Joe Stipe's outer circle. He attended fights and afterward savored the valor of the dogs. He gained spiritual enrichment from their struggles and triumphs. The fights were awesome spectacles and the man who put them on... Joe Stipe was magnetic, a dynamo. In all Buncombe County, no man save Stipe could quiet a crowd just by grunting. Or with a single word banish a reveler from all he held dear.

Stipe's circle was wide at the bottom, but narrow up top.

Ernie thought of Joe Stipe a lot.

Ernie's small stature caused him to compare himself to other men.

Early in his life his mother noted his behavior and said it was the root of his mischievousness. Left with no obvious comparator, fate forced him to dissemble. His want of superiority predisposed him to deceit. He sought the hidden qualities by which he could transcend his peers. He learned to notice minutiae. Flaws. Some men found inspiration in other men's greatness. Ernie Gadwal drew inspiration from unearthing what haunted them.

It was a short leap to trade on these faults.

Ernie studied men like a broker and treated faults like commodities. He traded information for favor like so much specie. He hoarded secrets. He traded up, ever seeking the exchange that would vault his stature.

By some perverse fate he earned a reputation diametric to his goal. In the overheard words of his mentor, Stipe, he was a conniving little prick.

Ernie would state it differently. He had learned to isolate the weaknesses other men sought to fill. He discovered their core motivations and the easiest levers by which to steer them. His guiding calculus was that knowledge of what men craved was valuable, because men lost discernment when making deals for the things they deeply wanted.

Baer Creighton had been leaning against a tree trunk, dozing. Then he rose, and studied the terrain. Then he reached inside the tree and deposited something from his pocket.

Ernie wondered about that, then in a flash of realization he connected Baer's visit to the bank and the gold dealer.

Now, looking at a tree ostensibly full of money, Ernie thought about what to do with the knowledge. He didn't need wealth. A trust left by his grandmother paid him a seventy thousand dollar a year stipend. What Ernie craved was the standing that accompanies men of action. It wasn't by Stipe's dollars that he commanded respect.

What Ernie now saw would be worth something—though not to a man as wealthy as Stipe. This little nugget fit someone else's desires far better.

Who among Ernie's poorest acquaintances was most embarrassed by his poverty? Who dreamed of wealth? Everyone, of course. But which friend had something to offer in return? Who, by his proximity to Joe Stipe, might bolster Ernie in the hierarchy? It was a complicated strategy, but Ernie Gadwal was a complicated man.

He waited. He stepped sideways, whispered "Patience," but his excitement grew. Would it be gold? Or silver?

While observing Creighton over the last few weeks, Ernie learned Creighton preferred solitude. He thirsted only for the company of a dog.

A deer broke cover and bounded off, not thirty yards away. Baer reached for his pistol and turned. His eyes searched for some other animal that might have spooked the deer. Creighton was wily, but Ernie wasn't afraid. He had surprise. He was unknown. He was invisible.

Baer Creighton walked away from the tree and Ernie shifted behind a hemlock. The darkness varied from shadow to shifting shadow. He cocked his ear toward the vanishing sound of Creighton's feet on dry leaves. Ernie stepped closer.

He should wait. Couldn't be too eager. Observing Creighton earlier, Ernie had seen Cory Smylie fire a few shots at him. Cory ran right before Creighton arrived waving a pistol in the air and returning fire into the cave. Cory tripped and stumbled over roots and rocks, and was lucky to have escaped.

Afterward, Creighton rigged mantraps around the cavern Cory had hidden inside.

What kind of traps had Creighton set around his deciduous bank account? Pits filled with spikes? Deadfalls suspended in the trees?

Ernie leaned against the hemlock. Would it make more sense to approach in daylight and risk being seen? Or dusk, and risk not seeing Baer's inevitable traps?

He knew a man who was close to Stipe, yet conscious of his poverty. Burly Worley would be more than happy to go after the gold and he wouldn't fear the dangers.

Burly Worley was close to a mule already. Ernie recalled meeting him. A frustrated dog owner had pulled a pistol and shot an already mortally wounded dog. Entertaining carnage, but afterward the man fired twice more into the air. Called the owner of the victorious dog a cheater. Ernie's nervous laughter drew the man's gaze—and wrath.

Burly Worley had acted upon the man's distraction, and dropped him with a quick punch to the neck. Later, he'd credited Ernie with being the only person there with the stones to act. Burly praised his coolness to Stipe. Since then he was welcome to linger after events ended, while the men stacked pallets.

Worley was honorable enough to edify another man. He was not jealous. He was close to Stipe, and he was unemployed.

Ernie backed from the tree and circled out the way he'd come in. This was good. This was unexpectedly good. A windfall that changed everything.

CHAPTER TWELVE

First I kindle the fire under the boiler. It'll take a while to get the coals glowing, but not so long that I can be idle while the tank sits empty. Every now and again I listen for the patter-rumble of a rock avalanche. The crack of a tree whip-snapping fifteen feet of barbed wire across some fool's nuts.

"Well Fred, we got to keep the lookout for a sniper."

Fine, Fred says.

"Or you could keep an ear out."

Yeah. I'll do that.

The fifty-fiver on the end is apple mash. Sits on blocks high enough to fit a bucket under the nozzle. Ants crawl all over it, sucking up sugar that seeps through no matter how tight I twist the knob. I fill a bucket and dump it in the boiler. Mash is sweet and rich.

Another bucket and that's all she'll take.

The trick is to keep the tank a quinnyhair above one hundred seventy degrees. Alcohol boils off while the water stays behind. Vapor slips out through the copper coil, rests in the doubler. Water condenses faster than the shine. Out the other side spits apple brandy. A man could burn it in his lawnmower if he was too dense to drink it.

Flames lick around the boiler. I clamp the lid and sit on a stump. Hungry enough to eat the quills off a porcupine, but food's at the house.

Suppose I'll drink.

It's been a few hours, but part of me is still in Mae's house. She lit up like a deck of firecrackers when the grocery boy Mike backed Merle's truck to the porch. Bree and Morgan screamed and ran back and forth. Joseph wanted in on the fun and let out a wail.

"What is this? What did you do? Baer? What's this?"

She had a half-mad look. I guess it was shock because she about suffocated Joseph in her arm while she was hugging me. Beating my back with her fist. I was afraid to tell her about the tab I set up with Merle.

The fire's died enough for some of the heavier logs to fit. I shove a couple, light a lantern and hang it from a jig in a hemlock. Throws enough light to keep the operation efficient. I sit on a stump thinking a watched still doesn't boil. Every twig that breaks or pinecone falls has me reaching for Smith.

A still makes a sound when it approaches the perfect temperature. Like a teapot before the water boils. You'll hear about operations where the stiller has welded a thermometer to his cooker. Valves all over. Truth is, all it takes is a place to cook and a place to condense. My operation is as basic as they come, built by an old-timer who died a long time ago. A ten gallon kettle with a fitted lid. I use a leather gasket and seal it with C clamps. The copper tube coils fifteen feet, and has a doubler midway.

The shine that drips out of the other end will hit a hundred-sixty proof. Plenty high for everyday consumption. Though another run would refine it almost perfect.

The boiler ticks, expansion sounds. Already vapor twists through the tubes, but without the pressure to keep it moving. Little longer.

Ah, Ruth. What's this all about? All these years and not a word? Your life ruined, and mine nothing but cooking mash in the woods.

They threw me out of high school in tenth grade. Seemed school was all about telling me what to think. I had my own mind. They knew when I looked at a teacher, I thought he was full of nonsense. The only thing worthwhile was Ruth—though I never once said hello. Her hair shined like a sunset off water, and her smile would turn a regular stiffy into a baseball bat.

She was Larry's girl and everyone knew it. I left school and didn't think about her. Found a job pumping gas and changing oil. Had free rein over the junkers in the back lot. Larry and Ruth were together almost two years. I wondered if I'd ever do anything more than pump gas and clean windshields. I had a muscle car and an attitude, but after buying the car, couldn't afford to move out my mother's house.

Larry went to college. Ma said he would marry Ruth when he graduated.

One day Ruth swung by in the car the honorable Preston Forsyth Jackson bought her. Oh, how she missed Larry. She talked like we'd been pals since God said light. She smiled. Locked her hands and straightened her arms, and poofed her chest between her elbows. She twirled her hair. Parted her knees and rubbed shin against calf. My eyes about fell down with them.

Larry and I looked alike, I told myself. She sure missed him. But there was nothing in the world so beautiful as the curve of her calf.

Of course she knew what she was doing. All women know men are hard-wired. May as well run electrodes from a man's brain straight to a billy goat's nads. She knew that.

Later I heard her father had warned her off Larry. The only thing for Ruth to do was track down another Creighton, the gas station greaser with a black Chevy Nova. She knew what she was doing. But I didn't. To me, she was a walking, talking pinup girl, but different from every other person I'd ever known.

With Ruth, there was never any red. Never any juice. She had a harlot's heart, but unashamed and unpretentious.

So Ruth swings under the gas station canopy in this cherry mustang, paint gleaming. Chrome dripping off both ends. She sits behind the wheel and does that thing with her arms.

"You're Larry's brother," she says, pouty.

I don't say a word, and that's what she wants. She wants my eyes buried right where they are.

"I'm empty," she says. "You want to fill me up?"

"Uh."

I stumble to the gas tank, and I'm looking off the other way because I caught her eye in the rearview scoping me scoping her. I'm adjusting my mess because it's bending my trousers.

I'm twenty minutes from shift-end. There's a drive-in theater a mile down the road.

"You want to catch a flick?" I still haven't met her eyes except on acci-dent. I want her so bad I could spring a leak. "There's an Eastwood movie," I say. "Hang em High."

"A Western... "

"I'm done in twenty minutes."

She looks at my greasy hands. My clothes with sweat stains at the pits and grime across the belly.

"I can take off now and meet you in a few."

She purses her lips. "Or we could meet at the lake."

The lake. When we were real young, Larry and me used to go there looking for panties and bras. Girls left them in the trees and on the rocky beach.

The lake.

I'm cool now. I found my cool. "The lake?" I clear my throat. "An hour?"

"Make it two. Those hands better not have any grease on them," she says. "Where they're going."

She drove off. I never collected money for her gas—shelled out for it myself.

Boiler's got a ring that says the mash is gleeful and saucy. A spit sound comes from the copper tube, and I'm in business. In a few minutes, the jug under the copper will fill with the fieriest brandy in the county.

I stir the coals. Add a chunk of dried cherry.

The lantern sputters. Leaves rustle. Squirrel.

All that with Ruth is ancient history.

Now I have to think on Stipe's dog. I have to figure out if I can win a war against Joe Stipe.

CHAPTER THIRTEEN

Mae packed Joseph into the car seat. The chest harness clasp was tiny and stiff and the belt safety clip chafed his thigh. She cushioned his leg with a Tempur-Pedic mattress sample she'd received in the mail.

She wouldn't have needed to make the trip if landlady Smotherman had ever answered her phone. The check came in the mail and as long as it did, the house was fine.

But the house would collapse sooner rather than later, with Mae and the kids inside. It was a rattrap. It had mice, not rats. And plumbing issues. The shower drain took Liquid Plumr the way Cory took Coors. The kitchen sink burped like a baby after a bottle. Her landlady, Mrs. Smotherman, had apparently put her money into bribing inspectors instead of fixing the house.

Mae had delayed paying once, in protest. She'd stationed pen and paper beside the telephone. For two weeks, every time she remembered an item in disrepair, she jotted it down. You want your rent? Fix the roof. A leak soaked the statistics text on my nightstand. I left the book open. Didn't wake until water had been dripping on it for hours. Even after I dried it page by page with a blow dryer, the print looked like an Escher watercolor. So fix the roof and replace my statistics textbook. And the shower drain—Liquid Plumr won't touch it. I step into a shower and climb out of a bath. Disgusting. Especially three days a month. And I'm sick of that buzzing in the walls when

I flip on the living room light. The wires are going to short and burn the house to the ground with my babies and me inside. Have you no conscience?

The phone call never came.

She received a letter from Smotherman stating she had notified Experian and TransUnion. Further delay in payment risked legal action. Mae responded that further delay in fixing the house risked legal action, too. Days later she worried about her credit score and her future as-yet-undecided business. She used fourteen staples to affix a check to a polite screw-you letter.

"Heading out?"

Mae rapped her head on the car ceiling. Baer stood behind her.

"Hi, Uncle Baer." Mae hugged him, smelled whiskey. His brow was wrinkled and his eyes had a perpetual squint. Like their job was to categorize, and they were skeptical from the outset.

"I was going to the grocery," she said.

"More groceries?"

"For greens. And I was going to see the landlady."

"You ought to. This place needs tore down and put up new."

"That would disrupt her cash flow."

"Something particular need fixing?"

Mae extracted the list from her purse. "Items one and four."

"Says here the drain and the roof."

"The shower drain is clogged. Liquid Plumr won't touch it. And the roof over the bedroom. I get splashed with cold rain one more time I'm liable to find a gun and shoot her."

"You don't have a gun?"

"No, I don't have a gun."

"Kids in the house? Single woman, don't have a gun?"

"What would I do with a gun but shoot somebody?"

"That's exactly what I'm saying. What'll you do, comes time to shoot somebody and you don't have a gun?"

Mae watched his eyes shift to her cheek. The swelling was down and her makeup covered the bruise.

"You had a gun yesterday, he wouldn't have done that."

"He would've taken the gun, like the money."

"Nah. See? You can't shoot somebody with money."

"Uncle Baer... "

"Tell you what. You want me to walk over and see Smotherman, get this mess straight? Or you want me to take an hour and fix the roof and the drain myself?"

"An hour?"

"'Bout that. After I get a couple supplies."

Mae hugged him. "Oh wait. I still have to go to the grocery. You want me to take you into town? What kind of supplies?"

"No, no. I'll walk. Keeps me young. I'm headed to the hardware. And the grocery. You going to the grocery?"

"For greens."

"You got baking soda and vinegar?"

She nodded.

"I'll get everything I need and be back in a half-hour. I'll visit Roy Maple, and he'll hook me up fine."

"Roy Maple?"

"Main Street hardware. You young'uns go to the Home Depot. Us old'uns go where we know people." Baer turned, and stopped after a few paces. "Back in a half-hour, so."

"Thank you, Uncle Baer."

Mae returned from the grocery. She opened the car door and the sound of a hammer greeted her. Baer hunched on the roof, his back to her. She looked for his ladder—he must have placed it against the back wall.

Mae worked Joseph free of the seat clasp. She led Morgan and Bree inside carrying a bag of greens and other produce. Merle had been sweet—other than the entire conversation between "Hello, Mae" and "See you later, Mae."

He'd grilled her on how strange Baer had been acting. That his dog had been almost killed and he'd given Merle money for her groceries. And Baer was quiet.

A fight was brewing. Merle saw Stipe and his boys talking with Baer on the sidewalk. You can see when Stipe's boys are looking for trouble. Every time you saw them.

What was Baer into? That's what Merle wanted to know.

"I haven't noticed anything strange," Mae said. She glanced out the window. Studied her wristwatch for a prolonged ten seconds. "Will you let me interview you and look at your income statement for an MBA class I'm taking?"

"Income statement? I file a ten nine nine and a schedule C, same as anybody."

Merle took the hint. He gave Mae the original slip with seventeen dollars and a handful of change deducted, and she left. Stepped past sweet old yammermouth Cora Winetraub. The woman's brow hinted the delight she'd experience gossiping that Mae had a line of prepaid credit at the grocer. Funny how the bluehairs clutching their Bibles never read the section on gossip. Wives be not slanderers.

Cora was a spinster; that was it.

Merle, sticking his nose in. And running the store's expenses through a Schedule C was like asking Richard Petty to race Talladega in a Model T. Of course he'd win, but it would be a marvel.

But what was Baer into?

Merle's observations about Baer's dog, and the fight brewing with Stipe, were enlightening.

Cory attended those dog fights. He'd told her it was sport and the dogs were like men. They loved fighting, if only for the glory of battle. Barbaric, she'd said, one more link to our caveman past. And Cory said, well, then your daddy's a caveman, and that makes you a cave girl. He'd flashed his dimples. It was time to get laid.

The steady thunk of Baer's hammer on the roof reminded her she'd had a headache all morning. Acute coffee deficiency. She opened the front door and led her tribe inside. Put away the groceries and five minutes later went outside. She stood back far enough from the wall to see beyond the eaves.

She called up to the roof, "I'm putting on a pot of coffee. You want to stay for supper? I'll cook something special."

"'Preciate you," Baer said. He continued hammering. "But I got to look on Fred."

Who would name a dog Fred?

"You sure? I'll cook some of that chicken. With collards."

"Tempting." Baer laid the hammer on the roof. "All done."

"All done? That fast?"

"It was a problem with the seam between the regular roof here and the gable. I caulked it but good. Lifted up under where the shingles was loose, replaced a couple the worst. Only real concern's falling through."

"Where's your ladder?"

Baer nodded at an oak tree with a limb that hung close to the roof.

"You climbed the tree?"

"Well sure."

"How will you get down?"

"Same way I come up."

Mae shook her head. "This is crazy. You need any help?"

"Help? What for?"

"I don't know. You want me to call the ambulance?"

He waved her off. She waited on the porch. Watched him climb down the trunk, limb to limb, holding a caulk gun and a hammer in one hand and the tree in the other.

Cory would pee his pants if he had to climb that tree with both hands and a safety harness. That was the difference—one of the thousand—between Baer and Cory. Danger simmered in both men, but with Cory it was only likely to boil over onto a person or thing weaker than him. With Baer, Mae sensed he was a handyman competent at any task he chose, including violence.

She held open the door. He placed his tools on the porch.

"I'll have that chicken in twenty minutes. You can visit the girls. They've been through every room in the house looking for a window to see you on the roof."

Baer glanced at the driveway.

"They aren't going to be young forever," Mae said.

"You hope."

"Uncle Baer!" Morgan crashed past Mae's legs and into Baer's. He swept her up and stooped for Bree, immediately behind. He pulled them to his face and scruffed both with his cheeks at the same time.

Any other man only wanted to do that with tits. "Come in, Baer. Come on. Playtime."

"All right girls, Uncle Baer's going to teach you to fix a drain. Mae, you got that baking soda and vinegar?"

"Just a minute."

"Grab a plastic lid, like from a tub of butter." Baer deposited Morgan on the floor. "Run outside and find me a rock the size of your foot, okay?"

"Hunh?"

"Go on."

Morgan bolted. Mae presented Baer a lid from the drying rack by the sink.

"Upstairs bathroom," Mae said.

Baer tossed Bree over his shoulder like a sack of grain. He carried the wriggling, giggling girl and the drain-cleaning supplies upstairs. Morgan raced inside with a rock.

Mae slapped a package of chicken breasts into a skillet. Washed collards. Laughter from above, then the rapid thud of footfalls as Baer bounded down the stairs. Only one set of feet, though. No doubt the girls rode his arms or shoulders.

If they weren't going to have a father in Cory, or a grandfather in Larry, at least they had a great-uncle in Baer. At least.

How long would it take him to check off every item on her list, if he set about fixing the house?

He stood in the kitchen entry bearing a conqueror's smile. Pioneer handsome. Rugged and focused. Smelly.

Virile.

Mae said, "When's the last time you cleaned up for a formal supper?"

His face was still.

"I mean, nothing against scruff and all... you're welcome to the bathroom. I could run your clothes through the wash real quick—I know you spend all that time in the woods. I... oh, dammit. I don't mean anything by it. I'd like to do something nice for you, but I don't have a lot I can do. Unless you want me to look at your stilling operation's books and dig into your supply chain management. I'll do a Six Sigma on your moonshine operation. Don't look at me like that, Baer. I'm trying to be nice because you've been so nice to me. I feel about as dumb as I ever felt in my whole life."

He stared at her, judging her. Mae looked back at him as plainly as she could, skewered by his eyes. He saw straight into her soul and in a moment would decide if she was worthwhile. She waited for an expression she could read, a twitch.

Nothing.

"You're some kind of silly." He came across the kitchen. Took her close, and squeezed like she was... what? Lost for a thousand years and they'd been lovers. She felt his ache through his arms, his broken heart through his chest. "Something else. You got to put on a saucepan of water. Get 'er to a boil, and in precisely thirty minute, pour it down your shower drain." He size matched hers. His chest, shoulders, the spoon between, perfect for her head... he said, "Any clog you got'll be gone. If it don't drain quick, have Morgan or Bree show you how I done it."

He pulled away. Held her at arm's length.

"You're one helluva good girl." He kissed her forehead. She smelled

70

what? Sandalwood? Iron rust? Oats? She wrapped her arms around him and in that exact moment he withdrew. "You're welcome for all this... fixing stuff. I'll come by and work on your list, time to time. And you don't got to do no man's laundry, you hear?"

He stepped back. In a moment he'd announce he had to look after Fred.

"Baer!"

"Huh?"

"Don't go! Stay! Please? Fred'll be fine. I'll drive you home to make up for the time you stayed for supper. Stay?"

"Uh."

"It'll mean so much to the girls."

Baer grinned—almost a frown. He'd seen through her. It was barely a lie.

He pulled Morgan from the floor beside him. And then Bree. "Girls, you got to show your ma how we did that drain upstairs, okay?"

"Baer... you can't go now. I wanted to show you all about the degree I'm taking. At Penn State. Online."

He was still. My God! His eyes!

"I wanted to tell you about the program. The business program... it's the best in the country. I mean so good that companies offer jobs because of the university's name. I get my MBA and all this... this house, these problems... go away. All that famous American opportunity is going to be mine. I want to show you the Internet. How I take classes from home. You have a couple of minutes, right?"

Somehow, he knew everything before she said it. She could see.

"You'll finish that school," he said. He kissed Bree on the cheek, then Morgan. Placed them on the floor and pushed them off toward the television.

"You're probably tops in class. I have to get back to Fred, before all this... gets out of hand. You're a good woman. And about this schooling, you remember. I don't know if it was the Bible or Darwin that said it, but people is lower'n worm scat. They'll lie and take what's yours, and step all over you. And smile while they do it. So my advice is, you want to make a living in business, you own the business."

He closed the step between them and dropped another kiss on her brow.

She clutched him, pulled, threw her chin over his lapel.

~

"Whoa, now!" I scoot back. Drag my sleeve over my mouth like I'm afraid she gave me cooties. "Whoa, Little Princess. Easy, now. This ain't what uncles do."

Just as wrong as two boys scrogging.

Her eyes are full and bright. Sometimes you see a woman has something in her head so firm it'll take an oxcart full of no's to shake it loose. Mae comes after me again, without a hint of red or electric, and she's shameless. It's the most natural thing for her, and it doesn't make a lick of sense—but I'm half snookered anyhow. She gets up close. Instead of planting those pudding-soft lips on me, she buries her face in my jacket. Throws her arms around my back.

We've retreated, us two. Back to family-type salutations. This's the familiar goodbye hug. Or could pass for it.

"Mae, I got to go. That chicken needs flipped."

I have to run. There are people waiting in line to shoot me. Something.

~

He was gone, like that. Mae checked the chicken and the collards. The chicken was fine.

CHAPTER FOURTEEN

It's colder out than most October afternoons, but the walk to Bleau's has me hot. Pete Bleau cut my liquor and said Henderson did it. I've thought on how he talked about cutting my shine, and the signals he gave. Nothing unusual. I catch cheats all the time.

Bleau knows Stipe, Larry and all them. His cohorts make him liable to know something about what happen to Fred.

Bleau being Bleau, he won't volunteer information until I shake it out of him. So we have to have a prayer meeting.

He lives a mile out of town in a shack like the thirty beside it, tall skinny slum houses. I'm good and loose from a half-flask of my new apple brandy, and a little shook by Mae's kiss. It took a quarter mile to walk off the willies.

Pete Bleau's truck is in the drive. Paint is Jersey-cow brown, but I peek at the tailgate anyway. Circle and glance at the undercarriage, and all along the drive. No oil.

He stores last year's Christmas tree beside a row of trash cans against the house. Stone steps up to a wide porch. Curled paint, wet-rotted boards underneath. Wonder how Bleau hasn't yet fallen through. I beat the door. His dog barks inside.

Floor boards rumble. Pete's coming.

Lock slides. Chain dangles. Door swings open. Pete looks like he expected someone else. Behind him, his German shepherd growls hello.

"Shut up, Butch," Pete says. "What you doing?" He looks beyond me to the yard, houses opposite the street. He spits in a potted plant by the door.

Nothing yet, for red or electric. "Ran apple last night. Some of my best."

"I guess it's that time of year."

"High dollar." I shove a flask to him. "Can you move twenty gallon?"

"More'n last year, huh?"

"Stepping up production."

"I'll move sixty," he says. "A hundred and sixty."

"Then it's time to double the price."

"At double price I'll move half as much."

"There you go, Sparky. I got ten now. Another run in two week. Ten bucks. Oh, and you cut my apple brandy… I don't want to go there."

"Nah. We got an understanding now."

"You know I got a dog?"

"Fred? Sure." Bleau drinks.

"Who stole him?"

His eyes glow from the sides and the color is hot. I get sparks between my fingers and if it gets worse I wouldn't believe him if he said I have a ten-inch tool.

"What?" Pete says. He throws the flask back and swallows a couple gulps.

"What I said."

"That's potent." He wipes his mouth with his arm. "What's this about your dog?"

"Someone fought him at Stipe's the other night. What you hear?"

"I don't go to them fights."

"You like that apple?"

"It's plenty good."

"I'll pour it in your eyes unless you get straight with me. We both know you're fulla nonsense and I'm someplace you don't want me to be. So you better un-ass some truth. What you know about Fred?"

The charge goes from my skin. His eyes cool into white-lie territory.

"Stipe run out of dogs. Hard to have a fight every week when you run out of dogs."

"How you know?"

"I talk to everyone."

"So who stole Fred?"

"Dunno. Just got word to keep Butch locked up."

"Who give you the word?"

"You wouldn't know him."

"Try me."

"Don't think I will. Don't matter who said it—truth's plain enough. Stipe fights ten dog a week, but only pits. Week in, week out. Even a dog that wins is licked for a while, and as many as five die each week. You got to have a lot of dogmen breeding them animals. And if you're stealing 'em, you got to have a broad sweep to stay flush. Only natural he'd run out."

"Step out on the porch with me, so your dog don't run out."

Bleau squints. Pokes his head outside and looks up and down the street. Steps to the porch in slippers and ragged jeans and closes the door. He takes another slam off my flask.

"Who give you the word, Bleau?"

"Don't—"

I swipe my flask out his hand and shove him to the jamb. Got him pinned with one arm, leaning with all my weight. I hold the potion over his face. "You want to flush your eyes in hundred-sixty proof brandy? Or you want to say who give you the word?"

I pour a little on his forehead like to baptize him.

"Ahhh! Don't blind me!"

He shoves hard and wipes his brow. We stand apart a few feet. I'm poised to throw punches and he's trembling like a ten-year-old getting picked on by the big kids. Liquor won't blind him—leastways not this stuff—but he's ignorant, confused with the wood alcohol.

I press my elbow to his throat and get him pinned again. Pour a handful of apple shine in my free hand and mash it into his eyes.

"Baer!" Bleau heaves, pulls me back into the house. That big dog slinks up. I trip Bleau and he drops. German shepherd growls low and the teeth marks in my neck start to ache. I draw Smith and hold it on the dog, and he gets wise. Cants his head. The hair on his neck stands straight and he looks like a duffel bag of teeth.

"All right, Bleau. You're going blind and your dog's getting buried in the back yard. Who gave you the scoop on those dog fights?"

He shakes. Moans. He says, "Cory Smylie."

"Keep talking until I tell you to stop."

"Cory's been working for Stipe. Gets his bait."

"Bait?"

"Cats and dogs. Cory drives all over looking for strays or animals he can steal without any trouble."

"Bait."

"Yeah, bait. They throw them in with a bunch of fighting dogs. Keeps them edgy and looking to kill, I suppose."

"And Cory give you the heads up on when he's doing the stealing?"

"Well, I don't think Butch'd make a good bait dog. Nah. Cory said Stipe paid money—called it a finder's fee—for anybody that brought him a fighting dog. Cory didn't want anybody else to make off with Butch."

"How's come you and Cory Smylie's so tight?"

"Now that ain't got nothing—"

I kick his belly flab.

Bleau groans. "We got other business arrangements."

My face is flat but I judge him with my eyes and he sees it. "You move his drugs to the shot houses."

"I'm not saying any more. Pour that whole flask down my face, I don't care."

"Or is it the other way around? You bring Cory the drugs from cities?"

"You dig much more, you'll have men from all over hunting you." Bleau eyeballs me. "I heard you shot Stipe's dog."

"That so?"

"Shot him in the eyeball. That dog was Achilles—Stipe's latest, greatest champ. Stipe's planning a biblical retribution. So you want to add every kingpin in three hundred miles, you keep digging."

"You hear something about Fred, better find me. Don't make me come pour shine in your eyes again."

Why not visit the Law?

"Chief Smylie, you know that fight the other night? That illegal fight you was at? Well, someone stole my dog and fought him…"

Don't think I'll talk at the police chief yet.

Chief Smylie and me—we have an understanding. It's the only way a man in my line of work can keep avoid fines or jail. Want the freedom to do whatever work suits? Pay the thug. That's the way of things. Chief knows he can come by for a jug when he wants. He swans over three times a year. First week of buck season, when he gathers his boys and they go to camp; July four; and his birthday in August.

Smylie joked one time that he'd make Fred a law dog, what with the crooks smuggling dope through Gleason. That was Chief shooting the bull after extorting a jug. Well, Chief doesn't have a white truck, and though he cozies up to Stipe, I can't see him bringing a dog to the show.

Another difficulty with Chief Smylie—he knows I have the still. I make trouble, he makes trouble. Time being, Chief's out of the picture.

Right this second, I'm thinking Cory Smylie stole Fred.

But I need to see about Larry's truck.

The only reason Larry would do it is pure spite. That's very possible.

Larry doesn't need money. After he stole back Ruth he put himself through night school. Wound up cooking books for Big Ted Lombo, the restaurant man with connections. Larry buys a car every two years, has a boy who mows his lawn every week. Even had the fashion to ditch Ruth and scrounge a second wife—a girl I remember from school. She was a few years behind and had a personality like wet burlap.

By the time I get to Larry's, the sun says mid-afternoon. He'll be at his office making numbers lie. His woman Eve will be in the house sucking a martini.

The house is plain vanilla expensive with a row of daisies by the sidewalk. A tree out front, pruned round.

I approach the garage doors. They're glass on top. I gander inside. It's plenty dark, but I make out his truck's outline. Light color; can't tell which. Truck is here because he drives a snappy sports car around town, looks like Snoopy's nose.

I try the big door. Locked. Side door's locked too.

"What you want, Baer?"

"Hello, Eve." I face her. "What, you stand at the window watching for people to swing by?"

"Something like that."

Her eyes are big and her stance is mousy. She either has a clamshell under her eye, or Larry's corrected her. She holds a drinking glass that looks like it's full of barbershop comb disinfectant.

"Larry at home?"

"He's at work. You know that. He won't be home for a couple hours. If he wants."

Larry and me don't talk, and it's been five years since I saw Eve. Downhill? Her looks fell off a cliff and left her standing on top. She wears shorts that show the pock marks on her legs. Her nipples poke against her halter, and force a man to speculate on whether in her prime she made milk or sour cream.

"Why are you here?" she says. "Why are you looking in the garage?"

"Want to see that truck."

"I wish he'd sell it."

She takes a drink of blue juice and crosses her arms. Her glass sweats. I can't lie. I have nothing to say, and she won't leave me hanging around gawking through the garage window. She shifts. Looks at the ground, then me.

"Why do you want him to sell it?" I say.

"It's junk. All the time either at the garage or the body shop. What people must think, seeing their accountant in a vehicle like that."

"He put it for sale?"

"You here because you want to buy his truck?"

"Nah. Wanted a word with my flesh and blood. I'll stop by later."

"Well, he won't sell it anyhow." She shifts her weight and throws one leg forward. Elbow tucked at her hip. Invitation stance. "Why don't you come inside and have a drink?"

I'd rather eat an oak keg full of leeches than bounce in the sack with Eve.

But a drink...

"What you got in the glass?"

"This?" She sips. "Blueberry Kool-Aid and Bacardi."

"I'll have the Bacardi."

"Come on in."

I look across the lawn. The neighbors must be inside their houses.

Eve walks with the swagger of a woman who thinks a good wiggle erases thirty years. She holds the screen door open with her hip, and after I follow, kicks off her sandals by the coat closet.

"Make yourself comfortable, Baer."

She stoops to a base cabinet and I get the feeling she chose her angle to give me a straight view down her top. Eve comes up with a bottle and parks it on the counter. She opens a cabinet and I swipe the bottle from below her. Spin the lid on my flask and fill it.

"Help yourself," she says.

"Appreciate you."

A little spills on the counter. The bottle has enough to top me off. "You got a rag?"

"I'll get it."

I sip from the flask. She looks at the empty bottle. Forces her face into a smile. "Why don't we go in the other room?"

I pull open the curtain on the front door. Nod at a neighbor across the street, standing with crossed arms behind a picture window.

"I did that, people would think we scrogged."

A quarter mile gone, I turn and look back. Woman make a man shiver.

CHAPTER FIFTEEN

I t's dusk. I sit on a stump and watch the fire under the boiler. This isn't a pickup night; I don't expect business, and I haven't had social company since God shat the town of Gleason.

With all that's gone on between Stipe and me, I suspect something's coming.

I keep my head hunkered into my shoulders. The hair on my neck stands anyway, on account of that cussed sniper out there, somewhere, watching. Or maybe Stipe has something else up his sleeve.

Mae tried to kiss me like I wasn't family. And her ex, Cory Smylie, has been getting his drugs off the same man that buys most of my liquor.

Sometimes life is so interesting, you can't bear it.

Every girl I ever knew had a screwed-up head; Mae's no different. Wonder how she'll feel getting grocery money from me, since I turned away such a bold invitation. She ought to feel like a dolt, but I hope she doesn't feel so stupid she lets the kids go hungry.

The steam-rattle's a few notes shy of perfect. Inside the boiler, corn mash bumbles around excited, and alcohol bursts into steam. The water part's a little more lackadaisical, and that's stillin. Pure magic is about to drop from the copper tube.

If I had any sense I'd fetch Smith off the sleeping bag and reassemble it. Doesn't do any good in clean pieces. Fred wanted to come out from under the tarp and I got sidetracked.

I drug him out, crate and all. He has good ears, and if Stipe's boys are in the woods, Fred will make sure I know. He keeps his face toward the heat. He appreciates the smell of fire or the orange glow teases through his scabbed eyes. He sighs a lot and I sigh with him. No such friend as a loyal dog. Never in a foul mood, never holds things over my head, like it was my fault they stole him and fought him in the pit.

Though it was.

I broke my Mickey Mouse watch when I was a kid. He had big-gloved hands that swung around his body. I was tom-fooling on my bicycle. Saw something coming I didn't like and clamped the front brake. Flipped. I wailed until Ma come running out to see how many bones I broke. I was made of rubber. I cried and showed Ma my busted watch. She gave me a good shake and when that didn't work, laughed at how silly I was. She said, "I seen some stupid fish, but you're being a dumb bass."

I knew she'd saved up for that watch and it was special, her being able to give it to me. She played it off like nothing, but it was my hijinks that broke it.

A man can't rely on another person's grace to get him out of deserved guilt. So when Fred grumbles as I rub between his ears, and beats his tail against the crate, he's got a lot of grace going to no use. He was my responsibility to look after. It's my fault he was stolen, and fought, and blinded, and left within an inch his life.

You have to own guilt. Even when it doesn't sit well.

The copper coil spits into the jug and the sound rattles me loose. The logs under the boiler glow red. I shove a couple chunks of split maple and nudge the last with my toe. Take the lantern to the jug and watch the shine drip out like from a spigot with a bad leak. Not a drop, not a stream, but a bunch comes out together, and stops until the pressure builds, and then spurts some more.

That jug will fill in fifteen minutes. I'll strain it through charcoal to pull out the oils. Looks iridescent and purple-tinged if you don't. Anybody who doesn't know his shine will have a case of the ass over you selling booze that'll make him go blind.

That's ignorance. Those oils are nothing and sometimes I drink raw shine out of pure happy laziness.

But get boys thinking they'll go blind, and you'll see how attached a man is to his eyes.

A horn bleats up at the house.

I have the fire just right and the mash cooking. Liquor dripping in the jug.

Horn sounds again, the long steady blare gets louder until the whole woods is ready to shut somebody up. I grab a stick, push the fresh logs off to the side of the fire.

"Guard the fort, Fred,"

Right, says Fred. I'll keep a lookout.

I head for the house with a dim flashlight. Prefer to do business in daylight but when a man wants shine, he lays on his horn until the shine man comes. I sneak inside from the basement, and climb upstairs.

It's a white truck.

I slap my hip and find I left Smith at the still site. House is dark. Don't keep anything in here but a rifle, but that'll work. You don't conduct liquor business without something that shoots bullets.

The horn bleats again. The door slams. I slip down the hallway, pop the lock on the cabinet and pull out a three oh eight Winchester. Nine power scope set over open sights. Like I'll need either. Crack the bolt, check the brass.

Business calls.

I throw the front door open and from his shape it's flesh-and-blood Larry.

"Ah, big man with a gun. You son of a bitch," he says. "Come after Eve like you come after Ruth?"

"Nah. I scrogged Ruth."

He steps toward me with fists like mallets. Stops. "What do you want, coming by my place?"

"Came by for you."

"But you went inside with Eve."

"You backslid, brother. I don't want her." I ease down the steps and he shifts sideways, like he'll jump one way or the other to keep me from scooting past.

"What you driving here?" I shine the flashlight to his truck.

"What?"

"What kind of truck you got?"

"You—what the hell? My truck?"

"I came by your place for a look. Eve said it's a piece of junk, mostly in the shop."

He's quiet while I approach, and his eyes start to glow. I feel a tickle all over my arms and the back of my neck. He came to raise Cain and now he's playing defense. In so many years watching some of the goat-humpinest liars you ever saw, they rarely do it cocky and strutting. I could count the times on one hand. Most folks lie when they backpedal.

The rifle sets Larry back, and he's thinking deceit.

Or, I ask about the truck and he's all of a sudden leery?

Should have come right out with, "You steal my dog?" But now that he's red and sparking it doesn't matter what he says, it's all suspect. I hold the flashlight to the truck bed. The grooves are wore to the metal. No blood.

"Get away from my truck. Or are you going to screw it, too?"

I get on my knees. Look up in under. Flashlight's dim enough I can't get a good read on the grime.

Footsteps, quick. Larry's boot finds my gut. I'm sucking.

"Damn, Larry."

"Stay away from Eve! I'll bust every bone you got."

My fingers are twisted in the trigger guard—caught a rock and peeled skin. Get my hand out of the metal and I'm on all fours, ready for the next. He stands back.

"I mean it," he says. "You've been a snake your whole life. You come around my woman again and I'll kill you."

I'd like to kick him from here to the lawn chair but I have another thought.

He climbs into the cab. The window is down. "You ain't going to shoot me, snake?"

"Nah, I won't shoot you."

He grinds the shifter.

"Larry?"

He looks.

"Turn in the yard there, so you don't back blind onto the road. The turnabout's there like it used to be… just grown up in weeds."

He holds my look, and if ever there was a time I was spewing red and shooting enough juice to spark a powder keg from twenty feet…

Larry finds reverse, pops the clutch, and swings the truck over the weeds. Blows rocks out his back tires and spins to the road. It's been enough weeks the moon's near full again, but it isn't up yet. Tailgate's all the same color, but without the moon, the angle, who knows?

But at the turnaround I shine the flashlight on the weeds, and spot oil.

.   .   .

Back at the still, Fred says, I worry.

"I do too."

Yeah, he says, but you can see them coming.

I settle on the stump and his words sit on my shoulders. Kick logs back deep in the embers. Tap the boiler. Five, ten minute she'll make steam. But why wait on the fresh stuff when there's vintage under the tarp?

Wailing on a car horn, again.

Larry? Nah—doesn't sound like a truck. Sounds like a rabbit feeling a wolf's teeth; blares that don't stop. Fred perks.

"I'll go see. Don't trouble yourself."

He rests his head. One day I'll fix a leash so he does more than lay around all day. Once he heals.

I put Smith back together in four seconds and slip the gun to my hip. Grab a gurgle of shine. Head for the house. Inside, I look through the window. Headlights are off—beat-up Tercel.

Mae.

The vehicle backs away. I step outside, down off the step. She doesn't see me until she's back to the road. The car sits. She's going to make me walk all the way. Never know what a girl's got on her mind. Not after she tries to plant a smooch, and you back away.

She rolls down her window and I stoop. She looks ahead but the angle doesn't conceal a fresh beating.

"Cory do that?"

She nods. Stares.

I look. All three kids are in the back seat. "Pull in the driveway here and let the kids out to play. Then you can tell me exactly why Cory Smylie needs murdered."

"Don't say that."

"Yeah, he'll stop on his own, will he? You expect something different, but I been telling you five years."

"So now you get to say you told me so?"

"Come on back to the house."

She reverses to the step and parks. Kids tumble out, rattled. Not in the mood for play. I sit on the step and hold my arms out to Bree and Morgan. Mae has Joseph.

"C'mere, girls. C'mere."

I coax them in my arms. Plop them on my lap. Nuzzle each.

"Guess you two saw some ugly today."

They are silent. Heads press to my shoulders.

"You know by now, the world ain't made of candy. But this's what you got to understand. Bree, Morgan—look at me, now. Look in my eyes." Reluctant. "C'mon girls. You need to know."

They look, eyes big unblinking moons.

"Your momma will be safe from here on out. And so will you. Cory won't do this no more."

They bury their heads again and I rub their backs. Mae leans on her trunk.

"Tell you what, girls. It's about time for the lightning bugs to come out. I'll give you a dollar each if you can catch me one."

Neither stirs.

I lift the girls off my lap. "Catch me one of them lightning bugs, girls. Catch me two. There's a Ball jar in the shed, bottom shelf. Run along."

They wander away.

"It's too late in the fall for lightning bugs," Mae says.

"I'll give each a dollar anyway."

Mae pulls her skirt closer to her knees. "I wish I knew where all the men like you hide."

"Woods. Stills. You call the police?"

"Gleason police don't want anything to do with the police chief's son."

"Yeah. You got a gun?"

"I've said enough about guns. Not with kids in the house."

"And you won't let me go string him by his nuts from a tree? That's out, right?"

She smiles, coughs, and that presses out a fresh batch of tears. "Violence doesn't solve anything."

"Dumbest words ever said. Enough of it does. Every time."

The air is still and the girls straggle across the yard, stumped. At least the pursuit takes their minds off what they saw.

"What do you want me to do? I'm no good at doing nothing."

"I don't know," she says.

"Suppose you could haul the kids to Mars Hill for a couple days. Give things time to shake out with Cory."

"You're going to go after him, aren't you?"

"That's why you came, Mae. Don't tell me different."

"It's why I came."

"Uh-huh. Visit your mother a couple days. You come back, you won't have problems with Cory Smylie."

CHAPTER SIXTEEN

It's been a week since I fell out of the tree while watching Stipe's dog fight. If I had a sack the size of a three-week cabbage I'd have gone to work on that crew of dog-fighters with Smith.

That's where my mind is at.

Naw, I won't go there and pull a six-shooter on twenty men, surly from watching dogs rip each other to pieces. Rich with liquor.

I'm going there to talk. See if I can't get a couple pieces of information that'll make the endgame clear. Stipe won't kill me with all his boys around. I'm banking on it.

There isn't a trail between my camp and Stipe's fight circle. I follow the crick, turn off, and hoof a mile or two until their whoops and hollers guide me in. Gather my nerves with a healthy snurgle of shine. Sit on a boulder overlooking the lantern glow, and the men who came to see dogs die. They dance around like leprechauns or gnomes or what's his name... Rumpelstiltskin. Evil.

Pure evil.

I ease up to the edge of the lantern light. Fight ended. I look over the faces. Half of these men have bought my liquor at one point or another. Lucky Jim Graves, Pastor Jenkins, Chief Smylie, Stipe—he didn't buy it, only took what I offered. George. I know most of these men.

Henry Means carries a limp dog in his arms. Someone opens the pit gate, an oak shipping pallet. The man says, "He died game," and Henry nods, solemn.

"What you doing here, Baer?"

It's Lou Buzzard, a regular buyer.

I swing a jug of shine. "Stipe here says I can come anytime, long as I fetch a jug."

"I said two," Stipe says. He tramps to me, clamps his jaws tight. All the men are silent. "But that was before you murdered Achilles."

"Brown dog? Bullet hole in his eyeball? I never seen that dog."

Stipe takes the jug from my hand. "You come for a dose of sledgehammer?" He looks around at the men, then meets my eyes again. "You got some gall, Creighton." He comes close and leans into me. His voice is a whisper. His eyes are red and I get the electric all through me. "We got business to settle, you and me. Fire and brimstone."

He smacks my shoulder like we're old friends, and though I brace I'm jarred two feet. I was right. He'll kill me later. Not now.

I'm close enough to the pit I can smell it. It's a place of death, and the odors are everything that happens when a body dies. Blood, from weeks and weeks of spilling. Piss stamped into the mud so the circle stinks like a witch's kettle. Throw in a couple bat wings and chicken livers, the right woman could cast a spell.

"I want to know who stole my dog."

Stipe's face is flat, white like a can of Crisco. Somebody drew a line across for a mouth and poked two fingers for eyes. "Make yourself at home, Creighton." He grins, backs away, and points. "Get Stinky Joe in the pit, Hank. He's up against Panzer."

Stipe gestures and a man I know from way back steps beside him. Stipe leads him a few yards away, leans to him and says something. Stipe looks at me and the man looks at me. He crosses his arms and nods, and wanders toward me.

"How you doing, Burly?"

"Better'n you, I suspect."

Meanwhile, men shuffle at Stipe's orders. The one called Hank nods, but comes for a hit on the jug first. Stipe pulls the cork and holds the mouth to his lips. He sputters and passes it. Hank beats another set of grasping hands and I'm all but certain everything'll shape up the way I want. For Fred.

I move a few feet and Burly Worley stays beside me, half watching me, half the goings-on.

A truck engine starts and reverse lights flash. The vehicle stops shy of the pit and with exhaust fumes tumbling along the ground, the driver gets out. He drags a big wood dog pen from the front of the bed to the tailgate. Has it mounted on skids. Inside, between the slats, a pair of feral eyes glows. It's the first time I ever detected a dog that was a liar.

"That Panzer?" I say.

Burly says, "That's him."

"I'll bet he fights dirty."

"How'd you know?"

The dog's master pulls a long handle—like from a rake—out of the truck bed. Rope loops at the end and feeds up the handle. The tool's purpose is evident. Lasso the dog's head, cinch the rope tight, and the handle will keep him far enough he can't chew off his handler's face.

The man bends to the crate door, unfixes a latch and cracks it ajar. He works the handle back and forth, muttering. I watch Panzer through the slats and shadows. The dog shifts sideways like a ghost, white and gone, there and no more, and finally his owner says, "All right, easy, boy. Easy now."

Panzer's every inch a fighter. His eyes glow like backlit blood and he keeps his head low. He shifts back and forth, like it's him against the whole world. Muscle ripples under his coat, and his neck's bigger than his hips. He's a brute.

Stinky Joe shrinks against the opposite side of the ring. His master stands beside him, not even bothering to put him on a rope. Is that how Fred looked? Disoriented, scared at the smell of arena mud and the stench of booze coming out of men's pores?

Panzer leaps from the bed of the truck and his master hops down with him. Men part as the dog approaches. His eyes fix through the pallet slats on the quivering wretch at the far side.

"Ten to one against Stinky Joe," Stipe barks.

Who'd name a fighting dog Stinky Joe? Call him Artillery, or Bullets, or Bone Crusher. Or Achilles, like that devil I killed.

Stinky Joe faces Panzer and drops his head low. The men hush and Stinky Joe's growl trips across the ground. It falters.

He's backed against a wall and his enemy comes.

I think of Fred, mauled and blind, and the Smith on my hip feels like the better way to go. But if I can be patient, I'll make these men feel like God dropped them deep in the Old Testament.

I scan faces one by one, curious that Cory Smylie isn't here, nor my brother Larry. Did Stipe tell them to lay low? Do these men have something more planned for old Baer? Do they think they're delivering justice, now that Baer brought his bullets?

Good questions when surrounded by men packing pistols and knives, gulping a hundred-sixty proof shine.

Burly watches me, but he'd rather keep his eyes on the action in the arena. Standing center pit, Stipe works mud from one boot with the toe of the other. "Ten to one against Stinky Joe. Last takers?"

The men are quiet.

"All right," Stipe says. He exits the circle and hovers at the edge with one arm raised.

Since he's been in the pit, Panzer's been occupied rattling Stinky Joe. Panzer's owner has his forearm across the dog's chest—he's removed the pole and rope contraption. Stinky Joe searches for escape between gaps in the pallets.

Stipe drops his arm.

Panzer leaps across the ten-foot circle.

I turn. Burly gazes at the fight. I work away from the pen, unminded. Men jostle closer.

I can't see the fight, but from the growls and yelps, low-tenored and breathy, I imagine what's going on. Back among the trucks, I search tailgates for any that seem brighter on the left than right. There's one with wide tires, but it has dark paint.

A shout comes from the pit and I look back. The men boo and cuss. Stinky Joe flashes past me, heading into the dark woods. He's jumped the wall, and with what I know about these men, he better never find his way home.

Burly figures out he lost sight of me and spins a full circle, looking. He shoots me an ugly look and starts working back to me.

Stipe pays money to the winners and says, "Time for King George and Gravy. Dogs to the ring! King George is a seven-time winner, undefeated. Never turned—not once in all his fights. King George is fighting in place of Achilles. You all know what happened there. Gravy... this is his first fight in this circle, but he's got two wins down outside of Charlotte. You can tell by his size he's going to give King George a mess of trouble. Three to one, King George. Who's in?"

Is Gravy like Fred? Like Stinky Joe? Given a made-up name and a pedigree from a distant town?

What name did they give Fred?

I gulp shine from my flask and yank Smith. Point at the moon and pull the trigger. Smith barks and flame flashes.

Men halt. Stipe stares. Burly is five feet away and I point at him. He steps back a half-dozen feet.

"You boys is a bunch of assholes."

Chuckles.

"Shut up," Lucky Jim Graves says.

I point Smith at him. "Hey, unlucky."

Murmurs die. Eyes flash red but their intent wavers, and the color fades.

"I don't know which of you recall a dog from a couple weeks back. White pit didn't have the sense to hop the pen like Stinky Joe. But one of you dead men fought him." I point Smith at Jenkins, the pastor. Then Lou Buzzard. Then George from the lumberyard. Come to a stop on Stipe. "Who was it?"

Stipe spits. "You sore about a dog? A coward dog? You murder my champ and cost me real money, but I don't go waving a gun in people's faces."

I keep Smith trained on Stipe's triple-chinned head. I didn't think before pulling it and I don't have an inkling of what to do next. But if I put the gun away, these boys will beat me silly.

George from the wood mill emerges from the group with his hands in the air and confusion on his face. "What's this about, Baer?" His eyes are plain; he wants to be the honest broker. He eases close. Reaches toward my left shoulder.

I shift aside.

"Don't think I can make it plainer. Who tossed my dog in this ring?"

"Put that piece away, before someone takes you serious," Stipe says.

All this time, and since I pulled Smith, I haven't seen a bit of red anywhere, nor felt a single zap, except at the beginning. I step back and listen to the sounds behind me. Leaves in a breeze.

I lift the barrel and squeeze off another shot above Stipe. He jumps, snarls.

"You're good as dead," Stipe says.

Eyes glow. All at once, every one of them, like I riled a nest of demons.

CHAPTER SEVENTEEN

Footsteps rush from behind me. Something like a sledgehammer drops on my gun arm and my hand's empty. Arms around my shoulders; men wrestle me down. More boys rush up. Kicks to my legs and guts. A boot catches my shoulder blade. I reach and can't find Smith. A heel stomps my hand. Boot in the mouth. I taste blood.

I need to get home.

Home's where I have a solution—but I relish the honesty in a groin kick, the alley tactics. They hate me and act with pure integrity. Their plain-dealing is nice for a change. I curl my knees tight to my chest but a couple kicks to my back have my muscles in a knot. These boys won't let up.

"Enough!"

The kicking stops. Men part. Stipe stands close.

"Get up, Baer."

Feels like every bone is busted, but it's the muscles doing the complaining. Burly bends over and yanks me upright.

"I brought your jug, Stipe."

"I don't got to tell you not to come back," Stipe says. "I don't got to mention next time you come prowling around here or my house or my dogs or any thing associated with me—"

He censors himself. His eyes are hot and his brow tight. He looks across the watching men. Something passes between him and Burly, who now leans against a black Suburban. Bumper sticker says, DEPENDS ON THE DEFINITION OF TREASON.

I spot my Smith a couple feet away. Grab it and pull the hammer back with my thumb. Their eyes are normal; their faces flushed. I point Smith toward them, wave the barrel back and forth. But before I grabbed it there were already a dozen men with guns in their hands.

Burly Worley's gone.

"You already proved you're an idiot, Baer." Stipe says. "Put that away and don't ever come back."

"I come here to give you boys a chance. This ends tonight. No more fights around these parts. Or I'll murder every one of you."

I point at the sky. Ease the hammer forward. The air is thick and humid and the breeze is cold. Moths around the lanterns have fluttered off. I catch one man's eyes after another, then snatch a quick look behind, and back away from the group.

Every muscle screams, but I don't have any new teeth marks in me, and I have a clear conscience. I gave these boys the chance to get right. I called out their evil, and delivered my message.

They want to die sloppy... up to them.

I'm a hundred yards out and it's darker now than when I set out a couple hours ago. One of their kicks to my head has messed with my vision. I keep a hand up deflecting branches from my eyes and feel along slow with my feet. The forest floor's irregular. I slip and catch myself on all fours. Pause a second with the silence. Look up to a moon perched on a beech limb.

A plodding noise comes along from behind. Crunches through leaves and twigs like it doesn't give a royal rat's rear who hears. Black bear, like me, headed away from the fight circle. Had her fill of watching beasts and smelling blood. She isn't but a dozen yards away, and looks like a tank bowling over scrub.

A stick snaps, back the way I came.

I stay crouched and search the dark forms. Tree trunks are solid black voids and the space between is gray with silver frost on the moon side. There's a shape like another bear coming, a few steps, then he pauses, then takes a few steps more.

But this one's upright.

It's Burly Worley—homed in on the bear, thinking it's me. He has a pistol in his hand, un-aimed.

I reach back slow without rustling a single brittle leaf and pull Smith.

If I had time, I'd dig a hole, fill it with spikes, slather them in dung. Stretch a line across right in front, ankle high. Fix a knife to a sapling and bend it back like a two-hundred-pound bow, set with a figure-four catch. Lot of ways to make sport on a man in the woods. But as he's coming now I have twenty seconds, and then it's plain old Smith.

Ten feet.

Burly stops, lifts his pistol arm and points. He sniffs. Ahead, the bear stumbles into a log and thrashes it, from the sound. I hear her snooting in the rotted wood, looking grubs for a midnight snack.

I can almost feel Burly's confusion.

The man is so close I can smell him. He likely lives in a house but doesn't bathe regular—a lot of folks don't.

Now that I look steady, I see the bear again. She's a big son of a gun—there are dog bears and hog bears, some with high bellies and some with low. This gal's a hog bear.

Black bear generally don't want anything to do with people. You want trouble with one, you have to make it.

Burly sidesteps, as if to circle the beast up ahead, and shifts two feet toward me. His face looks forward, with a red glow about the eyes. Hasn't even glanced my way. If I make a noise, he'll spook and shoot me.

I lift my leg.

A leaf crinkles.

Burly faces me—swings his gun arm level at my head. He had me all along.

"Hello, Baer."

"Hey, Burly. Doing all right tonight?"

"Better'n you." He steps closer. Places his pistol to my temple.

I feel the cold metal through my hair. "I don't think you'll miss. You want to give me an inch? A half-inch?"

He eases off. "Let's go. Careful. Don't trip, don't jump. I might get scared and shoot you."

"I guess Stipe sent you out to put me down? That it?"

"Nah, just to have a conversation. Let's both back away from that black bear, and we'll talk a bit."

"Let me ask one thing."

"Move, dammit. Nice and easy."

"Do you feel the red coming out your eyes?"

"What?"

"It gives you away."

My gun hand is halfways aimed at the bear; it's a subtle move, pulling the nose a little higher. I point at her backside, best I can, and squeeze the trigger. The muzzle flashes orange and I spin away from Burly's barrel, knock his hand with my elbow. I jump to the closest tree and start scrambling. The bear grunts. Comes quick. Burly stands still. I claw up a six-inch smooth-bark tree, maybe elm. It's slippy and each time I gain a foot I slide back half. Ready to give out, I grab ahold the lowest limb.

And drop Smith.

Burly faces the bear. Steps backward. He talks low-voiced and guttural. "You sure do look pretty tonight, baby," he says. His precise words don't matter; bears don't speak English like dogs, and their females don't flatter anyway. It's all in the tone. Burly's playing it right.

I spot his gun on the ground. I must have knocked it from his hand.

Black bear stands on her hind legs, waving her head back and forth, only ten feet off. With the breeze against her, she can't smell, and bears are halfway blind. So she steps closer.

Burly knows bears like any country boy knows bears. He can't turn his back, and he doesn't want to kneel for his gun.

"You stay back, you ignorant, overgrown pretty-pretty hog," Burly says, low. "Why don't you shoot her for me, Baer? Shoot her in the head this time."

"You better watch I don't call her in."

If that black bear wanted to charge, she'd have done it after I shot her. I'm thinking I missed, and only startled her. She's mighty inquisitive— most would have run off after a surprise like that. She'll go on her way once she's satisfied Burly isn't a threat. Or food. And then it'll be Burly and me again.

My gun sits not three feet from his.

That bear takes off, Burly has two guns. I'm up a tree. Bullets climb faster than bears.

Black bear lowers to all fours, begins a lumbering turn sideways.

I let go of the limb, drop silent. Right arm high, coming down hard with my elbow. Burly swings his noggin at me and I catch his temple. He's knocked dumb. I land on my feet. He staggers and grunts. The bear has seen enough. She scoots into the black night.

I swing with my fist and clock Burly in the temple. He drops to the ground and sighs from his throat long and slow. The noise has a groan of voice in it, like a life moving on.

A sound that makes you think you've gone too far.

. . .

I kick his boot.

Burly Worley hasn't moved nor made a sound in five minutes. He has one leg folded under the other, and his gun arm is twisted under his back. I shake with adrenaline and mull the logic of retribution. If a man does you ill, setting things right means giving back the same, and a little more for punishment. Burly is part of the group that made Fred suffer, and deserves to be dead. But him deserving it and me putting him in the ground? Though I promised it an hour ago, my mind hasn't yet made the leap.

I point Smith at Burly's head. Get on my knees. Lean on one arm and stick the muzzle against his temple. He so much as twitches, his head will meet that beech in pieces.

I park my ear above his nose and listen.

"Come on, Burly."

I smell whiskey like from a mouth fart.

I ease back, but keep Smith ready to lend instruction. Burly mumbles and I'm about sure half of his problem is the whiskey he drank, not the popknot I put on his skull.

Burly Worley will be fine, so long as he wakes before that bear gets hungry. But I never heard of a bear that eats asshole, so he'll be all right.

I wait ten more minutes and Burly snores. I'll not babysit any more of this. I set off slow, so my feet don't rouse him.

I follow the crick bank, careful not to slip. The water's eaten away dirt and sometimes walking too close you get a squishy feel. But that's where the deer path goes, and I follow it because the brush gets thick elsewhere.

Ruth and me was a thing all right. While Larry was off at school we fooled around every night she could get away. It became more difficult for her as the weeks went on. Her daddy wanted Ruth to be a trophy wife, like to marry into royalty or something. Nobody but some law-school boy set on ambulance chasing or politics was good enough. He must've had in the back of his head some greaser was boffing his daughter. She had to get clever to see me.

One day she came with a faceful of tears. Crazy like the world was at end.

"What is it? Let's scrog. You'll feel better."

She turned her shoulder. "I'm pregnant."

I trip on a tree root and my knee catches a rock right where I landed on my binoculars a couple days back. But I'm buoyed by hip-deep memories. There wasn't a feeling in the world like Ruth telling me she was knocked up. That baby meant we'd end up together. Doing the right thing lined up pretty well with my life's ambition. I'd marry her and work like a fool to keep her happy. Wanted to.

But the right thing to her daddy was bound to be different, and that's what had her bollixed.

I came up with a plan to handle Preston Forsyth Jackson. This was deep in Larry's first semester at college—November, memory serves. I'd been paying attention and learning at the garage. Wasn't anything with an engine and wheels I couldn't fix, and getting laid all the time made me affable. Especially with folks who'd talk gasoline and metal. Made a friend of a trucker that passed through every week, and I thought to make a career move with his help.

I drove my Nova to the city and tracked down the company he worked for. Got a mechanic job and came home to tell Ruth.

The still site is quiet except Fred grumbles, I know it's you.

I cover Fred with a blanket, scratch his ribs. I'm ready for the bedroll, but have one more errand. The river rocks I heat for the bathtub are cold as the ground. Fire's long dead. I start another.

I told Ruth I had a job. She looked at the floor.

"What is it, now?"

"Nothing."

"Well, fine. I'll tell you about my new job."

"I'm not pregnant."

It was all a scare, she said. A misunderstanding.

Fred says, You want to keep the mumbling to a minimum? Trying to sleep.

"I don't feel so good, Fred."

Know how you feel, Fred says. One thing. Did you learn what you went to learn? Is the plan going to work?

I nod. "Think so."

You have the balls?

I remember not being ready to shoot Burly. "I don't have a single clue."

CHAPTER EIGHTEEN

My body's beat good and if I'd feel any better in the sleepsack that's where I'd be. But a man doesn't rise to a lofty height such as mine without uncommon dedication. I stretch my bruised muscles and drink away the aches. Add a couple heavy logs to the fire.

So they liked your likker? Fred says.

"They did."

Didn't you learn that from the last time they beat you silly?

"I get mad. And they didn't beat me silly. That time I fell out a tree."

If good men don't get mad, it'll just be the bad ones, Fred says.

"You said a mouthful. I'll be back after bit."

Cory Smylie lives in a good part of town, up on Ketchum Street. I would've gotten in his face before going to the fight, but those fights are only one night a week. Cory's always a bastard.

There's a black man name of Harry, runs a shot house on a hill in Swannanoa; serves booze all night. Used to buy my liquor before Fletcher Rose sold his cheaper. I visited a couple times and Cory was there, on account of the women, or selling drugs. It's a long shot, but worth a walk.

Every muscle I have back-sasses each step.

The shot house sits atop a wooded hill. Nearby houses were built when this was the rich part of town, and they're mansions. But they haven't tended yards in decades, and scrub trees grow right up next to the siding. Feels like walking through the woods with a town dropped in the middle, and nary a tree cut to make room.

It's deep after midnight. A car moves slow up the hill, cigar cherry inside. People in the back seat have big hair. Giggles.

Men take women up the hill, get them sloshed and then go back down the hill. At two bucks a shot, these customers get a deal. Put my shine— or even Fletcher Rose's—against house liquor at a regular bar, and it's twice as potent for half the cost. Tastes like a gulp of bonfire; numbs your pipes from smile to smudge.

Though women say it goes straight to the gizzy.

A car parks outside a small cabin with an open door. The joint is packed, though there are only four or five cars outside. Smoke hangs at the ceiling and voices carry fifty feet. A pinball machine lets out a bunch of pings and zaps. Men swap stories on the step. There's a pinkish glow from every eye in the joint—but friendly, like lies at Christmas.

I wade in.

The men and women are black and white. Floor's wood. Walls need paint. No windows. There's enough room to wedge an elbow. I look over the faces but Cory isn't here. His truck isn't outside and Cory Smylie doesn't have the ambition to walk five miles.

I recognize a couple faces, no one I want to talk to. But Harry waves, and waves again, with vigor. The throng blocks me and Harry nods toward the door. He slips out the back and meets me at the steps.

"Sales call?" he says.

"Looking somebody."

"Whodat?"

"Cory Smylie. White kid. Ain't worth a whiff of—"

"I know'im. Uh-huh."

"Well, I see he ain't here. Still getting your shine from Fletcher?"

"Thassaight."

"Had a couple yourself t'night…"

"Uh-huh." He slaps my arm and bends over, laughing, and his eyes glow on the white-lie setting. He pulls my arm with the strength of a mechanic. Takes me into darkness.

"You bes' watch your back."

He's sober.

"Yeah?"

"Stipe's boy Barrow been out twice, last two week. Fust was t' see if I bought from you. I says no. He leave. Week later, he come back and says,

'Okay, who does buy from him?' You know sometimes you can tell a puhson got they ill will going on? Get the sense he's looking t' get ugly?"

"Know what you mean."

"Well, Barrow got his ugly on. That mean Stipe do too."

"'Preciate you, Harry."

"All right. Let's drink."

He leads me into the shot house from the back. Grabs a jug from twenty under the bar. Fills a glass and like the good people he is ignores my handful of money. I gulp the fire.

"Next you see Fletcher Rose, you shake his hand for me."

"One more," Harry says.

I oblige so I don't insult the man. While he isn't looking I drop my money on the floor behind the bar. Slap his shoulder and he winks. He does the drunk act good but he drinks like a stiller and I know he's putting on a show. I slip out.

If brains was leather I couldn't saddle a June bug. There are enough places Cory Smylie could be, I was foolish coming here. But I'm sure he'll he wind up back home with his useless parents. I reckon it's two more miles. Plenty of time to think on who stole Fred.

My flesh-and-blood brother and me have been cruel to one another, for one reason or another, most of our lives. But the dust settled twenty-some years ago, the last time I talked to Ruth. No reason for Larry to strike up a feud now.

Cory Smylie? Years have passed since I wanted to shoot his window on account of the deer he hit with his truck. Fred was gone before I dropped Cory to get the fifty-spot back for Mae. Anything he did was out of the blue, a crime of opportunity. Just looking for a dog and saw mine. Maybe he thought Fred was bait.

Stipe?

He's behind everything, all right. But it's the prime mover I'm after. I want to know the first man to conceive of Fred in a fight circle. That's the devil I want to pray with.

Years ago I came from the woods to a blaring horn to find three men in the driveway. I never had anything to do with Stipe. Knew he was a businessman, but not much more, and didn't learn these boys were working for him until later.

"We're buying you out," one said. It was Huck Barrow, a fella with a neck as red as his eyes.

"You ain't buying dick." I walked away.

I heard the pop of a little pistol. Fella on the side had a twenty-two caliber pointing at the sky, and wore a grin liable to split his head at the ears.

"Better work on your aim."

He pointed at my head, and Barrow said, "Not yet, Willie."

His face glowed. I felt juice all through me and I figured, it's been a good ride, but it's over. Twenty-two caliber bullets make clam soup out of brain. He said, "We got the money to make it square. We buy your inventory. The rig, the customers. You'll come work for us."

"Don't think so."

I walked away sure I'd feel a bullet, and I hoped the lugnut had the skills to hit my head in the middle. But I reached the house without dying, and by the time I poked a rifle through the window, the men were gone.

Subsequent, I carried Smith walking to the edge of camp to take a leak.

Shot house Harry's story about Barrow asking questions doesn't surprise me. You make a good thing, somebody will try to steal it. But Barrow coming back right now challenges the way I understand coincidence.

Long, long walk. Those four shots of Fletcher's finest were an unexpected delight. Now I have two flasks to hold me.

Headlights splash like water from a bucket. First thought—I want to jump in the woods and run. After Stipe's last promise, I'm more jittery than a regular moonshiner ought to be. The vehicle passes. Ahead fifty yards, the brake lights flash. White reverse lights, and a Cadillac truck revs back.

Stipe's boys don't drive Cadillacs, but I'm wary and the hair on my arms stands. Not the juice... just old-fashioned distrust.

I ease to the driver's side. Window zips down. Cigarette glows. "That you, Baer?"

"In the flesh come down from the mountain."

"Howya doon? Get in." He pops the door open and the dome light goes on.

I circle behind and climb in. Big Ted Lombo's across the seat. One of those men who make it his business to know everybody.

Larry does his books.

"How's the restaurant business, Big Ted?"

"People got to eat. How's your business?"

"People drink whether they eat or not. What brings you out, middle the night?" I fish out my flask and offer it. "This's special stuff. Plum shine."

"Brandy?"

"Nah, shine. Corn, barley, and wheat. Double-stilled, then a touch of plum brandy. Tastes better'n plum gasoline."

"Never had neither."

"Take my word on both."

He grabs the flask. Spins the cap with his thumb.

"Keep both eyes on the road. You'll want to close em."

He gulps and the truck drifts to the white line. "Whoooeeee!"

"Ain't it good?"

He wheezes. Rights the Cadillac. Hits his chest.

"Coupla friends got a card game. You know Mickey, right? And Franky? I tell them every week I be there, but I got the rest'rant, yeah? So they start late for me."

"Appreciate the lift."

"Why ain't you got a car? I got a friend make you a deal. You know Guilio Salandra gots the Dodge dealership on Merrimon? I tell him 'Make my friend a deal,' you get anything you want at cost. I make the call tomorrow."

"Don't make it yet, Big Ted. Got to gather up some resources, you know."

He nods. I crack the window. I never seen a vehicle with so many lights and dials. The air's cooler now that I'm moving fast through it.

"So what's these crazy stories?"

"Which crazy stories, Big Ted?"

"Fight the other night. And that thing with Stipe's dog."

"Saw the lights. Truck come out the woods where there's nothing but scrub, and in my line o' work, a fella wants to know his competition."

"Uh-huh."

"You go them fights much?"

"Nah. Once, twice. Don't like violence."

He looks sideways. A white-lie rose color comes from his eyes. He laughs.

Got a question stuck in my throat: You know who stole my white pit and fought him a couple weeks back? But Big Ted plays all sides. He'd tell me, and before sunup he'd tell who he told on, like I had the info and slipped and told him what I was thinking. I'd be no farther ahead, but he'd call it a debt.

My flask is in his hand resting on the shifter. Think I'll make a grab—
and he upends it again. We are a mile out of town, and past the turn for
the quickest route to Cory Smylie.

Big Ted giggles, beats his chest and hands over the flask. I weigh it.

"You keep them eyes peeled to the road, Ted."

"That's good stuff. You know, I could move some. I got friends always
lookin' hooch like that."

We enter Gleason. "Where you going?"

I grab the handle. "Here's fine." He swings to the curb. I pop the door.
Light goes on in the cab. His face is flat.

"You don't want to go back to them fights, Baer."

"No?"

"None of my business, getting mixed in family… situations. But that
crew out there… You don't have friends."

"Larry?"

He shrugs.

"Thanks, Big Ted."

I close the door like a scrawny pencil necked geek and it don't latch,
and I have to do it again. Inside, Big Ted already has a cell phone in his
hand. He pulls off as the dome light fades.

I tramp back the other way. Out of town, I cut right. The clock in the
Cadillac truck said it was two thirty-eight. Normal bars have stopped serv-
ing, and now I think I would have had more luck waiting at Harry's shot
house. He doesn't close until the party does.

But sooner or later, Cory Smylie will come back to Mom and Dad's.

I approach the Smylie place easy and slow, shadow to shadow. Cory's
F-150 is not in the driveway. A minivan sits next to a Blazer. Opposite, the
houses are sparse, with maple windbreaks between. Not dense enough to
hide a man in the day, but at night, the shadows are deep.

I'm warmed after the walk, but sitting next to a tree in the middle of
the night, the chill presses in. I work flask number two until it's gone.

Lights.

The vehicle passes the Smylie driveway without slowing.

I remember being Cory's age. Spent all those years wishing things
were different with Ruth. Wishing I didn't have my talent, my brother, my
nature.

By and by I let my head droop.

．　．　．

A door clunks. I look. The F-150's in the drive, nose toward the road. I'm awake like I ran a mile. I can see his shape. Cory Smylie. Has that muscle-bound slump to his shoulders, and walks like a pimp. He makes it to the truck bed.

He's messed up.

I pull Smith. Come up on him from his back right, while he's hunched. Glide over dewy grass as Cory gags on puke. I'm right behind, but I wait until he finishes yakking on his tire.

He climbs back up the side of his truck and wipes his mouth with his sleeve. He coughs. I grab his right arm and lever it behind his back. Press Smith to his head.

"Whoa—whoa," he says. "Dude. What's going on?"

I smell his upchuck.

"I got your attention?"

"Dude!"

He coughs.

I twist the gun barrel into his skin. Press hard, so his head moves back. "You mark my words. You listening?"

"Easy now... I'm listening."

"Touch Mae again. See Mae again. Think of Mae again, I kill you. Savvy?"

"I get it."

I smash the butt to his head.

CHAPTER NINETEEN

M ae leaned toward her crummy sixteen-inch computer. It ran Windows 98, and connected to the Internet via a 56K modem. She reread the sentence.

Thick.

She glanced at Bree and Morgan sitting too close to the television. Or had they changed that whole thing about sitting too close to the television?

She'd made mistakes. This MBA program could give her a fresh start in a new town. No one would know she had three kids by a dope-peddling loser named Cory Smylie.

She'd met him her freshman year at college. He had dimples, was boyish and troubled, and only used his brooding smile to get laid. Years later, he hung around her life like a noose.

How would it work when Morgan and Bree were twelve and ten? Would Cory make them push product at the playground?

The question opened an interesting supply chain management topic... a parenthetical diversion for her Age Diversity in the Workforce paper. She looked at the clock. The paper was due in eleven hours.

Mae glanced at Bree and Morgan, on the floor, and at Joseph, asleep on the couch. He was like a dog, sort of, always asleep on the couch. Always. As if he had a problem.

She went to him, touched his back, felt his shallow breaths. They were always shallow.

Bree twisted from the television and smiled at her. Mae slipped to her knees and pulled her close. Together, they collapsed beside Morgan, and all three snuggled on the floor. A cartoon reviewed how to count from one to ten.

Bree buried her nose at Mae's side and giggled. Mae squeezed her. "Mommy has to get back to work," she said. "I love you both."

She attended classes through Penn State, happy to be in an online MBA program that attracted recruiters. But looking at her second-hand computer, set off by the water-stained wallpaper... Did another forty-seven thousand dollars of debt make sense?

Would she graduate and be unable to find a job because she lived in Gleason, North Carolina?

She wanted a fresh start, away from Cory Smylie. Sure, she could pack the Tercel and head into the sunrise. Spending the money she'd saved by shopping at Goodwill, and feeding her kids with food stamps. Taking medical care from the government. She'd reach Charlotte on the first tank of gas, and then Research Triangle Park with the second. And then she'd be broke.

But finding a new place to rent? Covering old debts that were threatening her credit score? A move now would only ruin her chances at getting a business loan when she finished school.

Was she going about everything wrong? Should she start a business now, without her MBA? The only place that was hiring was Cory's Pharmaceuticals.

She sat at the computer.

Hold on, she thought, until everything comes together. Lots of moving parts.

Outside, a door slammed.

Cory?

"God," she said. She looked at the clock. "Turn down the television. Turn it off!"

"What?" Morgan said.

"Do as I say! Turn it off now! Hush! Pretend we're not here. Let's play a game!"

At the door she peered through the fisheye lens.

"Who is it?" Morgan said.

"Uh... Wow. It's your grandmother."

· · ·

108

Mae studied her mother. Ruth had lived in Mars Hill since the divorce. Though only thirty miles distant, Mae hadn't seen her in several years. The last time they were together was an awkward, man-less Christmas. Ruth served ham, reheated with a single clove pressed into each cube, and baked sweet potatoes. Sparse conversation flirted at the edge of being meaningful, but never penetrated it.

Mae held the front door open, mindful of blocking Bree from bolting outside. Her mother's face had aged decades in mere years. Her hair had turned gray. Crow's feet became dinosaur tracks.

"Hello," Ruth said. Her lips formed a thin smile.

"Come in, Mom… come in!" Mae backed away from the door, glanced at her computer, and the single paragraph of her midterm paper. All that white. So few words. So much research.

"I didn't call," Ruth said. She stared across the living room, beyond Mae.

"You should have called. I'd have made something." Mae shifted her weight from one foot to the other. "I'll make coffee."

Ruth followed her into the kitchen. Mae glanced at the grime on the shield above the stove. Did her mother see it? Or was she looking at the jelly bonded to the kitchen table, underneath a scattering of salt.

"My, look at that."

Mae turned with a can of Folgers in hand.

Ruth studied the open cupboard. "You come into good fortune?" Ruth opened the refrigerator, the freezer. A cabinet. She closed one cupboard and opened the next. "Look at this. Canned chicken and turkey? Soup? There must be thirty cans of soup. Did WIC buy all this food? Or did Cory? You still with Cory?"

Mae filled a coffee pot with tap water. "No."

"Why? He turned out all right, didn't he?"

"Mom, why'd you come? What's wrong?"

Ruth dragged a chair from the table. "This table is like the one I had growing up. Aluminum was the rage. It's Larry and me. We're having problems."

"You've been divorced eight years."

"I need to talk to you about your father."

The first scent of coffee drifted through the air. Mae leaned against the counter and crossed her arms. "You know he doesn't want anything to do with me."

"There are things you don't know. That I want to tell you, now."

"Was it the milkman?"

"Don't joke. This is hard enough."

"Have a cookie."

Joe Stipe drove a GM double-axle with a step side. He had a red, white, and blue bug deflector and a black POW-MIA bumper sticker. For his sixty-first birthday his wife had hired a local artist to airbrush an eagle on the tailgate. In her eyes, Stipe carried the weight of the world on his tax-bearing shoulders. It was right to proclaim his patriotic superiority to anyone following him. Hell, he paid their taxes, along with half their neighbors.

Stipe felt no need to correct his wife for considering him a hero, but he did find the eagle a little ostentatious.

"Don't forget to pick up an apple pie at the grocery," she'd said this morning.

Stipe drove slow, unhurried by the Honda Civic riding his bumper. The car swerved across the center line but an oncoming pickup stymied the pass. It veered to the other lane again but backed off in the face of a blind curve on a hill. Stipe checked his side mirror and his rearview. The Civic was completely hidden behind the GM's tailgate.

Stipe thought of the pistol tucked under the seat. He tramped the brake and waited for the thud. Tires squealed. The Civic squirted into the passing lane, and with a zip-rattle sound raced ahead. The car sat too low to grant a view of the driver, but Stipe noted the plate. 2FST4U.

The car zoomed around a bend. When the tinny exhaust faded Stipe was alone with his thoughts, elbow out the window.

He was going to see Chief Smylie and had a feeling he might have to lean on him. Smylie was fond of Baer Creighton's whiskey.

Of the half-dozen men in the county who stilled moonshine, Creighton was the maestro. Stipe had been to Creighton's still, after his man Huck Barrow had failed to convince Creighton to join Stipe's cartel. Stipe went to tell Creighton he would either join or be beaten out of the business.

Creighton wasn't there—only his dog. Stipe had sized up Creighton's operation in a single glance. It was a boiler and a copper tube.

Stipe got the feeling Creighton was like a pool hustler. He'd use a warped house cue to school a yuppie with a five-hundred-dollar stick.

Stipe had pried information from stillers as they folded their operations into his. Creighton's expertise resulted from his indenture to an old master. Gunter Stroh had been a chemist for the German government. In World War I he refined the manufacture of wood alcohol. He immigrated to the United States in the sixties. Took on Creighton as an apprentice in the early seventies. While Stipe served his country in Vietnam, Stroh taught Creighton to be a master moonshiner. When the old master died, Creighton took his place.

Creighton was known to dump imperfect shine into the dirt rather than sell it and despoil his name.

Topping Creighton's quality was out of the question. The only option was to help him arrive at a new understanding of his best interest. Through his proxy, Stipe had made Creighton the same offer as he had all the other local stillers. They'd enjoy ostensible autonomy, distribute through him, and receive monopolistic price controls. Stipe would skim a portion of the enhanced revenue and everyone would make more money, for organizing.

Stipe had anticipated offering Creighton two stark alternatives. Join, or face an ultra-competitive market pricing him out of business. Though he failed to meet Creighton he decided to fire a warning shot. He lowered the cartel's prices.

Then he learned most of Creighton's buyers were as happy with what he charged as they were with what he produced. Creighton had the better monopoly: brand loyalty.

Years passed and Creighton enjoyed prosperity at Stipe's expense. Stipe upped the cartel's prices, but doing so without increasing quality only drove more business to Creighton, where the quality was superior and value fair. Creighton forced Stipe to maintain forever-low prices. He was not gaining the profit his scheme was due.

To make things right, he designed this last round of manipulation. He'd bend Creighton until bones snapped, and if he didn't relent, Stipe would break him in two.

From Creighton's behavior with the dogs, Stipe suspected Creighton would end up dead. He all but sealed that fate when he killed Achilles.

Men grew attached to dogs. Stipe had been fond of Achilles; the way he moved across a fight ring was something to behold. Whirling, flipping —he was an acrobat. The dog was wily from experience. Achilles was a brute, and sure to be the founding stone of a new line of champions. Stipe loved him. But what was lovable about Creighton's wretched coward?

Dog turned tail. No gameness at all. In fact, the fight was so lame the men lost interest. It would have been an embarrassment to any organizer. Stipe had ended the match early so the men wouldn't leave. There was no way to compare a dog as miserable as Creighton's to a warrior like Achilles.

Stipe had delayed studding Achilles when the bitch Medusa had gone into heat. He waited, affording Achilles more time to pile up exploits. The more he accumulated, the greater the value of his eventual progeny. Besides, Achilles was in no real danger. Stipe organized the fights. There were only a handful of animals of Achilles's ability, and Stipe could ensure they never met.

But he never considered the possibility that Creighton would sneak into the compound. Put a bullet in Achilles's head. Muscling Creighton cost money, but now it was more than a business challenge. Creighton's retribution was an affront.

In having Creighton's dog stolen, fought, and abandoned, Stipe had a singular purpose. Convince Creighton to join the cartel. The only alternative was absolute destruction. To convince a man like Creighton, Stipe knew he had to be willing to go all the way.

In visiting Chief Smylie, Stipe would set the conclusion in motion.

Creighton's habits were his weakness.

Stipe pulled into an empty space beside Chief Smylie's Suburban.

If Smylie had a problem accommodating Stipe's request, well, he'd throw in a choice pick from Medusa's next litter. And if that didn't work, Smylie would learn of his son's connections in Baltimore and Washington. The risks he was taking.

So often, good business was a matter of reminding men what they had to lose.

CHAPTER TWENTY

I t's morning and I'm late to rise. Took a leak at sunup, gandered through the woods, looking for an early-morning sniper. Wondered if I ought to check the traps I set by the Hun blind.

Fred snores. While I was up I snuck a hand under the wool blanket and he was plenty warm. Besides the blanket he sleeps on, he has another around the whole box, and then another folded on top of that. Not taking any chances with his condition making him weak, though truth told, he gets up as much as he wants. What's it been? Three weeks? He breathes natural, and soon I'll pull the stitches out of his chest. Rest of him, save his eyes, looks normal. He's not quite right in the head, but his body's come along.

Fred can sleep as much as he wants. Me, no matter how I twist there's a gap in the sleeping bag that lets the sun creep through. Once I wake, I can't lay more than a few minutes.

That beating the other night didn't break me. Anything but. Those boys thought they'd teach me something about my place in the world, and they did.

They beat me silly and now they think I'm broke. All they did was steel my mind. My place according to them is eking out a living selling shine, and one day I'll die in the woods and no one will be the wiser. But I live in the woods because it beats what the world has to offer. I come and go as I want. Answer to nobody.

I'm thinking all this from the warmth of my bag, angry at sunlight.

A horn lets out at the house.

I climb out of the bag and set about getting my clothes. Now I feel the full measure of the beating I took. My chest and back protest. Kidneys push a sick feeling through me. Sitting up, all my blood sluices to my feet and I'm dizzy. Brace hands on knees.

Once my heart realizes I mean to see about the house, everything steadies out.

I strap on Smith.

Each step brings out another grumble or deepens one I thought I had a handle on. Time I come upon the house, I doubt there's a single stretch of me not bruised or busted.

From inside I look out the window. It's Pete Bleau. There's a passenger in the truck, hidden in cigar smoke. No red comes from either. No juice.

Must be after the apple.

Pete rolls his window and cigar smoke billows out. His passenger is Butch, his dog.

"You got to know I don't appreciate you dumping that brandy in my face. But it turns out moonshine don't make you blind, even straight in the eyes."

"Uh-huh."

"Come after that brandy," Pete says. He looks me over head to toe. "You look pretty well worked over."

"How many gallon?"

"Six for starters."

I hold out my hand. "Money first."

His eyebrows dip. He squirms his arm behind his back. Comes out with a wallet and fishes bills. Counts thirty-six. Butch twists away from looking out the side window. His eyeballs are bloodshot.

"You said six gallon," I say. "That's sixty."

He pulls more bills and hands them through the window. "What happened to you?"

"Roll down the other window. Your dog is stoned."

Inside the house I grab jugs from a downstairs rack against the cement block wall. If they knew how easy it would be to rob me, a lot of men would. Never lock the doors and I spend ten months a year in the woods. Make a point of always coming out of the house, but the chain of thoughts gets me musing.

"You get lost in there?" Pete says.

"Shut up, Pete."

I tuck the jugs in the hay on the truck bed. Pete has rolled down the side window for Butch. I return for the last jugs. When I come out with them Pete has a thought taking shape on his lips.

"What?"

"This ass-beating you took… anything to do with that dog of yours? And Stipe?"

I tuck the last jug under straw. "You talk to Stipe? That it?"

"Ain't seen him."

His eyes say he's playing it straight. "Why you bring Butch today?"

"It ain't that anybody would take him. But why take the chance?"

"They bust into people's houses?"

"Why not? Stipe has the police chief at the fights most every week."

"You'd think they'd steal dogs from some other town."

"Nah. This is the town they got sewed up."

"Yeah." I push off the truck. "Something else on your mind?"

"They beat you the other night, didn't they?"

I don't answer.

"I was at the barber shop this morning. Heard bits and pieces."

"From?"

"Frank."

"Frank?"

"Murdoch."

"Ah."

"They got more in store, Baer. They plan on hurting you but good."

"How's that?"

"Dunno. But it's big. Murdoch made it sound like the end times for one man only. You do something special, set them off? Seems like a lot of trouble for one man, 'less he helped make it."

"I ask myself why someone would want to steal my dog, and all I come up with is some folks enjoy evil. Some men slap around their women. Some start wars. Anywhere you go there's men unhappy without they got a foot on another man's neck. But I haven't done anything special. Been minding my own business thirty—"

"What?"

"Nothing."

"Yeah. Well keep your eyes open." Pete starts the truck engine. "You got them boys riled."

"Thanks, Pete."

He nods, and backs the truck. His grimace says he thinks this's the last he'll see of me.

CHAPTER TWENTY-ONE

W alking helps my bones. There's no particular ache worse than the rest. They will all require considerable spiritual intervention to rectify. So I brought two flasks of the spirit, and the first is already empty.

Brisk day. I keep my hands in my pockets and my eyes on my feet. Lots to think about on the way to see Mae, making sure Cory Smylie hasn't retaliated.

She always had the brightest hair. That's the first thing I thought when I saw Ruth holding her.

I'd gone to the city and found work rebuilding diesel engines on the big rigs. They put me in a bay with a set of tools and a 1962 F-model Mack. Told me to tear it down. By the time I'd put it back together, I'd have my schooling. Boss was a crusty jarhead who served in Korea, and liked to get to the point of things. I didn't have anything better to do than work. I was there all day, every day, close to two years. Found a bunk-house nearby and saved every penny.

I stood looking at Ruth holding Mae. Larry came to the door beside her, and my fingers tingled. I thought about a score of letters Ruth had written, declaring her loyalty. Asking me to come home.

I thought about the one time I did.

She stood with Mae in her arms and her eyes sparkled with tears.

No red at all.

A truck rolls by, slows as the driver takes a long look at me. It's a chubby girl in a Nissan. Her chin reminds me of those flat-faced Mack trucks I worked on, with a chrome bumper all the way to the ground. I don't know her and she keeps moving—but even seeing me on the road shoulder, she's brewing deceit.

Lies and treachery. The world is a thundercloud that moves as fast as a soul walks, and no faster.

Larry stood beside Ruth and he glowed red. Sparks shot from my fingers; my joints had an extra jolt, like the juice made me stronger. I don't remember crossing the dirt. Only got off one punch before Ruth cut between us, with Mae in her arms. Mae screamed and Ruth wailed, and Larry bounced off the wall.

Ruth said I needed to leave. Looked at me like the things that needed explaining weren't ever going to be.

I shook, befuddled. Couldn't ask a question. The electric was all the communication I needed. I stepped back from the porch and missed the plank. Landed on my back and it rattled me loose from wanting to murder my brother. He came around Ruth and stood above me, shaking. Blood on his lip. Ruth stepped farther into the house.

I was on my back, up on elbows. I fished all the money I'd saved in two years from my pocket, peeled two twenties off the roll and threw the rest at Larry. It bounced off his chest. Landed in the dirt.

"This's my house now," I said.

"You can't have it," Larry said.

"If I get off the ground before that money does, one of us is dead."

Larry studied me. Ruth stood behind the screen. Larry wasn't moving, and my blood was boiling. I pulled my legs back and shifted to my side.

Ruth came out the door, jostled around Larry, and swooped to the money. A small diamond gleamed on her finger. She pulled Larry by the arm. I sat and listened to them argue inside the house, and tried to add facts that couldn't no-how go together.

All those letters. Lovey-dovey words. Faith-filled poems. Stories of recent small town events and updates on the weather. She'd never once said, "I went back to Larry and had a baby. So go to hell and get out of my life."

I got in the Nova and backed into the turnaround. Sat on the hood and smoked a cigarette. Larry came out with a box and Ruth followed. Back and forth, they loaded his truck.

Pulling out of the drive, Larry slowed beside me. Without meeting my eye he said, "I didn't want this rathole anyway."

He was gone. She was gone. I had the house.

I spent that night in the woods.

I'm at Mae's. The driveway is empty. I rap the door and Morgan pulls it open. She's in my arms, twisting my hair and nuzzling my neck. Now Bree's here—with purple jelly on the sides of her mouth. She puts a finger to her lips and shushes me. Hugs my knee, steps on my feet. I walk her inside.

Mae's doing dishes. Joseph sleeps in the other room on the sofa, snugged against the back pillow. There are two glasses at the table and two plates with the remains of a PBJ-and-milk lunch. Mae finally brings her eyes to me. Must be brooding on that kiss.

"What happened to you?" She dries her hands in a dish-towel and comes closer. She hesitates.

"You got a little time?"

She takes my hand.

I say, "You keep up with your mother?"

"Why? Did she do this to you?"

"What to me?"

She touches my cheek with her open hand; eases her thumb across my cheekbone. Aches.

"That's nothing." I ease her hand away.

She squints like a mother.

"Wanted to ask about Ruth."

"What are the odds?" She shakes her head, gives a smile that reads like a wince. "Mom's been by."

"Been here? I don't reckon I come up in the conversation?"

Mae takes Morgan from my arm and stands her on the floor. Leads me outside.

"She say something bad?"

Mae sits on a lawn chair with frayed nylon straps. I take the other.

"She hasn't known what to make of you for years. Why are you asking now?"

Why am I asking? I want to know if there's any hope of redeeming a love affair that died the day I saw Mae in her mother's arms. I'm getting old. Had the snot beat out of me. Considering action that'll land me in heaven or hell, one. Reached my breaking point, and ready to holler so loud they hear me in Idaho.

"Nothing special. I think on her now and again."

"You two were an item, back in the day."

"You heard about the day?"

"A little."

Mae gleams pink, and it's unusual enough I need to study her eyes.

"What, Uncle Baer?"

"Nothing." The pink is faint like mother-of-pearl, and kind of pulses like a heartbeat. "You can tell me the truth," I say.

The pink vanishes.

CHAPTER TWENTY-TWO

"She thinks she still loves you."

I stand. My knee pops. The lawn chair falls over. Mae isn't one to lie much but I won't believe it. Should have braced myself for some such stupidity, on account of seeing the pink. Could be they're both liars. Something in the blood on her mother's side that makes a full-throated falsehood look like a whisper.

If that was true, maybe one time she'd have written a letter. When I walked all the way to Mars Hill and watched her for three days... Finally struck the nerve to say hello... That would have been a fine time to say, "Hello, Baer, I love you."

If she was in love all this time, she wouldn't have bedded my pencil-pushing brother.

"What's gotten into you?" Mae says.

I go into the house and check the cupboards because that's all I can think to do. Make sure she has enough food, then she can go to hell. Bree's got wide eyes and Morgan looks caught doing something wrong. They study me keen.

"You two got enough food?"

Course they do. Never ate better. Every cupboard's like I left it. Only been a few days... Ruth's in love with me my royal English ass.

Footsteps. Mae's at the kitchen.

"Baer!"

"Cory Smylie been here?"

"No."

"Good."

I shoulder past. Leave the front door open. Otherwise, I'll throw it off its hinges.

I'm a mile down the road and her words still play. "She loves you."

Well who are you to know?

Don't recall asking.

So I guess I'm not the only one who can't see when she's lying.

Well, what if I don't love her any more?

What if I never loved her, and all we had was a bunch of car sex?

I can't remember anything else. What if I hang onto her memory so I don't have to write off the whole human race, and I don't want her to love me back? Did you ever think of that?

Meddling woman.

I'm three hundred yards from the house and the still, and a windshield glints through the trees. Somebody's parked in the drive, and another truck is along the road.

A rifle echoes. I pick up the pace. Another shot.

Fred.

Somebody came back for Fred.

Smith flaps on my hip. I yank the grip. Move fast as I can without stretching a run. In the back of my heart I know I'm late. Someone got two shots at a blind dog. Not likely he missed.

No, my hurry's to make sure he doesn't get away with it. That's what I tell myself so I can ease off my pace and lighten the strain on the pounder in my chest.

The truck on the side of the road is white.

I duck into the woods. Weave through brush. Metal clashes on metal and two more gunshots echo. First noise was an axe, someone having a good time with my still. Second blast was a shotgun.

I'm fifty yards out, coming from behind. Three men—two with long guns and one with an axe. The axe man has knocked the cooker from its blocks . He's going to town on the sides.

I stop at a tree. Aim with both hands, shaking so bad I rest my left wrist against the bark.

That isn't Stipe's crew.

That's Mercer. He works for both the revenue service and the state force for liquor law enforcement. Don't know the other two men. Mercer might have borrowed them from some other jurisdiction.

These men might not know Fred's at home. He's more than likely shivering inside his box under the tarp. Surely these revenuers didn't come to whack a dog?

I point Smith at the ground. Ease the hammer forward and slip the gun into my holster. Anything wrong with Fred, they'll be teeth in the dirt. Hands up, I step out from the tree. "Hey, boys."

The two gunmen draw stocks to shoulders.

"Easy, Mercer," I call. "Easy."

I cover the distance slow, let them gather their minds. They have the power and know it, so I don't see any red.

"Hey, Mister Creighton..." Mercer says. "Thought you'd have run."

I come within the circle. The still's full of shotgun and axe holes. The copper tube's hacked in pieces, nice clean cuts, like he rested it on a log for support. Doubler is split. They cut four mash barrels through with holes. Fermented corn and apple spills out and soaks the ground. The air stinks of rot, sweet with sugar and heady with undistilled shine.

I meet Mercer's eyes. He's a young man, stocky like a log of firewood, and his small bald head sits atop like a bead of bird shit. I let my arms drift to my sides and check inside the tarp. "Mister Mercer, I hope you didn't shoot my dog."

Fred's head lifts above the diesel turbine crate. His ears are up.

One of Mercer's boys points his rifle at Fred.

"Mister, that dog's half dead as it is. Blind as a bat and can't hardly walk. If you need to be afraid of somebody, point the rifle at me."

He obliges.

I tromp to Fred and whisper as I come. His tail beats the crate.

"You're under arrest, Mister Creighton. You know how this goes. You're coming with us."

I kneel at Fred. "You all right, stud? These knotheads shoot you?"

I run my hands over his coat. Look at the crate for BB holes. Fred makes a couple throat sounds and I'm so happy I kiss him.

I face the men. "Guess you don't like me wearing this."

With my index finger and thumb, I dangle Smith from my hip and step it to the closest man. He takes it without changing his law enforcement scowl.

"Mercer—this is the standard deal, right?"

"You work with us? We book you today. Judge fines you tomorrow, you rebuild this copper contraption tomorrow night."

"Fair enough. Let me feed Fred and get him covered. Don't want him to freeze."

Mercer nods.

He didn't give me any red nor juice, but under the tarp I figure I may as well plan on nothing he said coming true. I fill Fred's dish with three eggs, and use my saucepan for another bowl, and fill it with dry dog food.

"One more thing," I say. "Lemme run over the house."

"Looks like you got everything you own here."

"Look here, Mister Mercer. I didn't run. Give you my gun. Just asking a little help."

"Roy—you done with the still?"

"Yup."

"C'mon, Mister Creighton. Lessgo."

I lead through the woods to the back of my house. "I got to go inside."

Mercer follows, alone. I stand before the rack. All total, there's a hundred gallon or more. Some are special blends, corn, wheat, barley, but flavored with fruit. Makes fruit whiskey, if you can noodle that. Mercer's eyes shift along the rows and he licks his lips.

"What was all that stupidity about?" I say.

"We had to hit you," Mercer says.

"Had to?"

"When Chief Smylie hisself phones in the tip, it trumps."

"Chief Smylie, huh?" I grab a jug and wipe the dust from the shoulder.

"What you doing?" he says. "You can't have liquor in jail."

I shake my head. "Later on, why don't you come back and help yourself to a couple jugs? Special stuff's on the end. See this 'G'—that's grape. You got plum here, strawberry, apple, pear."

"I'd a thought 'P' woulda been for peaches."

"Don't do peaches."

"Peach'd be nice."

"Peach is for pussies. We good?"

"We good."

Jail cell's down a hall, not like the Western movies where you sit and jaw at your jailer.

Chuck Preston (I knew his daddy, but not that he had a boy this old) leads me in cuffs, for show. There's nobody around. I could brain him and walk across the county before anyone figured there was a jailbreak. But that isn't how we do things.

The code is simple. They come on a stiller and he sees them, he has the right to run. They make mincemeat of his operation and don't come back for a while. But if they bust him, he doesn't fight. There's no sense shooting the lawman when he'll only put you in jail a night or two. The biggest pain is they smash the still beyond the restorative skills of even the handiest hillbilly.

Well, I don't have to explain turning myself in. I let them keep shooting, they were liable to poke a hole in Fred.

Mercer took the jug I carried out of the house. I chose plum—the only jug in the whole basement with the official liquor stamp on it. There are a lot of stillers in these parts. Judge is liable to have run across all sorts of bribes, but plum is an unusual fruit. Not many stillers have the patience to tinge a gallon with it. In all I'd say apples are the most common. You get to strawberries or plums and you're dealing with high-dollar squeezins.

Any judge would know that.

Also picked plum because it has a little something else in it. How that something else came to be is a story any Carolina judge will appreciate.

Chuck Preston slams the door behind me. I'd prefer one of the old-style jails with bars. See freedom on the other side. Keep it fresh in mind. But nowadays they don't want men stewing on liberty. Your view is a cement wall and a thick metal door painted light brown, like a rich woman's pants.

I sit on the bunk sixty, seventy years, and they finally shut the light off. I wonder if some animal smells Fred and knows he can't hardly defend himself. We have coyotes now, and a pack would give a blind dog trouble, pit bull or not.

I think on Mae and her crazy words. If she believed what she said, that Ruth was in love with me, she doesn't know her mother. But she didn't believe those words. She was pink before she said them.

What would I do if it was true?

Sitting in a jail cell, nothing. I can ponder the future, but without a blade or spoon or chisel or hacksaw...

At least I have the sense to close my eyes and wander a bit. Sitting in the cell, stretching out on the bench and folding my hands into a pillow, I let go of the whole world. For tonight. I can't protect Fred from here. I can't make sure those dogfighters don't steal some other dog and fight him into hamburger. In this cell, the most I can do is get my mind right.

What would I do if Ruth was in love with me? Real love, like neither of us ever knew?

I'd take her hand. Put it in both of mine for a long while, and I'd try to smell her hair without her knowing what I was up to. Wait for the air to carry the scent. And once I got that perfume and I had her hands all warm and used to mine, I'd slip to her elbow and bury my face in her hair. Breathe it in so deep—

Bunch of nonsense. Mae's out of her mind. And the rock-bottom truth is, I don't know what I feel for Ruth. All I've been doing is writing letters and wishing I was still young enough to get laid in the back of a Nova without throwing a hip out.

Stretched on the jailhouse bunk, I get sleepy quick. No stars or trees whispering back and forth, or the crick keeping somber time. All the stuff that would make my heart beat fast and fill me with worry is gone, stuck on the other side of the wall.

This is Stipe's doing.

Back and forth, each time worse.

CHAPTER TWENTY-THREE

They trucked me to the courthouse in Asheville. Brought me through the back, where the court connects to the jail. My nose runs with the morning nip. I'm not dressed for cold weather any better than I was yesterday afternoon. I wipe my schnoz on my sleeve and it leaves a streak. That's all I need, have the judge see that streak turned into a silver crust flashing sunlight at him.

Us criminals sit on a wood bench. We six are a surly lot. More whiskers and hair than all the rest of Asheville, now that it's booming yuppies. I know Buck Hedgecock, down on the end, last in line, but he isn't sober enough to recognize me. The man between us folds and unfolds an Allis-Chalmers cap. First time in court, I can tell.

Worst thing about sitting next to these boys... every one of them is going to start thinking about the lies he needs to tell the judge. It's going to feel like they slapped me in the electric chair. Soon as they start thinking their stories.

And the body-stink. That's kind of raw.

A man in a crumpled suit shuffles to the man on the other end of the bench. "Charlie Crystal?"

"Thass right."

"You guilty or not?"

"Who the hell're you?"

"Public defender."

"I ain't done nothing."

"Right. Okay. Not guilty. You got any proof?"

"That the way it works these days?"

"Well, that's the county attorney over there. He's got nine witnesses ready to swear you were drunk and smashed six windows on Merrimon last night. You want to say you didn't, you might have some evidence that goes against his."

"I got my rights. I want a trial. Jury and all, like the Constitution says."

"Sure. Of course. But in a minute, Judge Omar Bradley Hickory's going to climb up to that bench, and you'll think you're looking at God. You'll want to piss yourself. My advice? Say you did it and you're consumed with remorse. Judge Hickory will give you a fine, order restitution, and send you home."

"I could use a dose o' restitution."

Ruth.

Mae said Ruth was still hung up on me. Wouldn't that be a barrel of titties?

Doesn't feel good leaving Fred like I did, but circumstances in this world are rough, no matter intentions. I don't begrudge folks doing their jobs.

But I have a considerable problem with the meddlers that made it against the law for a man to sell homemade hooch. If I take apples and make them drinkable, and other folks are thirsty for apples, I ought to make money. Crystal clear. Don't see how it's different from a man that cuts a tree into boards, or another digs coal out the ground, or oil. They act like rednecks are ignorant and liquor is evil. But if that was the case, I wouldn't be able to sell a hundred gallons a week, peak season.

Naw. Bottom line, they decided long ago to pick one thing a lot of people want and won't ever do without, and tax it. Comes to it, Judge Omar Bradley Hickory will get an earful. It'll be the first unvarnished truth he hears all day.

If it comes to it. But I'll stick with the plan, until.

Mercer comes in. I can't see his hand from my angle. He better have brought that jug. He meets my look and dips his head.

Defender stands above me with empty eyes, as if the real courtroom work is lofty and beyond. He has the look of a man who wouldn't notice a red ant chewing his ear at a picnic. He stares at the sky, thinking about the sanctity of the law.

"Baer Creighton."

"I surely done it, but the law's plain nonsense. How do I plead that?"

"That falls under 'guilty.'"

"Fair enough. Can I go first?"

"Judge Hickory will follow the docket."

"You sure he's gone?" Burly said.

"I watched Mercer haul him away." Ernie shifted sideways in the Suburban seat. Burly sat behind the wheel. They were approaching Baer's house. Ernie's gaze dipped to the knife on Burly's hip. He'd been uncomfortable since he'd climbed into the Suburban. If he'd seen the Bowie knife, he wouldn't have gotten in.

"Good," Burly said. "You look at the still? Cut up pretty nice?"

"More than that. Lot more."

Burly slowed as Baer Creighton's house came up on the left. He looked out the window and Ernie noted the corded muscles in Burly's neck. The house was unchanged.

"We ought to burn it down," Ernie said.

"Don't get ahead of yourself. Stipe don't like freelancers. You've already made him uncomfortable."

Ernie thought of Creighton's still site, which he'd visited right after the revenue boys hauled Creighton away. "Didn't I give him good information? Isn't that what friendship is all about?"

"Yeah." Burly swung the wheel to the right and the Suburban plowed over the grassy drive of the Brown farm. He parked. They sat a moment, both leaning forward, studying the house. "Thing of it is, Stipe don't trust nobody. So you come and say you been following his enemy and got an idea, and suggest bad things... how does he know you're not setting him up?"

"Come on, Burly. You know me. Didn't you tell him I'm okay?"

"Yeah, well, I don't know you too well either."

Burly opened the door and stepped outside. Ernie followed and they walked toward the house together.

Stipe being suspicious was bad news. Ernie had been too excited, maybe too aggressive in his approach. He said, "Then why are you even here?"

"How do you know Stipe didn't already have things in motion?"

Ernie stopped and Burly kept walking. The Bowie knife slapped his thigh with each stride. Ernie hurried to catch up. "I'm just trying to help the guy out. Man in his shoes needs information, and I wanted him to see I can get it for him."

"Everybody knows Creighton's been robbing the Brown farm since the old man died."

"Well, I got to ask again. Why are we here?"

"What do you think?"

"I'm in trouble."

"Maybe. You didn't think you'd make the man wonder? Show up at his house and tell him how to kill his enemy? You got to be real close to a man before you suggest murder."

Ernie considered the ramifications. He imagined what the Bowie knife might feel like dragged across his throat. "Does he like my plan? Because I'll do it. That way it was all my idea and everything. He didn't know anything. I'll cover my own tracks and that's that."

Burly faced Ernie. He rested his palm on his knife. "What's your angle?"

Ernie stepped back. "No angle." His mind raced. Burly was a big man. If he lunged and managed to grab him, Ernie was as good as dead. But if he could keep a few feet away until he could think things through...

There was the gold in the tree, but he didn't want to dangle that in front of Burly just yet. Not now, when he could no longer trust him. He decided on the truth.

"No angle," Ernie said. "Burly, I want what you got. You rub elbows with the man who controls everything worthwhile in the county. He runs the dogs, and he's bought about every still. Stipe's the swingin' dick in these parts and I did him a favor. That's all."

Burly pulled his knife.

Ernie took another step backward.

Burly pressed the blade into a siding board and angled the blade downward. Wood chipped. He snapped it off and turned it over in his hand, then tossed it to Ernie.

"Awful dry."

Burly kicked yellow grass growing close to the house. He walked alongside and turned the corner. Ernie trailed him, but stopped before rounding. He listened until the sound of Burly's feet rustling the grass grew distant, then eased past the edge.

"So how long's it going to take for Creighton to come over and steal every piece of copper out of this house?" Burly said.

"He's got to get out of jail first."

"He'll get three days."

"Then he'll be here that night."

"You know Creighton's ways that well, huh?" Burly said.

"He'll be here that night. He's as cheap as they come. He won't spend a penny if he can help it. You wouldn't believe what he does with—"

Burly stopped at the next corner. Drew his hand across the baked and splintered wood. "You come get me when Creighton shows up. And here on out, you got information for Stipe, run it through me first."

Judge Omar Bradley Hickory's no slouch. Been up there fifteen minutes and found two men guilty. Another is back in jail, pending word on his sanity. The other two are out a thousand bucks each. Plus they have to go to the anonymous alcoholics, and do a hundred hours of community service. Hickory looks like a school textbook picture of the abolitionist John Brown. White hair and a scowl built into his forehead. I heard cowboy boots clonk when he come in.

Only thing is, when these other men stood and lied to the judge, I didn't feel hardly a thing. Couldn't scope their eyes on account of their turned heads. But I'd have thought with me being sober as a skunk and sitting right next to them, I'd have felt sparks.

Bailiff says my name and the defender says, "Guilty, Judge."

"Creighton. Says here you run a still out of Gleason."

"That's right. Say, Judge? You remember Lou Creighton?"

"No. He kin of yours?"

"Uncle."

"He a stiller, too?"

"If he was, he'd be a good one. Mostly he just tells stories."

"Stories, huh?"

"You ever hear the one 'bout Mabel Kinney? Down Old Fort?"

"Doesn't sound familiar."

"Well this old girl could still. Had her an operation size of the Daniel Distillery, all in her tobacco barn. Everyone that drank shine from here to Boston preferred the Kinney label."

"Yeah, I've heard of Kinney."

"She was in the barn bossing orders—and I can tell all this because you law fellers put her in jail and she died there. So I'm not breaking the code—well she was in the barn snapping orders. Now, everybody knew she was right intolerant about tobacco."

"This is pertinent to the proceedings, of course?"

"If you like your liquor stories, it sure is."

"Do I look bemused, Mister Creighton?"

"Well, if you look that way all the time, I'd say no."

Hickory smiles flat. "She was right intolerant about tobacco."

"So one of her boys has a mouth of chaw and he don't think she's looking. He lets a spit loose into a floorboard knot-hole, in the corner where he always does. Mabel Kinney sees this big ol' string of goop out his mouth, and comes stomping over. Says the habit's disgusting and foul and if any of that spit ever got in the whiskey mash, it'd be the end of her."

"This a true story?"

"Well, that man with the chaw was Uncle Lou."

"Don't waste the court's time, Creighton."

"Mabel lit into him—beating, pulling hair, pushing and shoving. Lou was a firecracker 'bout my size. Way he tells it, he's about to lay into her, since she was more man than woman anyway. He said, 'I'll spit my whole chaw in that whiskey mash, and you won't do a thing 'bout it.'

"He breaks loose of her and starts edging to the vat. Mabel looks at the rafters like for God to intervene, and sees old tobacco leaves hanging from the beams. She goes pale as piss. Bosses Lou and some other kid up there to fetch down those tobacco leaves. Throws them in the mash and that's how come, soon as a man tries Kinney Shine, he's stuck like he smoked a pack of Camels."

Hickory shakes his head.

"Judge, I don't mean to be impertinent, but I thought you might like a jug of them squeezins. Mercer, you got that jug?"

Hickory shifts. Eyebrows float.

"Now judge, this ain't illegal shine at all. You can see the stamp from the liquor board. They only sold fifty-seven of them stamps since they been out, and I bought the first twenty. I'd like you to take that jug as a token of my appreciation of the court, and the fine job y'all do."

"Bailiff, bring me that jug."

Bailiff takes the jug from Mercer and carries it. Judge Hickory bites the cork and pries it loose. He sniffs.

"This tastes bad, I'm holding you in contempt."

"I hope you're a rye man, Judge, because that's rye whiskey with a touch of tobacco."

Hickory upends the jug. Adam's apple rises and falls one solitary time. The jug hits the bench top with a thud. Hickory beats his chest. Coughs like his voice is gone. Waits. Coughs again. Wipes his eye.

"Creighton, you innocent or guilty of the charges today?"

"Guilty, but the law's pure ass nonsense, Judge."

"Well, it's our law, and we stick to it. Stand up, Creighton."

I stand. He's a stern old bat, and like the public defender said, I want to piss myself.

"I'm finding you guilty, Creighton. Sentence is a three-thousand-dollar fine. One year imprisonment."

His hand moves to the jug. I can't breathe.

"You have any more of this?"

"What I don't got, I can make."

"Sentence reduced to three days minus time served. But you still owe me three grand. Bailiff—"

CHAPTER TWENTY-FOUR

Cory Smylie was forty-five minutes away from Gleason. He eased his F-150 past a house in the sticks, outside of Hendersonville. His lights were off. His windows were down. A large black dog bayed at the end of a chain attached to a doghouse. It was at the edge of the yard about thirty feet from the house. Closer than Cory liked, but doable. He drove until a wedge of woods blocked his view, coasted to a stop, and turned off the engine.

Cory lit a joint and sucked in the smoke while the dog barked.

The routine was predictable. In a minute, the porch light would flash on. The door would open. A man would curse in his underwear, scream the dog's name, and slam the door. The light would go off and the dog would shut up. It wouldn't matter, because the man wouldn't come back within two minutes. That was all the time Cory needed.

He gripped a Taser he'd stolen from his father. The clown had actually asked Cory if he'd seen it. Gee, Pop, what would I want with a Taser? His mother, quick to Cory's defense, suggested deputies had absconded with it. A year before there'd been a scandal in Hickory, or somewhere east. Deputies had tazed one another while drinking beer at the hunting lodge, and one of them sued.

The Taser was comfortable in his hand.

This was his first stop of the night. He reached for the door handle and paused. Yeah. He was forgetting something. He switched his dome light to the middle position so the light wouldn't turn on, and then stepped outside.

The Labrador still barked, though his master's cussing had stifled his enthusiasm. Cory crept along the road, still sheltered by the woods. He sucked a final hit from the joint and tossed it to the pavement.

Cory turned along the lawn's edge. The dog let out a volley of sharp barks.

Dogs were tricky. They moved fast. This Lab was big and ornery. Cory grinned. He could do anything.

The Lab went silent. Cory walked closer. He was twenty feet away, too far for the Taser. The dog dropped his head. He growled and stepped toward Cory.

"That's right. You come to me."

Cory raised the Taser and sighted along the top. It was always easier to shoot a dog broadside, but they rarely afforded the opportunity. Dogs liked to face danger head-on.

Cory continued walking. "Hey! That's right. It's all good."

The distance was right.

The Lab launched. The chain jangled and the dog sailed toward him. Whoa, Cory thought. Teeth glinted. Cory adjusted his aim and jerked the trigger.

The dog kept flying.

Cory missed. The dog bowled him to the ground. Cory raised his arms to shield his throat. The Lab bit his wrist, then darted past his arms and snapped shy of his face. Cory pushed back. Swung his arm to his side and with all his might shoved the Taser into the Lab's side.

The contact points blasted fifty thousand volts.

The Labrador grunted and collapsed. Cory rolled to his feet and when he had his balance he kicked the quivering dog in the ribs.

"Don't die. You ain't worth nothing dead."

Cory put away the Taser and carried the dog to his truck.

Stupid animals. Cory slammed the window in the back of the cab. Turned on the radio to drown the growls and whimpers coming from the crates in the bed of his F-150. He'd been prowling the outskirts of Hendersonville half the night. There had to be a better way.

He'd tried to "adopt" several dogs from each shelter in Buncombe and Henderson Counties. Each facility was more than eager to have him take the animals, but they wanted seventy bucks apiece. "To spay or neuter."

"Well, these two won't need neutered. I'll do it."

That didn't go over.

It would have cost seventy bucks a dog. Stipe paid from twenty to a hundred depending on the animal—but a neutered dog wasn't exactly brimming with fight. Cory would do better working at McDonald's.

Plus, how many times could he go back to the same shelter?

He'd surfed the Internet and found a woman operating a nonprofit called Adopt-A-Friend. He took two Rottweilers that both still had their nuts. Stipe paid two hundred for the pair, leaving Cory a profit of sixty dollars. Cory scoured the web but hadn't found any other organizations like Adopt-A-Friend.

There were hundreds of kennels listed in the phone directory. He staked out a couple. Chain link fences. Baying dogs, constant commotion. Hardly easy street. Stealing one would raise such a ruckus he'd end up in a shootout.

The only option left was cruising the streets at night with the windows down. He listened for barking dogs, and tazed them.

Cory shook his head. What was he wasting his time for? The real money was in drugs, not stealing dogs for Joe Stipe. His plan had been to use the work as a stepping stone, like starting out in the mail room. Eventually he'd prove himself and advance deeper into Stipe's organization.

Drugs, he thought. He'd make a hundred bucks an hour, not a night.

But if the drug world offered real money, it also exposed him to real risk. He'd already served time, and another strike would put him in prison until he was forty. Judges were cracking down. Plus, you never knew when some kingpin would go nuts and whack you. You wanted to play in the underworld, you had to be comfortable living on a razor's edge.

Stipe offered a different path. Cory would enjoy the powerful man's protection and rise through the ranks while Stipe took the risks. Cory only had to be the muscle.

He imagined himself as one of Stipe's lieutenants. Stipe asking his opinion on a difficult matter, nodding gravely at Cory's advice, and saying, "Are you sure?"

"I don't see any way out of it."

"You're the best I got. You handle it, son."

That's what he'd say. Cory would nod. "It's going to cost money."

That beat some Columbian slitting his throat with a machete.

Approaching Stipe's trucking compound, Cory slowed. Stipe had hired a crew to build a chain-link fence around the entire place. The posts had fresh dirt tamped at their bases. A pickup sat with tools in the bed. A new gate blocked the approach.

"How do I get in?"

Cory jumped out of the cab, leaving the engine running and the headlights on. He looked inside the compound to the mechanic's garage, and to the house, set back off to the right side. Though it was after two a.m., lights were still on inside both.

Stipe had insisted on face to face communication. Cory didn't have a phone number for him.

A dog growled from inside one of the wooden crates in the bed of his truck. Cory slammed his palm on the top of the crate. "Shut up, Meat!"

"You there!"

Cory raised his hands. He turned his head and saw a man on the other side of the cab, on the inside of the fence, with a rifle aimed from his shoulder. Security?

"Who are you?" the man said.

"Cory. Here to see Mr. Stipe." The man's build looked familiar. He was big, with a belly. "That you, Worley?"

The man slung his rifle over his shoulder and swaggered in front of the headlights. It was Burly Worley after all—the man who'd asked Stipe for a job that night at the fight. Sourcing bait dogs wasn't Hollywood, but it sure beat rent-a-cop security.

Worley produced a key and opened a padlock. He swung the gate open. "You know where to take them?"

"Yeah." Cory hopped into the truck and drove inside.

"Let's see what you got," Stipe said. His eyes were watery and he smelled of alcohol, though he hadn't brought a drink outside. He'd exited the house as Cory pulled in, as if he'd been up waiting. Cory stopped the vehicle and met Stipe at the front porch steps. Stipe was a huge man and walked like it. Cory followed a pace behind.

"Got a big-ass Labrador, a boxer, a pit, and two of them little wiener dogs."

"Two chew toys—and did you say a pit?"

"A female."

"Which crate? Let me see her."

Cory opened the cab and withdrew a long flashlight, also courtesy of the Gleason police. He directed the light beam at the crate closest to the cab. The white-and-brown dog snarled.

"You put her in a pen by herself," Stipe said.

"You ought to see her. She's a blockhead. Beefy as hell. Top-dollar dog."

Stipe grunted, moved sideways and leaned closer. "No bloodline, boy. What, you thought I'd breed her?"

Cory shrugged. "Yeah."

"The breed is the starting point. But then you need years of pairing only the gamest champions. You have to cull weakness from the line for twenty generations to get a dog that won't turn. Have the big lungs, the thick neck, the speed. You don't start off with some mutt."

Cory allowed the light beam to drift.

"Give me that." Stipe snatched the flashlight from Cory's hand.

"What?"

Stipe pressed against the bed and placed the flashlight between the slats.

"That's your pit, huh?"

Cory looked. "That's her."

"That's an American Bulldog."

"Looks the same."

Stipe shined the light into the other crates one by one, grunting at each. Finally he handed the light to Cory and drew out his wallet. "Hundred for the lot."

A hundred. Cory thought of taking the money, wadding it, and shoving it down Stipe's throat. Instead he leaned against the F-150. He'd take the money. He'd drive to Baltimore and connect with some people he knew, and in two days turn that hundred into a thousand.

"What?" Stipe said. "You got a different opinion?"

"I have to do better than that."

"A hundred dollars is a favor. You don't like it, take them back where you got them."

"I got bills. I got kids."

"I know you do. Funny time for you to tell me about that."

"What?"

"Come here smelling of reefer, eyes like two mud puddles. Kids at their mother's, and you don't have a clue what she's doing, do you?"

"This time of night she's in bed."

"Yeah, Cory. But with who?"

"Who?"

"Like you care. Mother of your children involved in the worst kind of sin. Your kids growing up in a house with pure evil. Very hand of Satan rules that house, and you'd rather smoke dope and steal dogs for a living. And you don't even take that serious enough to learn the difference between a bulldog and a pit bull. Only thing the same is half the name."

Stipe offered a hundred-dollar bill. Cory grabbed it.

"Pull these brutes to the back and get them unloaded. Pick up another set of crates—"

"Who's Mae with?"

Stipe stared. "You don't want to know. Give you another thing to snivel about when you go home."

"Who?"

"A man wants to make sure a woman stays his, he got to put a chunk of metal and a rock on her hand. He got to get a job, Cory. He wants to raise a nest of children he's got to work from sunup to sundown. That don't sound like you. That's hard work. Fact is, you turned your back on your responsibilities and it don't matter who she's with."

Cory withered. Stipe was watching him through narrow, appraising eyes.

"It's her uncle nailing her! Her uncle."

"Baer?"

"Same man knocked you cold that night in your driveway. But you was too drunk to notice. Tell you anything about her feelings for you?"

Blood rushed in Cory's brain.

"Take these animals to the back."

Cory leaned against the vehicle and lifted his head enough to watch the big man stride away. He sensed a crisis—that this moment should be something more. He'd always thought of himself as a kid, a boy. He'd never wanted to be a man, never wanted to assert the title and all that came with it. But this moment of truth was more important than hearing the judge say, three years. This was more important than the first phone call he made on the day of his release. The first joint he smoked that afternoon.

Cory stepped from the truck and it felt good. It was a departure. He felt radical. He would either shrivel from life or he would seize it.

"Stipe!"

Cory hurried after him. Stipe stopped.

"You got to bring me in. I'll get these dogs if that's what you want. I'll get on my belly and crawl across that lot if that's what you tell me. I'll go put a bullet in Baer Creighton's head. But you got to tell me what to do. You got to help me get all this right."

Stipe exhaled. He studied Cory, then resumed toward the house.

Cory jumped into his path. "I'm serious. I'll do whatever I have to do."

Stipe latched onto a handrail and swung his rear end onto the steps. "Sit down."

Cory sat and placed his elbows on his knees. His head drooped. He closed his eyes and his mind swam.

"I got a spy," Stipe said. "He watches Creighton all the time. He was there when you got stoned and shot all over the woods, and almost got yourself killed."

"I got a bad habit. A real bad habit."

"It's who you are, deep down. You're a coward."

Cory nodded. He brushed his forearm to his eyes.

"Being a coward means you only fight somebody when you can sneak up behind him. You never fight yourself or your worst demons because you can never get the drop on them. You think I'd have the truck company, a wife, grandkids, a few million in the bank, if I'd followed every foul instinct? If I never met my own weak heart head-on?"

"No, sir."

"Hell no. Self-discipline is how you get somewhere. It's the first law. It's like starting with the right kind of dog. There's a lot of work afterward, but discipline is where you start."

"What do I do?"

Stipe shook his head. He rested his hand on Cory's shoulder. "Get off the drugs. Get your mind right. Take them kids out of that house of sin, and let me see you three times in a row without bloodshot eyes. Show me you're serious, and we'll figure out where you go from there."

CHAPTER TWENTY-FIVE

Thumb out. Hitching. I got Smith back when they cut me free this morning, and now that Stipe and Smylie smashed my still I figure we're even. Time being.

Fred'll need a half-hour of story-telling and lie-swapping to get his mind straight. All that shooting. I've been thinking on Fred, and Stipe too. Chief Smylie called in the tip about my still. What would motivate him now, other than Stipe?

I don't know where things sit, morals and all. Mae said violence doesn't solve anything. One man does something wicked and the other comes back with something worse. Back and forth. It doesn't stop until one man gets hurt so bad he quits.

As things sit, Stipe and me are about square. If I called it quits, maybe he'd call it quits too. I don't like what he did to Fred, but I guarantee he doesn't like what I did to his champ.

Just thoughts.

Two days looking at a wall. Lot of time with no liquor. Things that were clear in one light look sketchy under a sixty-watt bulb. I come after Stipe because he's pure-ass evil, and had a hand in Fred's situation. But I'm no closer to knowing who tossed Fred in the weeds.

Another thing has me worried. I was stone sober and could hardly tell when a couple crooks told a judge they were innocent. Hardly any juice at all. At this rate my curse might be gone in a week, and I still don't have the truth on Fred or Ruth.

There's always been a connection with the liquor. I kept myself sloshed mostly to hold the curse at bay. Now the liquor's about killed my skill right when I need it. I often thought I'd rather not know everyone around me was a liar—it might be good enough to suspect it. But if this war with Stipe ratchets up a level, I may have to quit the liquor. See if I can't hang onto my talent.

How'll it be, first time I see a man and don't know if he's full of deceit?

Sunshine looks good but I bet Fred isn't happy. I hope he dug into my foodsack. I get home I'll cook him some eggs and Alpo; he likes that. Get on his good side again.

My feet are about peeking through my shoe leather. Gleason's coming up and I'm hungry enough to eat the grime out of a muffler and wash it down with antifreeze.

I shortcut town on the north side. I don't need to run into anyone. All this walking. Shoulder wound festering. That beating I took. Holes in my neck. I'm a clock losing ten seconds a minute.

Less than a mile from home. Old Fred—I can see him now, sorta, head above the crate and perking an ear. He has a gift, lets him know long before he hears feet crushing leaves or smells a man's armpits.

Come up on the still site from the woods. Everything's chopped and hacked, mash barrels tipped. Flies everywhere buzzing. Air is still and quiet, and smells like stale fire. Big stale fire. Old fire.

"Hey, stud. Guess who's home? I got some lies to swap. That's—"

Fred?

Step into a cloud of flies under the tarp. He's in his crate, covered in rolling black shiny wings. I swat 'em, smack 'em, shout at em. Run my fingers over Fred's coat.

He couldn't have starved in three days. No way.

"Fred?"

There's blood matted under his head. I see the bullet hole that did it.

"Fred!"

Somebody shot Fred through the scab that was his eye.

I toss up my guts. Fall over in the mess. Lay on the ground. I listen to the woods and every critter knows disaster has come. Every critter's silent, holed up, spooked off. Nary a bird has the stones to chirp.

CHAPTER TWENTY-SIX

Ernie and Burly had been waiting for hours in a neglected apple orchard. They'd parked between blackberry brambles, and sat in Burly's Suburban. The hill overlooked plowed-over fields that stretched like a mile-wide lake. Brown's decrepit farm was halfway across.

Other side of the road was Baer Creighton's burned house.

Like Ernie had promised, he'd sought Burly as soon as he'd seen Baer return from jail. They'd returned to stake out the Brown farm in case Baer made his move. So far, he hadn't.

After an hour of waiting in near silence, Burly said, "I thought you said he was ready to go to Brown's."

"He might have gone while I came to get you."

"Or he might not go at all. I have work to do. If you see him getting ready to redo his still, come get me. If not, neither me nor Stipe has the patience for games. It'll be Plan B—a bullet in the head."

Burly left.

Ernie waited in his own car.

Burly had made clear that Ernie's plan was too elaborate. He would rather sneak to Creighton's camp, pop him in the head, carry him across the road, and dispose of him that way. To his mind, the only thing gained by waiting on Creighton was that Burly wouldn't have to get blood on his clothes.

Ernie watched through binoculars. Hours passed and he dared himself to sneak closer. He walked the edge of the dirt road toward Creighton's house and then eased into the woods. Creighton was distraught. His dog was dead. That was freelance work. Stipe would appreciate it, even if Burly couldn't see the poetry of it.

Creighton would be off his guard.

Ernie approached a little at a time. When Creighton's camp was visible between the trees, he reclined against a tree. He watched through binoculars.

Plan A was much more poetic than Plan B, but it wouldn't matter in the end. Ernie would watch Creighton until he made his move. If he wandered off, Ernie would follow. If he had loose stools, Ernie would know.

Whether Creighton walked to Brown's or they carried him, he would go and not return.

The stench of burned wood and metal is heavy on the ground.

My house is a charred shipwreck shoved into a basement. Ashes. Burned two days ago at least, judging by the trickles of smoke and the black jutting boards. Burned shortly after they busted my still. The same time they killed Fred.

October leaves flutter yellow and red, lazy, and when they land it's just me amid all this ruin.

I'm going to burn you down.

Stipe let the shed stand. I grab a shovel. Head back to the still site. I look in on Fred almost like I'll find it was all a bad dream. But as soon as I see him I recognize part of the smell of rotted mash and stale ashes is dead Fred.

My knees go weak and I steady myself with the shovel, dry-eyed but so godawful broke inside I could die.

Only been three days but it looks like I've been gone a year, and the woods are taking over. Hundred years, none of this'll matter.

I meditate on my knees by the crate, hands on wood wore round by four generations of man's best friend. I look to the dirt beside the diesel turbine crate as if any tracks might help me cipher how Fred spent his time. There's enough paw prints I'll never know which was last.

Down by the crick, there are prints at the edge. He was comfortable getting his own water, and I'd been letting him build his confidence. Don't know which boot prints belong to Cueball Mercer and his boys, or which go with whoever finished Fred. One set of prints look to have come from a kid, they're so small.

A few feet from the fire circle I plunge the shovel into the dirt. Fred will rest here, in the middle of everything he loved. I jump on the back of the shovel and work it back and forth, and pull out the first big clump of black dirt. I stab the ground again and hit a root. I stab and stab and find the root's cut and I'm still stabbing.

Tearing out dirt is violent, satisfying work but I have to reel in the anger. Make it work for me. I have to set that shovelful down in a pile, not fling it off through the woods.

Three feet long and two wide. Four deep. I wrap Fred in his wool blanket. Climb down the hole. Kiss his cold nose and squeeze him like to bring him back.

There's a scream in my head but my throat's silent. There's rage in my eyes but they're closed. I'm calm and slow but my soul jumps up and down like to go to war.

Goodbye you old son of a bitch. I love ya.

Fred doesn't say anything back.

I lower him to the bottom. Backfill, and tamp the ground.

I talk to the congregated woods. "Fred was good people. Some dogs is like cats, all prissy and screw you all the time. But Fred was the kind of fella who'd give you a smooch and say the craziest things, just as you thought the same. And he never begged. He was as self-respecting a dog as ever was. And loyal. Good cheer."

I fight hard to not dig him up and hug him one more time.

I'm going to burn you down.

I have Smith. Even checked to make sure they gave me back my bullets. I trek into the woods.

Head up a hollow that curves into the side of a no name mountain. In twenty minutes I'm two miles from Gleason. Every step carries me someplace more remote than the last. No one comes this way. Used to think if I ever got fed up or had to disappear, I'd hide out here. I follow the crick back to a trickle over a couple flat rocks. Two-thirds up the mountain, a cave overlooks the grade. Man could sit and shoot squirrel all day. Buck or bear, if he had a mind.

Or anything else that wandered by.

With maple all over; a man would have all the sugar he'd need.

Oaks drop acorns like rain. Hickory and walnut, too. There's fish in the stream, and a glade where the sunlight pokes through and a man could grow potatoes and leeks.

Out front the cave is a chunk of metal all busted up and rusted.

This is where Gunter Stroh taught me to make shine.

He used to brood on his fire, rifle in reach. He'd lean and pitch wood under the boiler. His mouth watered soon as he heard the tinkle-rattle, the hiss coming out the copper. He'd smack his lips and spit, and his shaking hands would steady.

Long gone.

I used to come back this way with Fred.

I wander inside the cave and poke around. Rotted blankets, moldy threads. Bones from some animal, likely not a man. Maybe a cougar called this place home, though I've not seen cougar in thirty years.

With my house a pit of embers and the still cut up, and Fred... this cave has all the solitude a man could want.

I stumble down the hill.

Time I hit the flat ground, the stream's a bona fide crick, with pools deep enough for trout. I circle east, sweep the woods.

I call "Fred!"

Listen. My voice goes off to nowhere, and I half-expect Fred hears me on the other side.

Time to put the plan back on rails. The plan I thought of that very first night, when I set one empty barrel aside from the rest.

I have a tree full of gold. There's the one bucket hanging from the nylon cord, but two more dropped inside, full. I set that money aside, and if this ain't a rainy day I don't know what is. Time to fetch an axe.

I ease off my pace coming up on the still site. Stand in the middle next to Fred's grave. Thirsty. Kind of blank in the head. I set for the house.

Come up from the backside, like always, except now there's nothing between me and the road. House is level, collapsed in the basement. Smoke wanders across the ground, looking for answers. Roof's fell in. Shingles burned clean away. Only thing left is pieces of timber that look like wood at the campfire edge. Juts up, sides black and white with ash.

At the back corner I step to the foundation. The door's burned away. This must've been the hottest part by a long stretch. All those jugs of hundred-sixty proof liquor are glass puddles on the cement floor. This is likely where they started the fire. Loaded the pickup with liquor and busted the rest open, tossed a match, and skedaddled.

I'd hoped a jug survived the heat.

Back at the still site, I strip to my skivvies and grab a towel and soap.

Brook water's liquid ice. At the edge I kneel naked on a rock and scrub my pants and shirt and skivvies and socks like they did in the Bible. I hang drippy clothes from a dead hemlock branch and tiptoe into the water, careful on slippery rocks.

Walk past the tub. I got to feel something.

At the middle the water's only a foot deep; I sit on a smooth, flat rock and soap up, and splash my pits, and get my privates. Nads all up inside, huddled tight with my ribs, saying he's lost his mind. Again.

Ribs say, Naw. That's rage.

Can't stand the cold but three minutes and it feels like three years. I dry off so cold my guts rattle. Climb in my sleeping bag and zip it over my head.

Peek at all that busted metal, and the empty turbine crate.

I don't think I ever been quite so licked.

I wake and it's night. Late enough there's no crickets from the house, echoing through. No lightning bugs wandering in—but it's been weeks since they had the run of the place.

There's no sound in the crate, no Fred snoring.

Climb out the bag naked and cold and drag the diesel turbine crate on top of the fresh dirt mound. Grab a lighter from the tarp and set the blankets aflame. Huddle on the ground and watch the orange and blue.

I'm going to burn you down.

CHAPTER TWENTY-SEVEN

I got to whiz and my arm pressed groundside is asleep and tingly. Sun's out and the birds've come back. Have a little food here but most was in the house. Got some eggs. I cook them.

It's quiet without Fred.

Time's getting on for ending all this. Fight's in a week and it's divine providence the Lord made me a stiller.

I have a powerful thirst and water won't touch it.

Pete Bleau's in his truck.

Once in a bleau moon someone comes up while I'm at the house anyway. So happens I don't have a house now. I look at ashes.

This isn't Pete's day for liquor.

Meet him at the truck. He looks shiftier than usual but there's no red, no juice.

"Had a visit this morning," he says.

"That so."

"Huck Barrow."

"Why don't that surprise me?"

"Said they busted the still."

"They?"

"Revenue."

"Uh-huh."

"And Barrow said I'd want to run my business through him. They was willing to sell for five a jug."

"What a deal."

"This ain't the first Barrow's been after me."

"I know."

"Thought I ought to tell you. When you be back in operation?"

"Ain't thought 'bout it."

"You know I got to find a supply."

"I know it."

"I been saying for years I'd move twice as much, if you'd make it. See, this is an opportunity, Baer. You put in a modern operation. Double the size your boiler and run it twice as much. I got people clear to Philly buy whatever you make. Them shot houses is rip-roaring, what with the economics in the crapper for good."

"All that's true."

"You want me to wait on you to get your operation up again?"

When I first found Fred I made a decision. Renewed the vows last night. I'd park a pile of hell on Stipe's front porch, then drive until I find someplace nice, and stop there. I can see the road. Dotted line flashing under the hood. Trees zinging by. Wind blowing through open windows— maybe even with snow outside.

"Don't think I'll set up anytime soon, Pete. But I appreciate you stopping by. They steal your dog yet?"

"He's laying on the seat. Hey boy." The shepherd stands. Bleau says, "He don't go out the house except to take a dump, and that's with me watching."

"Bet he likes that."

"Take care, Baer."

He leaves me with my ashes.

I sit beside chunks of still and copper. Part of me wants to red things up.

I made a living with that still for years and years. All the time avoided the revenuers by working with a select group of men. A dozen drinkers and a couple wholesalers who moved my stuff to shot houses. They always said they'd take whatever I made, there was such demand from migrant labor down south. Always opportunities in D.C. and Philly. I never did it to get rich, only to live the way I wanted.

Now there's no way in particular I want to live.

Can't go back to those days, and even if I fixed up a new still and found a new pit bull pup, it'd never measure up. I'm a traitor to even want it. All these chunks of copper are an affront to the eye. Ought to bury them. The rest of me wants this place to stay like this until kingdom come. Let the rust and woods reclaim it, like that busted still at the cave.

And Ruth?

There's only one course left, for Ruth.

Quits.

I kick off my boots. Crinkle my toes and kind of work them back and forth with my fingers. The little one pops. Back before I quit school, Mister Ping told us toe bones ossify like the skull bones and the tailbones. I set about making sure my piggy toe bones never ossified. I've cracked them before bed ever since.

I pop my toes and when I got my mind where I want it, grab a pen and sheet of paper.

Dear Ruth—

On account of you never writing back, I'm done.

I scrunch the paper into a ball and chuck it at the fire. Go to the crick with a brick of soap and get the toe funk off my hands.

Dear Ruth—

I hoped you'd send a letter and tell me why our lives didn't turn out the way we thought they would, back at the start.

You know by now I've stayed stuck on you. But I don't know what I'd do if you showed up. It's too late. Things is going to happen that change the rest of my life, and I don't know which way.

But I like to think if you showed up, we'd take a car and drive all day and all night, and not stop until we got somewhere nice.

But this is quits. I'll say bye with that.

·   ·   ·

—Baer

I read it over and the words don't say half of what I want her to know, but if I haven't said it in all these years, too bad. Part of the responsibility's on her. She ought to carry some water if she wants a drink.

She doesn't want a drink, though, and that's why I'm through writing. After this's over, I may be dead and gone, I may be living in a cave, but either way, no more letters for Ruth.

CHAPTER TWENTY-EIGHT

Mae's heart jumped. Cory stood in the open doorway, gun dangling in his hand. Eyes glazed.

Don't take the fight to him. Don't challenge him now—he doesn't have the sense to think. But don't be one of those women who wind up on Oprah. Trying to explain why it was rational to submit while her babies watched her get beaten into the ground.

"You got things to explain," Cory said.

Cory was here to fight.

"Just a minute." Mae twisted to her computer and hit "save." She should have planted a knife in the desk drawer. She closed the document. Spun on her chair.

Should have asked Baer for a gun.

"Getting a little uppity, all this college." Cory stumbled on the rug. He waved the pistol and recaptured his swagger three steps into the room. "But you're a real smart girl. Real smart. Got all the men you want, and none the wiser."

"Girls, go upstairs. Go to your room and play for a little while."

"No! Stay here. You two want to see this. So you know the difference between right and wrong."

"Girls, upstairs. Now!"

Morgan took Bree's hand. They backed away. Their eyes moved from Cory to Mae and back to Cory, until they turned at the stairs.

Cory lunged, trapped Bree under his arm like a satchel of books. Bree screamed.

Mae jumped across half the living room, and trembled two feet shy of Cory. "Put her down! Cory, don't do this. Morgan! Upstairs now! Cory, listen to me. Put her down. Let's talk."

Cory strode past Mae. He swung Bree upright as he dropped into the couch, and plopped her beside him. Bree's face was terror. Morgan stayed on the steps, three high, shrunk against the wall.

"I want my baby girl to understand what happens to whores."

"What are you talking about?"

"I know what you been doing behind my back."

"Cory—you're not..." Don't tell a man he isn't sober. "Cory, not now. Let Bree go. We can talk all you want."

"Talk. You're good at talking. Never shut up. So why don't you start running that trap of yours and explain all that food in the kitchen. You got to 'splain four hundred dollars waiting at the grocery." He smiled. Rubbed his cheek with the pistol barrel. "You got to 'splain making out with your uncle." Cory pulled Bree closer. She wriggled. "Honey, I'm going to take you away tonight. In a minute we'll go upstairs and get your things. You won't have to grow up watching your momma be a whore."

"What are you doing? She doesn't even know those words! Let her go."

"You see, Bree—and I see you over there, Morgan. It's good for you to listen when your daddy's talking. You see, girls, your momma's been a bad, bad girl."

"Why are you here, Cory? I don't have any money."

"I wonder. I bet your daddy will be real interested in you screwing his brother."

Mae forced her mouth closed. With her eyes she urged Morgan to climb the stairs but her daughter stood transfixed. Bree's horror had become shock. Things were unwinding.

Mae wiped her eyes. "Cory, don't do this... please?"

"You never once said it wasn't true, Mae."

"It isn't true. He's my uncle!"

"You can't lie your way out of whoring. Guess it's in your blood. Yeah, I know about that too."

The gun barrel reflected light from the bulb overhead—it was like a star. Mae looked away. "I kissed him. Baer backed away and left five minutes later. You saw that too, right?"

He clenched his jaw.

"Yeah, you saw it. So what are you up to, Cory? Or did you take off so fast you didn't see what you thought? Put the gun down."

"Listen to you. Put the gun down. How about I use it instead? On you." His voice cracked. "But you got to answer one thing."

Bree wriggled. "Mommy?"

"Hush!" He clamped her closer. His eyes pointed across the room, to the floor, to the kitchen.

"What is it, Cory?"

He nudged Bree. "Look at your mother." He leveled the pistol at Mae. "You still love me, Mae?"

"You don't want your babies to see this, Cory. Send them upstairs!"

"I want them to see you lie to me. Do you love me, Mae?"

"Bree—I love you! Morgan—I love you!"

Mae stared into the end of the gun. The pistol wavered. Cory lifted it until he met her eyes over the sights.

"I don't love you, Cory."

"You're one dumb whore, you know that?" He closed his eyes. Inhaled deep. Opened his eyes and said, "Wasn't too bright, sending Baer out to jump me at the house." Cory released his grip and swiveled the pistol barrel toward the ceiling. "You haven't loved me for a long time. That's the truth. Now we're going upstairs. Pack some things."

"This is kidnapping, Cory."

"I'm not taking you."

"That's what I mean. You take them with a gun, there isn't a court in the state that'll let you keep them. Listen to me. Listen. You think you'll do better bringing them up, do it the right way. Not with a gun."

"Upstairs." He gestured with the pistol and stood between the door and Mae. "Upstairs, everybody."

Mae was still. Cory stepped to her.

His hand flashed. She saw it coming. She felt blood in her eye, carpet on her cheek. Morgan punched Cory's legs with fists light as clover bundles.

"Come on, girls. Upstairs."

☙

Last time I went to the Gleason post office I carried two flasks. Now I haven't had a drink in four days. I wait in line and avoid looking at anyone. My turn comes and I slap the letter on the counter.

"You can't carry a rifle inside a post office," Harry says.

"What? I'm gonna steal a letter? Here."

"Letter to Mars Hill," Harry says.

"Last one."

"That so?" He looks at me like I said a dragon squatted over my scrambled eggs.

I turn.

"So don't you want to know how long it'll take to get there?"

"So long, Harry."

I swing by the grocery. Merle's parked on the stool behind the register. I slap a gold coin on the counter.

"What's that?"

"What's it look like? Real money. By weight, that's eight hundred fifty dollars."

He lifts it. "A maple leaf."

"It's from Canada. They're fond of maple."

"What you want me to do with it?"

"Write eight hundred dollars in that book of yours for Mae."

"She hasn't used twenty dollars of the other you left."

"She will. She's got them kids."

"Why don't you take that down to Millany and turn it into money, 'fore you bring it here?"

"You don't know what money is. And I'm lazy, like you. Put down eight hundred on a slip for Mae. I'll take a ten-dollar jug of bourbon here, and five dollars of that cheddar-type cheese. So you get a commission for working with me, this one time. Right, Merle? Good with you?"

He nods and I go to the cooler. I stop by the register and he hands me a pint of Wild Turkey. Shoos me away.

Kentucky bourbon washes down cheddar better than water. After a few drinks I realize how dried out I been since the house fire cooked all my jugs. Now my brain's starting to work.

I head for Mae's, already thinking ahead to what I'll do if I see Cory Smylie there.

I've recounted the facts as I know them. I've replayed that night I found Fred. Matched the shape of the man that dumped him in the dirt to Cory Smylie and to flesh-and-blood Larry. I've thought of Cory's truck, that day he was at Mae's, and how it was or wasn't the truck I saw that night. How Cory washed his truck and there'll never be any telling if the tailgate was dirty on one side. I've thought on Pete Bleau confessing that Stipe pays Cory to steal dogs.

You can't know a man's done evil unless you know he's got it in his heart.

With Cory it's as sure as venom in a rattler. Five years ago, him and Mae started popping out kids. I didn't have anything to say about the way they wanted to work their affairs. I tried to get on, and be civil.

I was at the still one day and heard a horn. Went to the house and found Cory with his new F-150. Smashed grill. Thin streak of blood on the hood. Spider web on the windshield. He had a dope-headed grin and hung to the mirror for balance.

"You got a ball bat?" he says.

"I dunno. What for?"

"Hit a deer."

"You say you hit a deer?"

"That too. He's still alive and I want to club him."

"I'll get a gun."

"Look how he dicked my truck. I'm going to club him."

"I'll club you. Where is he?"

Cory pointed across the drive to a bend where deer cross from the wood to the field at dusk.

"Go on home, Cory. I'll handle it."

He studied me like a punk taking my measure. I watched him do the math. Add a little for experience, subtract a lot for age. The math always puts a punk on top. The longer he looked at me, the sharper the electric got, and his eyes glowed in the dusk.

"Yeah," he said. "Guess I'll head home."

I went in the house and came out with a thirty-thirty. Cory's truck was gone and time I reached the road, I saw him driving back and forth over the deer. Each time he hit the gas hard, the truck bounced and the body flopped. I swung the rifle to my eye. Lined the sights to put a chunk of lead through his cab.

But before I pulled the trigger, I figured it would end with me putting a chunk of lead through Cory too.

I set off down the road and he was long gone. It was a doe and he'd smashed her. Dead from the second time he hit her, most probable. I fired six times into the dirt to let off the steam, then dragged the doe to the woods.

In my book, Cory Smylie's a human septic tank. A man that'd treat one animal like that is about as likely to treat another. Maybe since he's hunted dogs for Stipe, he had the moxie to steal mine. Maybe Stipe put him to it, specific, because he was working some other angle. I don't know. But I know he's got the evil in his character, and adding everything else, I'm about certain Cory stole Fred.

I reach Mae's and rap the door, making sure not to knock it in. It's dusk, but lights are on.

She opens the door. Big old smile. Red faced and happy.

"Don't got but a minute," I say. "I wanted you to know I'm going away. Could be a long bit, I dunno. Left another eight hundred down at the grocery."

She stares at the porch planks. I look closer. Her eyes are wet, and her big old smile changes—or my understanding changes. Now she looks like she's been bawling an hour.

The bruises from before have progressed to a sick black yellow. And there's new swelling and a cut in her brow. She's tried to cover the damage with makeup. Bruises on her arms.

I turn away. Cory Smylie made a liar out of me to those girls—but I'm the fool that promised what I couldn't deliver.

"Was the kids here, this time?"

She nods. "He took them."

I punch the wall. "I did it your way. I shoulda cut off his head."

"I want my babies."

By Tercel it's not ten minutes to Smylie's house. I'll take the police chief and all, he gets in my way. I got the rifle across the back floor and Smith on my hip. Mae sits on the passenger side. She says, "I'm ready to do what I have to do."

"You don't have to do nothing. First we see what's going on. We'll get the kids back."

"I called Mom and she didn't answer. It's been two days. And I drove to your place and the house was gone. Burned. What was I supposed to think? Why didn't you say your house burned? I mean, what the hell? What the hell, Baer?" She faces the window. "Last I talked to Mom she said Larry was giving her problems. She was worried."

I look at her.

"Watch the road. You're speeding."

"Since when do you call him Larry?"

"Since now. Since he started giving Mom problems and threatening her."

"What kind of problems?"

"Coming around, like a stalker. She caught him watching her at night a couple times."

"He's married again."

"When did that ever stop a man?"

"When was all this?"

"Last week. I told her to get a restraining order."

"That won't work."

"She hasn't called back in two days."

Seems like words is useless. Between the time for saying and the time for doing is silence. We drive through it.

The Smylie house lights are off, like the whole family's gone. The upstairs windows glow from a nightlight, or a lamp left on, but the rest is dark.

"Where'd he take them?" Mae says. "I'm going to kill him!"

"Easy. You don't got to." I touch her shoulder then think better, and pull over beyond the Smylie house.

"What do we do?" Mae sniffles. "If there was ever a time I could break all the rules this is it. They're out with their high-price lawyers," Mae says. "They're stealing my babies."

"Quiet, now. I'm going to poke around. Stay put."

I leave the car without slamming the door. The minivan's in the drive. Cory's truck is gone. I slip alongside the house and the only noise comes from neighbors out back, with a fire pit and a circle of lawn chairs. A bug zapper. Old-fashioned marshmallow roast. The fire and bug light throw a glow on Smylie's back yard. I stop at a window. With no lights inside, anybody in there could see me—but there's nobody in that house.

Back in front of the house I stop to a sound. If those neighbors with the marshmallows would shut up for one minute I could hear it. Footsteps. Patter like raindrops so small it's like mist on leaves.

The knob's locked. I press my elbow to the glass pane—but the neighbors would hear it shatter. Other side of the house, I slit screens with my Leatherman tool and press windows until one budges. I pry the screen out and push up the window, all the way. I jump, ease through on my belly, and land on a sofa that smells like spice and flowers.

Little feet drum upstairs. I stand in shadows and get my bearings.

Smylie's got an organ against the wall, a coffee table right where a man would stumble on it. Maybe an alarm system tattle-telling the Gleason police.

"Morgan, Bree?"

Whispers. The stairwell's behind me.

"Uncle Baaaar?"

"That's right. I got your momma outside. I come to take you home. Anybody else here?"

"No sir," Morgan says, voice squeaky scared. "I don't think so."

"Where's Joseph?"

"In bed. Upstairs."

"Let's get him. Show me."

I come up the stairs and this whole setup doesn't feel right. Like I should have looked up and down the street for Cory Smylie's truck. Like I'm the man breaking and entering another man's house.

I pass Bree on the stairs. She clings to the rail. "Go downstairs and wait by the door. I'll be right there."

She nods. I'm high enough now I can see they got a night-light in a room down the hall. "Morgan—which room?"

My arm tingles real faint.

Morgan scampers ahead and stops. Points.

Any number of ways this could pan out. Cory's inside with a gun at the door, and Morgan's old enough to know Joseph's in trouble. But her eyes don't glow at all.

Or Cory's outside ready to catch a burglar in the act. Or he's downstairs stowed under a desk, waiting the right moment to drop me.

My curse is weak. I'm almost sightless.

The door is open. I swing inside, arms high enough to block a punch, but none comes. I twist around and the room's clear, save a closet. I grab Joseph—he lets out a cry and this's ten times worse than having a bunch of dogfighters rush you in the woods. I'm about blind, all these walls. I pull Smith, then holster it.

"Come on, Morgan. Let's go outside. Your mommy's in the car up the street."

I lead the way and the tingle gets stronger—as much a signal as I've got in the last week.

"Where you at, Cory? I know you're here."

I glance down the hall. Nothing. Shuffle along, fast. Outside comes a sharp red glow like four hundred liars. It's either the United States Congress come to order on the front lawn or police black and whites.

"Girls, c'mere! Out the window. Like I come in. Here we go."

I sit Joseph on the sofa. God's on my side; Joseph's quiet. I sit on the top of the sofa with Morgan. She wriggles through the window and I dangle her to the ground.

"Go the end of this wall and hunker down. Bree—c'mere!"

She steps up like a soldier. I get her out the window. "Go to the back and wait."

Now for Joseph. I'll probably break my back, but there's no good way. I sit him on my lap and swing my legs through the window. Lean back until my spine's about to snap, and slip down the sill. Vertebrae pop like Rice Crispies. My chin hits the window. I drop to the ground and freeze.

A flashlight cuts across the front lawn—a cop covering a lot of ground. I shrink behind a shrub and a man steps around the front corner. I have a baby in my arms and a cop twenty feet off looking for something to shoot. The beam flashes me in the eyes but how do you know if they see you? Got to wait.

The light shifts away and I'm half-blind, and there's raised voices far off—man and woman. Mae.

Flashlight comes back, parks on the open window. "Hey Bob! I got an open window. Think we got someone inside!"

You jest go on thinking that.

"Keep it covered."

I'm pinned. I make a break for it, I have a baby liable to scream and two girls that can't run in the dark. I have neighbors cooking marshmallows happy to holler, "He went thataway."

The cop with the light moves closer. The beam on the window gets tight. If I move, he sees me. He comes to the window. He's five feet away and only a bush between us. Then there's the girls. White, or light blue clothes. This cop's blind, not seeing them even through the hedges.

"Hey, John!"

The copper moves quick and the beam catches me full on and keeps moving. He's turned away.

"Yeah?"

"C'mon up front. It's Mae looking for Cory. She set off the alarm."

Cop John goes back around the front corner and I'm beside Morgan and Bree in three seconds. They huddle tight to the wall, arms around each other.

"You girls did a real good job," I whisper.

We're on the edge of the bug light glow coming from the neighbor's.

"Follow me, girls. Real quiet. Your momma's out front but the police is talking with her. She's got to tell them a story, and then we'll go."

I lead along another neighbor's house. They're upstairs, judging from the lights. We walk a line, turn the corner. Up front, I get low and scope the goings-on. Two police cars have flashing lights. One is in front the Smylie house and the other's behind Mae's Tercel. She's talking to four cops by her back bumper.

I have electric on my arms. I'm surprised Joseph don't yell for being shocked. This is the best juice I got in a week.

Morgan gasps and there's a one-foot shuffle.

Got a gun against my head.

"Hey, Cory."

"Hey, kidnapper. Put Joe down."

"What you want?"

"I want to paste your brain against that wall, but we got to wait a few minutes."

"You want to do that in front of your kids?"

"Don't you start, too. Morgan, Bree—stay right there."

Joseph gurgles.

"Shhh," I say. I get him up close, feel the metal press hard to my head. "You go easy with that gun." I rub my nose on Joseph and he gurgles a little, something not quite as angry as a shout, but not altogether happy. "You want to ease up on that thing? I got your son in my arms."

Cory backs off. He pulls another gun from his belt and I see right off it ain't normal. The front is big and square.

"Put Joseph on the ground."

"Cory, it's cold. This is your son—"

"Put the kid down!"

He straightens his arm and points a Taser at my chest.

"Easy, Cory." I bend to the ground and sit Joseph down. I stand.

I hear a zip sound and feel two bee stings in my chest and I got electric coursing through me for three full seconds. Feel like I'm a battery got plugged into the wall. Feel like a tired man ate a three-pound steak. My whole body shakes and I never felt so good and strong and surly in my life. The juice ends and then another juice, the kind I'm familiar with starts. The hair on my forearms shoots straight out inside my sleeves. Cory's eyes flame red like I was sober and saw Nixon say I ain't a crook.

Cory Smylie healed me.

He still has his arm stretched. I knock the wires loose, step in close and bring my fist from low and smash it into his jaw. Cory's head pops back and he drops against the neighbor's wall, then crumples to a hedge.

Joseph cries and I grab him off the dirt and nuzzle him to my stubble. "Hey son, you're all right. Yessir. Whooeeee." But he keeps on. Maybe the cops'll think he's with the neighbor's kids, roasting weenies.

Cory groans—the gun in his other hand points this way. I grab it. Bring the hammer forward, check the chamber. Dumb prick was ready to shoot with his babies right here.

I smash the grip to the back of his skull. He's stunned like a thumped rabbit.

The girls have run back the way we came.

I kiss Joseph's forehead and make a fart sound with my lips. Joseph giggles like he's on the edge of tears.

The neighbor's front light goes on. "Who's there?" comes the shout.

I tuck the gun in my pants while I run and stumble on the girls waiting at the back of the house. Again Joseph wails.

Mae gives the cops a hard time, or her voice carries better than cop voices. Joseph's liable to end this rescue if he doesn't stop his confused whimpering and giggling.

"Morgan, you got to settle Joseph."

I put him in her arms and it's a miracle. The little girl's already got the momma know-how. She coos and cuddles him, and it's pure-ass crazy, this whole thing. Out here with only the hardiest crickets still chirping. The moon out, and those marshmallow people. Four cops sassing Mae, and Mae talking smack right back. Cory knocked out cold. In the middle of all that, six-year-old Morgan has an infant in her arms. He thinks he's the safest critter in the night. Pure uncanny.

"Now girls, you listen good. Those police think your mother busted into the house to get you—and she'll let them think that so's we got time to scoot. We find a place we can watch, they'll let her go in a little bit, and we'll go find her."

Bree takes ahold my leg like I'm not getting away. Morgan looks up from Joseph.

"Okay, here we go. We got everybody in the neighborhood riled up, so we got to head straight to the woods. All the way through these people's back yards. We'll circle around and watch for your momma from up the road."

Safest bet is to cross well behind the houses. Morgan passes Joseph back to me and we set off. These people have back yards that used to be wheat fields. Goes on and on, and a hundred yards out, I cut right. There's no way they can see us. "You girls, if I say drop, you drop quick. I see a spotlight, they won't be no time to think, you hear?"

Police lights flash against trees opposite the road, and the houses between us. Bet the neighbors are happy. Bedrooms are discos again.

After a hundred yards, I angle at Mae's car, then hunker with Morgan and Bree. "All right, girls, you see that police car up there? Right in front, that's your momma's car. She's talking with em. We'll get a little closer and wait on them coppers. They leave, we go up and surprise your momma. I'll tell her you deserve a vacation."

Bree seems to doubt vacations are good.

I stay low long enough my knees are about to bust and I plop back on the grass. Joseph has little snores going on.

Morgan pulls my collar. "Uncle Baer—they're taking Mommy."

"What?" I shift a little sideways, roll to my feet and take a few steps. They lead Mae to the closest cop car. Put her in the back seat—do that number with the hand on the back of her head. Mae stares out the window at Cory's house. A streetlight shines in the back of the car. Mae looks about unglued.

"They're taking Mommy," Bree says.

The police cars turn around in different driveways, and they're gone.

"Where are they take Mommy?" Bree says.

"I'm cold," Morgan says.

"Me too," says Bree.

The sky's clear. Whatever heat's been sticking to the ground will leave soon enough. By midnight, I'm thinking frost. These girls have their shirts and pants and jackets on.

"Morgan, I want you to take your brother a minute. I'm going to the car. Be right back. You okay? Can you watch Joseph?"

"You coming back?"

"I'll be right back. You'll see me the whole time—straight to the car and straight back."

She nods somber-like. It's the first time in my life I wish someone had a wisp of my talent, enough to know there's one person that won't ever lie to her.

I set off quick and low, Cory's pistol in hand. Everything's quiet. Don't know if Cory's had the sense to go back inside the house, or if he might be along the police station. I listen at the edge of the lawn.

Mae's driver-side door is locked. Passenger opens. I unlock the back and grab the blanket covering the back seat. Try to yank it but this baby seat is on top, and now I'm thinking I walked square into another trap. Blind under the dome light, back half hanging out the door.

But the girls are cold.

I unclasp the buckle and that isn't enough. Another rig somewhere holds it down. I lean deep inside and see another buckle. Pop it loose, thread the strap through the hole, toss the car seat. Mae's cut holes for the seat belts but the blanket'll do. I poke around for anything useful and find my rifle on the floor against the seat. Mae must've thought quick and tucked it under the blanket draped over the side.

I worm back out the car, lock the door, close it. Expect to hear "You're a dead man" or some Hollywood nonsense, but it's just me in the dark. Street's quiet and the houses are dark. Isn't a dog anywhere got a problem with anything.

It's downright eerie, expecting to be caught, and not.

I find the girls where I left em. "I got a blanket, keep you warm tonight."

"Where we going, Uncle Baer?"

"Camping," I say. "I know a place where we can get warm and snug with a fire, and you girls can bed down. I'll tell a ghost story, or something."

Bree looks at me.

"Or not."

Mae sat in a straight-backed metal chair and squinted under fluorescent lights. She imagined her babies in Cory's parents' car, speeding to some distant state where she'd never find them.

Officer Randy James sat across the desk. They'd graduated from the same high school class. He'd asked her out six or eight times, and never acknowledged her disinterest.

He probed his incisors with a toothpick. "Mae, none of this makes sense." Randy removed his hat, spun it so she glimpsed the stained headband, and placed it on his desk.

The Gleason police headquarters was a narrow two-story. On the left, a travel agency. On the right, a boutique picture-frame store that survived on tourist dollars. Mae looked around the station. She listened to the deputies' voices coming from the hallway. Each member of the four-man force had been academy-trained. They all walked and talked with uniform rigidity. It was a good presentation. But Chief Smylie had groused in the newspaper that he didn't the budget to hold suspects in the basement jail. Though the deputies wanted to be legit, if a crime didn't involve a bucket of human blood, the accused walked.

"The logic don't make sense," Randy continued. "You say you knocked on the front door and triggered the alarm. But we got the open window in the back that did it."

Baer made it inside! "What I have said—over and over—is that I knocked on the door and the alarm went off. I didn't say that I triggered the alarm. I was never at the back of the house."

"The back side. It was on the side of the house. But you knew that, right?"

"No, I didn't know that. Was anything missing from the house?"

"If you don't mind, I'll ask the questions."

"I don't mind. Was anything missing from the house?"

"As you know, Chief Smylie and Mrs. Smylie are away all week at a conference. So we don't know what's missing yet."

"I didn't know they were gone."

Randy paused. Studied her with a trick behind his eyes. He grinned. "We pulled fingerprints from the window. Big ol' prints, clear as can be."

"Why am I here?"

"You know that, don't you? Come on. We've got Asheville running those fingerprints through the database. Why don't you tell me your version of the events one more time?"

"I don't have a version, Randy. You got any coffee?"

He stared. "Sure. Lots of cream and sugar?"

"Black."

He disappeared to another room.

Deputy Leroy Dupont entered from the hallway, trailed by Cory Smylie. By the addled cant of his gaze and the disgust on his lips, Cory had crashed from his high. He rubbed the back of his head. Leroy reported to Randy.

"Cory here says he was inside, asleep, and stumbled down the steps when the alarm went off. He likes to sleep at the top of the staircase.

168

Knocked his head on an end table. He went through the house, and nothing appeared out of order."

Randy sighed. "All that work on his skull come from a night table?"

"I'll have my dad check the alarm," Cory said. "Maybe get a nightlight."

Randy snorted. Shoved the form he was writing on a few inches away. "All right, for now."

Leroy led between the desks and paused at the front. Cory stood behind him. "You want, I'll take Mae back to her car," Cory said.

"'Preciate you," Randy said. "But I'll take her back. I want to look things over one more time. You understand."

Cory grinned. Dimples. "See you later, honey."

Randy handed her a Styrofoam cup of coffee.

Mae placed the cup on the desk. "I guess this means we're through."

"Let's get another look at your car." He remained standing.

Mae stretched her back. Saw Randy appraise her chest.

"Don't forget your coffee," he said.

"Styrofoam emits xenoestrogens. But thanks."

She rode in the back of the Chevy Caprice cruiser and her thoughts returned to worry. An image flashed to mind: three terrified kids looking through the back window. The car speeding into darkness.

She'd kill Cory yet.

The rifle! She'd left it under the backseat blanket.

Could she challenge Randy? Didn't a search require probable cause? Or had the Supreme Court decided cops could do anything they wanted? She'd talk her way out of it. Wait—if Baer had the kids, wouldn't he have taken them home in the car? Unless he wiled himself out of the thought. The rifle—she'd use Baer's logic. She had kids, therefore she had a gun. Randy would understand. Besides, it wasn't concealed... yes it was. Under the blanket.

Cory had been willing to drop the issue at the station. Did he still have the kids, or did he fear an investigation might escalate beyond his father's protection? The window fingerprint had to belong to Baer, and Baer owned the damage on Cory's head. But what if the children hadn't been at the house at all?

And what about the rifle in her back seat?

"You know, Mae, times are tough for women, and all."

"What's that mean? And all?"

"You got that cut on your face. We got Cory Smylie, back of his noggin looks like someone took a sledge to it. How long you and him been an item?"

"An item?"

"You don't like a word I say." Randy turned onto the road that led to the Smylie house. "What happened? He knock you around, and you come back for him? Maybe settle the score?"

"No."

"What happened to your eye?"

"I fell and hit it on an end table."

"No call to get smart."

"I don't appreciate harassment, Randy."

"Cory's folks are out of town. You ain't clear yet. Chief gets back and Cory gives him a different story, you don't want that. You'll be answering a new set of questions back at the station."

Mae looked through the windshield, saw her car beside the road. Randy slowed; Mae watched as they passed the Smylie house. Cory's truck was in the driveway, and he sat like a sleepy sentry on the front step, elbows braced on his knees. He watched.

"There's your boy right there," Randy said. "Waiting." Randy parked behind Mae's Tercel. "Anything you want to tell me before I search the vehicle?"

Yeah—that rifle in the back seat—Cory stole my kids, and if you hadn't shown up, I would've killed him. "I disapprove, on principle."

"Right."

Randy got out and approached the Tercel like it was a slumbering beast. He advanced to the passenger side. Cast the flashlight beam over the trunk, license plate. He knelt and shined the light on the tire tracks. Back to the car. The rust hole on the trunk revealed the spare tire inside. Randy leaned close to the hole, then continued to the back door.

He shined the light through the window. Tilted his head toward Mae, revealing a cultivated, professional frown.

Randy inspected the front seat. He held the light steady, studying the console, the floor. Hoping to find drugs, if she had to guess. He stepped around the front, passed the driver's door, and again blasted the light into the back.

Mae wilted. I have the gun because I have kids. No. I have kids; therefore, I have a gun. Of course I have a gun. I have kids. God.

Randy returned to the Caprice and opened the door. "You want to hand me the keys?"

"I don't want to."

"It's that, or back to the station."

She dug in her purse. They were at the bottom of the center compartment, but she missed them three times. Pulled out a plastic packet of tissue. A maxi. Chapstick. He'd seen the rifle; why else come back?

"Randy, what are you doing? Don't you want to go home, go to sleep?"

"Night shift. The keys. Or are you finally coming around?"

She passed him the keys.

"Stay put," he said.

Randy left the door open and walked back to the Tercel. He opened the driver's door. Reached back and unlocked the rear, and opened it from outside. He waved her forward.

Mae approached.

"You been robbed."

Randy stepped aside and Mae looked through the open door.

"I recollect a blanket on the back seat. It had a bunch of ducks and whatnot. Daffy and that. I got powers of observation, you might say. This vehicle's the site of a crime, Mae. We're going back to the station—"

"Over a blanket? Who cares about a blanket?" She snatched her keys from his hand and saw his grin. "That's wrong, Randy. Asshole."

She slammed the rear door. Jumped into the driver's seat.

"You drive safe, sugar."

She screeched into the first driveway.

Snapped the shifter to reverse.

Calm.

Now.

The blanket was gone—and the rifle with it.

Baer had the kids.

CHAPTER TWENTY-NINE

Sunlight breaks through trees, leaves fuss like cornhusks rubbing in a breeze. I haven't slept but a couple winks; spent most the night keeping the fire hot enough to melt lead. The girls never been in the woods at night, didn't like it a bit. Every deer or fox that wandered by in the dark, their eyes got big and white. Every story they ever heard about bears eating kids come back. Bree stood and pointed into the black, gutsy but trembling.

"The Boogeyman!"

"What's the Boogeyman?"

"He's made of boogers."

"Well, I'd be afraid of a monster made of boogers too."

Didn't calm her, so I went to the Boogeyman, a clump of scrub oak. I gave it a shake and she screamed. Next it was goblins and trolls. Never ended. I'm bleary-eyed and sober, not the best combination.

We bust camp first light. I cut the blanket in two pieces and wrap each girl in half, like they're Arabian princesses. That's what I tell them. I have Joseph in one arm, Cory's pistol in my pants, my rifle in my hand, and Smith on my hip. A single flask of shine and I'd take all comers.

The kids follow. They're so beautiful it puts the woods and sunlight to shame. But they aren't used to trekking and the going's slow. We avoid roads, follow a trail cut by four-wheelers and dirt bikes.

"I'm tired," Bree says.

"I'm hungry," Morgan says.

Joseph sleeps. Now and again I touch along his neck, down into his chest. He stays warm tucked in my coat and arm, but the girls...

"I'm tired," Bree says.

"C'mere." I go down on my knees. "You see down there?" I point the rifle. "See them houses? That's yours on the end. See your car out front? That means your momma's home, waiting on you. We got another ten, fifteen minutes and we'll be there, and you can raid the kitchen. I'm sure Mae'll cook some breakfast. Can you make it down the hill?"

Bree yawns. "My feet hurt."

"It's a little farther," Morgan says.

"That's right. A little more."

I walk a few steps. Turn. She hasn't moved. "This's the plan." I pass Joseph to Morgan. Take the rifle, eject the cartridge, and ease the lever closed with my finger in the breech so it doesn't feed the next. Pass the rifle to Bree. "It's empty," I say, and show her the cartridge. Slip it in my pocket. She takes the rifle. "All right, Bree. Climb on my back."

I get down on my knees. She climbs me like a horse, holding the rifle in front of my neck, pressed against my throat so I can't breathe. I hook her leg in my right arm, and take Joseph back from Morgan with my left.

"We ready?"

"Giddyup," Bree says.

We get to the house and I'm ready for a stretch on the dirt with my eyes shut. I put Bree down on the front yard. Morgan's already run to the house and Mae throws the door open before she hits the steps.

"Oh baby." She sweeps up Morgan and races down the steps for Bree.

"Ought to get out of town while matters settle."

"I can't reach Mom. I've been calling all night and morning and can't reach her."

"Uh."

"It's been three days now. I tried to call her yesterday, before all this. Something's happened, I know it."

"What's happened?"

"We talked the other day. Last week. About everything. About her, and you, and Larry. She said they'd been fighting and he'd threatened to come hurt me."

"Hurt you."

Mae puts Morgan and Bree on the ground. "Go inside. Hurry." She waits a second. "Mom's in trouble." Mae takes Joseph from me, checks his vitals. Temperature and heart-beat. Color. "I'm worried sick. I know he's done something to her. She doesn't stay out all night."

"You got your car keys?"

She tosses them. I chamber a round in Cory's nine. Hand it to her. "Pull the hammer back this way. Release the safe here. Squeeze the trigger and whatever you hit'll have a reasonable hole in it."

I'm in Mae's Tercel again—a chunk of fuel-efficient rust, spring-mounted on four bald tires. Shimmies like a heavy girl's knockers between forty-five and sixty, but evens out at seventy.

Mars Hill sits north of Asheville. Has a little college, a bunch of houses, a few businesses. Only been here a few times—the last was ten years ago after Ruth divorced Larry. I caught word from a man I sold liquor to, Job Harding. He did me a favor and dug into her address. Every liquor drinker wants a stiller in his debt. Wasn't much digging, it turned out. Him and Ruth lived on the same block.

I couldn't believe Ruth and Larry parted, so I snuck to Mars Hill and scoped her house. Saw her once, purty as ever. I ducked behind a tree and made sure she never saw me.

Been sending letters ever since.

Memory serves, I follow the main drag to the end of town and watch for a left. It isn't the road on her address because there's a turn after that. I get mixed up and drive back and forth a half-dozen times, left and right a couple more, and see Tilson Drive. Must have written "Tilson" two thousand times. Front and center on two thousand envelopes.

There. I stand beside the Tercel and stare. Ragged and overgrown, shingles falling in rusted eaves. A lightning rod leans sideways at the roof apex.

"Ruth's gone," a man says from the sidewalk.

Didn't even see him. His features is plain. Honest.

"Ain't seen her in a week," he says. "Say, you seen a Collie wander by? He just up and disappeared last night."

"Nah, I ain't seen your dog."

CHAPTER THIRTY

One day years back Job Harding came after a bunch of jugs and said they'd be his last. He was giving up the life and these ten cases were for personal consumption, to last until the day he died. I said if he got to the final jug and still felt spry, he'd better drink it all at once.

He lived on the same block as Ruth, but looking from one home to the next, I don't know which is his. Houses are dense like most of the town was done and the builders already tipped a few jugs. The foreman scratched his nuts and said, "We need space for five more houses."

I scan the street back and forth and try to picture Job Harding's pickup. It was an American model... an S-10. He used to brag it had a Camaro engine. Dark green. Chrome mags. Plus these psychedelic green plastic jiggies on his windshield wipers.

That's the whole nineties, right there.

I pass a house and another. No names on the mailboxes, only numbers. No vehicles in the drives. Comes to it I'll beat on every door.

End of the street I look back the way I came. Weather-beaten houses got one foot in the grave. Eaves coming loose, shingles in disrepair, paint cracked or flaked off. Big old gaps between cement blocks. Some of these folks don't enjoy lawn work. Big tufts of grass by the trees, along fences and foundations. There's grass all around a beat-up S-10...

I'm tromping straight for the door, realize it's the back of his house and he'll meet me with a gun. Circle up front.

"Job!" I beat the door with the side of my hand. "Job!"

The door rattles in its frame; I give it another pound. The door gaps open—

"—the sam hell's going on?"

"Job! Where's Ruth?"

He opens the door a bit more. "Hunh?"

He's thinking hard. His eyes cross.

"Job! It's Baer Creighton, out Gleason. You remember?"

"Baer."

"You remember. You bought the liquor. Job?"

"Bought the liquor. Right. Bought the liquor."

He don't know whether to scratch his watch or wind his ass.

"How you doing?" Job says.

"You remember ten year back, you told me Ruth Jackson lived a couple houses down? I'm looking for her."

His brows tighten. "Poor girl."

"How's that? Where is she?"

"Prob'ly in the ground, halfway to Pisgah. Who knows?"

"Why... why you say that?"

His eyes widen. "Oh! You're Baer Creighton... out Gleason way!"

"That's right, Job. What happened to Ruth?"

He exhales a long breath. Slumps to the jamb. "Larry Creighton happened to her."

"He take her away?"

"He beat on her, is what he did. I saw through the back winda, here. His truck was in the drive, and since I know the history, I watched close. Cracked the winda, case I could hear anything."

"What do you mean, you know the history?"

"Oh, goin' way back when she moved out here. She told me. Woman loved to talk. Loved it. And when Larry started coming around again a few weeks back, I paid attention. Half the time he'd park down the street and never get out—he'd sit there in the truck smokin' cigarettes. This last time he went in the house. I sat on the commode twenty minute. Then he come out, and she come out, and she's hitting him all over. Angry as a hive o' hornets. He's got his arms up and she's thumping him any which ways. She screaming gibberish and he's shouting back. Then he reaches one arm way back like this, I swear to you, Baer, just like this."

Job curls his hand into a fist and swings hard.

"Clocks her. She goes flat. She laid there, Baer. Dead as Lincoln."

I look behind me and to my side. Nowhere to sit, and my legs are about give out. I don't get a single shock and his eyes are plain white. "You saw all that?"

"Every bit of it. Larry looked all around, after that. See if anyone was watching. Then put her in his truck. You know how it is when a body's just a body and they ain't no person in it. Arms and feet dangling."

Cement comes up to my knees, then my hands. I swing my ass below me. My head tingles and my ears rush with noise. My mind steadies and I sit on the cold cement. Mae said Ruth still had a thing for me after all these years. I should have gone and found her five years ago. Ten years ago. Hell, I did find her. I should have come out from behind that tree and said I'll take you now, and we'll never look back. We have twenty thirty years left—let's run out west and spend them together.

That letter I mailed her today—I don't think I ever before said we could go away like that.

I breathe. For a few seconds, that's all I can do. "What kind of law you got around here? You tell 'em?"

"I told em."

"What'd they do?"

"They didn't believe me. They went over and knocked on her door, said she was out getting groceries. Walking her cat. I said she don't got a cat and they walked off while I was talking at em. One stayed in his car there at her house for a half-hour, then he left too. Ain't been back."

Ruth's door is locked. I beat on it and glass panes rattle. I wait on the step and think maybe she's coming to the door right now. If she answers... if she swings the door open right now, what will I say?

I rap again with a little less gumption. Look at the lawn and imagine Larry walloping Ruth like Job said. See her fall, knocked out. Knocked dead. And him carrying her into his truck. This back-and-forth with Larry —all these pieces start to fit a little better. I come poking around and talk to Eve, and maybe Eve says I come on to her, like any scorned woman might. So he looks at his hand, decides to raise me. I'll take your dog and the only woman you ever might have loved.

This won't stop until Larry and me throw down the cards and go sideways out the window.

I try the doorknob again. Job's on his front step, shaking his head, talking.

My coat sleeve's good and stiff. I smash my elbow through the lower pane. Rips my jacket and pinches the skin. I reach through and feel for the lock. In a couple seconds I'm looking over Ruth's living room. Coffee table, sofa, small television with rabbit ears. Telephone on the end table. I can see her curled on the couch with the phone, talking with Mae about all the crazy things women talk about. Pisses me off. She was my woman. That was my life—seeing her yammering all day and night. Me having to go to the other side of the house for a moment's peace. That was mine.

There's the kitchen beyond. I should've had the last thirty years of her banging pots and pans and roasting whole chickens. Thirty years of sneaking up behind her and giving her a squeeze.

"Ruth?"

My voice checks the rooms and echoes back empty-handed.

I breathe in deep and catch a cinnamon scent. Glance things over. Get the full scope of the house. If I miss something that might tell me what happened, I'll spend the rest of my years with another kind of guilt.

In her bedroom is a bureau with frilly things that smell nice. I pull each drawer and push it closed without molesting anything. There's a photo of Mae on the nightstand. One pillow on the bed. Closet with clothes, extra shoes at the bottom. A thousand. I look at her desk, with a mirror and lights above. An antique-painted monstrosity with a box of makeup that looks like a tackle box of fishing lures. All stuff a woman would take if she was leaving for a while, and it's the best evidence old Job saw what he saw.

I check the bathroom. Toothbrush in a cup.

Kitchen's fulla food… not a lot, but assorted. She was partial to Spam.

I'm back to the living room and on the coffee table spot a letter I missed the first time through. It's one of the handful I sent last week, opened, letter partly out of the envelope. There's a shoebox full of letters under the sofa.

I lift the box and thumb across the tops. In order, by date.

Job's still on his stoop. I head at him and he says, "Find anything?"

"Where's the police, this town?"

"Twenty-eight Main. That'll be the north end."

Six minutes I'm there. Step inside and smell burnt coffee. By the look, the day shift is accustomed to nothing going on. College kids might keep the night crew busy, but this town walks like it's got a stick in its ass, so maybe not.

"Help you?" the man says. He's got a beard and no mustache. Eyes lidded like a frog. Feet propped on the corner of his desk.

"Fella named Job Harding reported a woman missing a couple days back. Ruth Jackson."

"Yeah."

"Well, she's still missing."

He studies me. "Guess we can file a report."

"Thought you'd get off your chair and look for her."

He drops his feet off the desk but doesn't trouble to rise. "Last I looked, there was no reason to suspect any foul play. She up and went somewhere." He squints. "You got different information?"

"She ain't where she always is."

"You a member of the family?"

"No."

"Well then who are you?"

"Never mind." I back out the door.

"Hey!"

I get in the car and head out of town.

Cory Smylie realized Stipe had been correct. The foundation was self-control. He'd screwed up while intoxicated. He'd humiliated himself again. He hadn't been able to think, and a millisecond after a decision, he knew it was wrong. Yet he pushed through, and moment by moment his situation worsened.

He should have known Baer Creighton would mount a rescue. Creighton was Mae's hero. He should have foreseen a police response—his father was the police chief. Instead of slow anger and painstaking plans, Cory had raged. Acted on impulse. He'd been high. So much for invincibility.

The humiliation was real. He owned the respect of no man in the county. His kids feared him. His woman chose to screw her flesh and blood over him. Stipe had heard of the night's misadventures and by now had written him off as a failure. He'd done it to himself.

He would do things different this time.

He'd awakened the following morning with a knot on his head. A brain that felt flattened by a steamroller. He looked around outside for his gun and couldn't find it, but the Taser was in the neighbor's hedges. He went inside the house. Took four Tylenol with a glass of water and went back to sleep.

He woke at noon and lay in bed, staring at the ceiling. A dull ache filled him, the residual pain of a body fed poison. He wanted a joint to smooth things over. A cup of coffee and a joint and a beer. Between the three of them, his body would find the chemical it craved.

Then he thought of Stipe. How he'd placed his hand on Cory's shoulder. How his voice had softened. The most powerful man in Buncombe County had seen something in him worth saving. The moment was like being in church. Guilt. Hope. Stipe had told the truth. Cory was destroying himself. If he didn't get a handle on his addictions, it didn't matter how hard he tried to do anything else. He was sabotaging himself.

Cory rose from bed. His head throbbed. He stood with his hand on the headboard for a full minute while his blood pressure evened out. He couldn't continue like this. He felt like an old man.

Disgust washed through him.

Discipline. Cory closed his eyes, embraced the pain. I will beat you, he said. He thought of Mae, saw her in her uncle's embrace. Cory needed discipline to right his life and save his kids. He owed it to them. He'd been a coward too long. He would face himself, and when he had control, he would face his enemy.

Cory swallowed two more Tylenol and three glasses of water. He reached for a pack of Marlboros and withdrew one. Stuck it in his mouth and lit it.

He inhaled smoke.

This is what's destroying me.

He stubbed the cigarette in an ashtray.

He needed to go away. He could go to Baltimore, where he had contacts...

He shook his head and the headache stabbed. Wrong decision.

"My troubles are right here."

He squeezed the pack of Marlboros in his hand. He crumpled the box and worked his fingers back and forth, grinding the cigarettes inside. When the box was a ball and the aroma of the tobacco rich, he dumped the contents in the toilet and flushed.

Cory returned to his room and pulled a shoebox from under the bed. He'd never had to find a crafty way to hide his drugs because his parents never looked. He opened the box, removed a plastic baggie of pot, and took it to the bathroom.

He was being rash, but he also knew from the silence of the little voice that this was right. Drugs were killing him, not only his body but his mind and his hope of ever amounting to anything. Drugs were his perennial retreat. Drugs were cowardice incarnate. He dumped the baggie into the toilet and flushed.

Still in his boxers, Cory grabbed his keys, walked down the steps, exited the house, and opened his truck. He pulled a leather satchel from under the seat and carried it to the bathroom.

He stopped. Wouldn't he be better off selling it? Be done with it... At least get his investment back? He only had a few hundred dollars, and this bag was worth a couple thousand. The little voice said no. One by one, Cory emptied pill bottles and baggies into the toilet.

That was going to be one stoned septic system. He smiled.

He had faced himself. He was learning self-control. Once he reined in his mind, he would revisit Stipe's recommendations. He'd think things through, but one way or the other Mae and Baer Creighton were over.

He'd show Stipe he was serious. Cory had just the right idea.

CHAPTER THIRTY-ONE

Those dogfighters have the law. No way Horace Smylie will turn on his friends. That's not how the bloodsport clique works. It's an invitation-only affair. You need a ticket stamped by six of your daddy's cousins. Ticket says you're salt of the earth, death-lovin and blood-lovin and prone to keep mum.

They operate in secret because most folks—even being liars and cheats —recognize pure evil. These dogfight men say dogs are born to fight. They crave squaring off against another dog and seeing who's best. They say it happens every day in the wild, and most wolves don't die from old age, but other wolves.

I've had a bellyful thinking about what Fred endured in the pit. Maimed, so these men could guffaw and place bets. And that—whether the dogs want to fight or not—makes it evil.

I been thinking on Larry, and how my past with Ruth has things mixed up. She was with both of us, back and forth. I did wrong by Larry. But you can't turn your back on family like Larry did. You can't show disgust for where you came from without showing disgust for who you came with.

Ruth went back and forth. She had Mae and I took the house from her and Larry.

After that, I went out and found the house they'd rented. It was evening and Larry was at college. I gave the door a knock. Stood there with a clump of lazy Susans wilting in my hand. Ruth answered the door but wouldn't take the chain off, so I looked at her through a two-inch gap.

"I'm going to win you back," I said.

"You got to let things end."

"Hell I do. If it's money you and your daddy got to have, I'll get it."

"Don't matter if you do. I'm married. I'm a mother."

I had a hunch I could make money off my talent. Knew a fella from working the gas station. Lou Debenker. Drank beers and shot stick at the bar. He was working some insurance racket. Said he drove around all day and collected money off people. Only thing he did was ask each one if it was time to buy more insurance, every week when he saw em. He'd get the neighbors' names and sell the insurance to them too. Product sold itself, Lou said, if the salesman had the knack. No limit on the dough he could make.

Lou introduced his boss, playing pool the next table over. Permanent red coming out of him. He didn't mean harm—some folks broadcast they're cheats, and that almost makes them honest. Lou's boss was listening and said he'd give me a job on the spot if I'd ask every man in the bar if he needed life insurance.

Sounds easy enough. I go to the first five guys and each either looks away or says "piss off." Next man says no, but his eyes flash red and I get a shock. In those days shocks were live-wire hot. I said, "You know damn well you need life insurance, and it's been eating at you. Come talk to my buddy over here and he'll set you up so you can sleep at night."

Day later the boss showed me the ropes. Then I built my own system. A man would look at his wife and kids, and by the time his eyes got back to me they were red and he'd be done for. I'd push until he was honest.

After a few months I had a pile of money and the kind of prospects Ruth's daddy could appreciate. I had snappy clothes and green in my billfold. Went to see Ruth while Larry was gone again and she looked through the two-inch door gap.

"You can't come here," she said.

Her eyes glowed.

I about messed my drawers. Thought my curse failed. She was all the time honest and randy. I didn't figure she was honest because our desires were congruent until I thought on it a decade. One time, one big-assed lie. But knowing a woman has deceit in her heart doesn't tell you which words are the lie. I didn't arrive at her real lie until long after.

"I got money," I said. "Look at this." I opened my wallet and stood there like a fool. Might as well have had a fedora with a flamingo feather. Boots with my pant legs tucked in.

"You rob a bank?"

"I sell life insurance. Setting records every day."

"You're a life insurance salesman?"

"Ruth, you got no call flipping back to Larry. Don't you get it?"

She slammed the door. Locked it.

That was that. Didn't matter if I had money. Had to get it the right way. Inherit from somebody else or have a sit-on-your-ass job looking down on everybody. I quit insurance and went to see Gunter Stroh. Put my money into a still, and a few hundred pounds of corn, wheat, barley, yeast, and sugar. Wrapped my neck tie around a spruce pole and used it to light the first fire under my boiler.

Thinking of Ruth in those days doesn't come close to taking the ache off her being dead. I gave up on people, but I never gave up on Ruth. If I'd done that, life would have been hopeless.

Now that she's gone, I have to face the truth. Evil is everywhere. She had it too. She lied.

I know what I need to know.

There's killing to come.

I hope Larry's at the next fight. I'll kill him for watching Fred suffer, but he deserves it more for Ruth.

Cory stole Fred. Got the right color truck, took it for a wash so the tailgate was all clean after that night. Stipe paid him to find bait dogs and somehow he knew about mine. He knew about the Hun blind—that must have been him smoking dope in there and couldn't shoot for nothing.

Cory's flat got it coming—him and every other man that goes to dog fights. The men who keep the institution alive. Bet on it. Hoot and holler. The man who stage the fights. The whole crew. The ugliness goes on and on, until a man ends it.

I know what I know and I feel positively sanctified about the murder to come.

CHAPTER THIRTY-TWO

Cory Smylie was sober.

The first day was easy. His ill feeling reinforced his commitment. He kept his goals foremost in his mind. When he needed to focus his self-control, he thought about destroying Baer Creighton. Baer was the glue that kept Cory coherent.

Without chemicals corrupting his thought process he felt grounded. The right path was easy to spot and simple to walk. Self-control was the ultimate thrill.

But on the second day his thoughts were nebulous. He couldn't concentrate and every challenge left him frustrated. He tore the cereal box because the morons at Post used too much glue. His parents had been gone for days at his mother's business expo. No one had done the dishes, and he had to wash a cereal bowl and a spoon. The phone wouldn't stop ringing—deputies wanting to question him again. Or worse, his lame father wanting answers on an attempted break-in.

Man, he could use a joint.

In high school he'd wrestled. Long before he tried dope, he'd subjected himself to grueling team practices. He learned to crave the intoxication of sweat.

Sitting with his mind spinning out of control, he desired to exert himself. Feel a real blood rush. His lungs full with air. His muscles responding with strength.

He threw on sweats and running shoes.

Cory started out fast. His body hadn't felt this good for a long time. Adrenaline shot through him. His legs were pistons and his arms worked back and forth like locomotive rods.

Within a minute his lungs were on fire. His legs grew wobbly. He eased his stride and looked at his watch, gasping. Two minutes. He used to run for an hour at a time, fast. Way faster than this. He glanced at his watch again and looked up to see a cute girl jogging toward him. He grinned. His toe caught an uneven sidewalk slab. Cory flew against a hedge and rolled back to the cement.

He sat on the sidewalk with his elbows on his knees. His eyes rimmed with tears. The cute girl trotted by and he was too ashamed to watch her wiggle.

And then he got up and smacked the dust from his thighs. He picked a thorn from his palm and resumed the run. He wouldn't attempt a full hour, but he owed it to himself to do his best. To not quit at the first hardship. What else was he going to do? Smoke a joint?

Cory Smylie hadn't felt this kind of emotional stability, such cold blankness, for years. Every action resulted from thinking things through. He had time and commitment.

Cory crinkled the cash in his pants pocket. He'd taken every stashed dollar. He'd pored over every detail of his plan. He knew how to get close. He knew those woods almost as well as Creighton. He wouldn't make the same mistakes as last time.

He had been crazy to think that while he was high, drunk, and short on sleep, he could outwit an animal like Creighton. He was lucky to have failed, for if he had been successful he would have returned home with the murder weapon. He'd seen CSI. Mae would have thrown the spotlight on him and the police would have matched the rifle.

But not this time.

He stood behind a glass counter at Frankenmuth's Big Sports studying a row of Cold War–era rifles. He'd driven to Charlotte. In case there were cameras in the store, Cory wore a stick-on mustache. He'd dyed his hair black and covered most of it with a Carolina Panthers baseball cap.

He scanned the racks back and forth but his gaze kept drifting to a 1953 Soviet-made AK-47. The rifle looked rugged.

"It's a great rifle," the heavyset man in plaid said. He found a key from a ring of fifty and removed the rifle from the rack. He handed it across the glass counter. "What'll you use it for?"

"Targets."

"Any distance?"

"Two hundred yards."

"Well, it's a good gun."

Cory heard a subtle change in tone. "But?"

"AK's are known for standing up to abuse. That's because they're manufactured sloppy. You can charge it, shove a handful of dirt into the bolt housing, and it'll still cycle the next round, and the next. They're indestructible. But all that sloppiness costs you, especially on a fifty-year-old rifle. You could bolt this thing to an iron table and not shoot a ten-inch group at two hundred yards."

Cory nodded. "So what's better?"

"Anything, if you want accuracy." He lifted the AK from Cory's hands, replaced it in the rack and removed another weathered rifle. This one was older and had seen more use. The stock extended to the end of the barrel and the bolt handle stuck straight out the side. The man passed the rifle to Cory. "Take this Mauser. Fine German engineering. By the time they made this in 1898, they'd already had thirty-plus years to work out the bugs. Open the bolt."

Cory did.

"See how tight that is? No play at all. Smooth action. Now slam it home."

Cory slapped the bolt handle forward and down, a liquid action. The rifle balanced in his hands and the smell was rich like metal and oil. "This accurate?"

"Oh yeah. Two hundred yards is short-range. I hunt deer with one of these and bagged a ten-point at four hundred. They say they're accurate to a thousand yards. Way more than the average shooter'd know what to do with."

"Right," Cory said. "How much?"

"This one? We got a sale going on today. One ninety-nine. I'll make you a sweet deal on two."

"One will do the job."

Cory passed the Gleason interstate exit. He'd spent the two-hour drive from Charlotte dreaming of his Mauser's recoil and hoping it would be robust. He'd bought four boxes of ammunition and everything he'd need to sight in the rifle. He would work at it until fluent with the rifle's mechanics. He had two hours before dark.

His ears rang. They'd been ringing all day, but he hadn't realized it until he slowed coming off the Old Fort exit. His body missed drugs, but his soul was greedy for the coherence of sobriety.

Sykes Range was a few miles from a church-and-crossroads community north of Old Fort. Ten winding miles down the mountain from Gleason. It consisted of a small cabin attached to a fifty-foot indoor pistol range. The range only permitted dues paying members to use the indoor facility. Outside, they'd removed a wide swath of trees from the mountain approach. They'd placed rough-sawn posts and fence rails every fifty, then hundred yards. Each splintered and riddled with holes.

Locals used the outdoor range as they pleased. Most of the time they only came to sight their rifles before buck season. Cory had visited the range the year he graduated high school, and had a sense for its pace. With almost a month before deer season, he was unlikely to encounter other shooters.

But he had to be prudent. He motored over the gravel and rehearsed his cover story. "Coming in a little high last season. Thought I'd bring it in. What you shooting?"

Cory pressed down the sides of his fake mustache and threw on a ball cap. Trees along the drive obscured the parking area but so far he hadn't heard any gunfire. He slipped on dark sunglasses but the sun was already behind the mountain. Sunglasses at dusk looked ridiculous. He'd never noticed that, high. He tossed the shades to the console.

The driveway opened into the parking area. Cory was alone.

He parked and filled his pockets with a marker, thumb-tacks, and three boxes of cartridges. Carried the Mauser to the back of the Sykes building, and looked at a row of triangular shooting tables under a rusted sheet metal roof. A cold gust made his eyes water. An unanchored piece of metal tapped a post. Cory chose a table and placed his rifle on sandbags.

When he'd been here as a teenager, his friends had ridiculed him. He'd never shot seriously, for accuracy. But he'd listened to his friends' tips and watched their mechanics. He learned to control his breathing. He assumed the same posture every time, and found an identical sight picture. He fused his friends' lessons with his innate sense and over a short time became the best shot of the group.

Cory looked downrange with trepidation and regret. How much skill had he lost?

He emptied his pockets and carried the targets and tacks to the left-most fence at two hundred yards. He affixed a black bulls-eye and returned to the rifle.

When he'd come to this place as a teenager, he'd been steady and his eye was clear. Now his mind was ringing. His nerves were sharp from the absence of drugs. He was kind of spacey, kind of focused. He would hold a thought and realize after a moment that he'd been thinking of something different. At any moment he might penetrate some deep truth. He was conscious that he was conscious, and his self-awareness felt like an awakening. A turning point. He would choose what he wanted to be. He would be anything he chose.

He slipped a cartridge into the Mauser's open chamber.

He would be lethal.

CHAPTER THIRTY-THREE

E rnie Gadwal had watched through binoculars as Baer Creighton buried his mutt. He'd moved sideways a little and pressed his pants, shifting the erection below with the palm of his hand. Wished he could do something about it.

Misery drove Creighton's shovel into the dirt. Wrath pulled it out. Ernie had studied Creighton's motions. Mused on how Creighton would react if he knew his dog's slayer was so close.

Like Nietzsche said, build your cities on the slope of Vesuvius.

Ernie followed Creighton's long forest trek to the cave bearing the remains of an old-timer's still. He followed Creighton to his busty niece's house. Several times he'd thought Baer had spotted him, but his size and craft kept him safe. Ernie had never walked so much in his life, and when Creighton took off in his niece's car, Ernie had a use for the free time.

Burly scared him. But Ernie saw their eventual partnership as a détente. They each had more to gain by cooperating than by destroying one other.

Requisite to détente was the ability to mount a strong defense. Ernie had tired of fearing for his life every time Burly was around. If Burly was going to wear a Bowie knife, Ernie strapped a surprise to his ankle. A .25 caliber pistol he'd picked up at an Asheville pawn shop a year before. It wasn't accurate but Burly was big.

Ernie sat on the trunk of his car. He glanced over his shoulder toward town, watching for Burly. Then he looked over the other shoulder, watching for Creighton. Ernie had copied Burly's preparations. He'd stowed five-gallon jerry cans of gasoline in his trunk, right under him. If Creighton crossed to Brown's farm with Burly absent, Ernie would take action alone.

It had to work. Stipe would realize Ernie's value, and other elements would fall into place.

Overtaking Stipe would be a long, surreptitious operation. Ernie would be clever and endearing until Stipe was no longer useful. Then they would become competitors, and Stipe wouldn't know what hit him.

Ernie returned his thoughts to the present. He knew he could get Burly to imagine being more powerful than Stipe. But could he convince Burly success was only possible with Ernie as his partner?

Burly said Stipe wanted Creighton dead sooner rather than later. Burly would return, and when he arrived he would go to Creighton's and shoot him. Throw him over his shoulder, and carry him to his final resting pyre at Brown's.

Creighton would be dead whether Burly followed his impulse or Ernie's nuanced plan. The method of execution only mattered insofar as Stipe knew Ernie had conceived it. Ernie drummed his fingers against the car trunk.

The money would make a stronger argument—money, and a challenge to Burly's courage.

It felt like madness, giving half the gold to Burly. But in exchange Ernie gained Burly's most fervent labor. Ernie had considered all this before. He could steal every dollar from the money tree, and pay Burly by the hour.

But a wage man wouldn't toil like an equity man.

In the end, he would exchange half the fortune for Stipe's favor and Burly's labor. Wasn't that how empires were built? Strategic bets at opportune moments?

A distant, high-pitched sound came to Ernie and he glanced toward town. A dust plume chased a black sport utility vehicle up the hill. Ernie leaped from his trunk. He dashed across the fifty-yard stretch to the road and arrived as the Suburban crested the hill.

Ernie waved and watched for the Suburban's nose to dip.

It raced closer.

Ernie jumped to the center of the road and threw his arms wide. The Suburban swerved and skidded. Inside, Burly cursed and beat his fists to the dashboard. The window lowered and Burly craned his head out. "Get off the road, jackass! Move!"

Ernie looked downhill toward Creighton's place, a half-mile away. He motioned with his hands for Burly to keep his voice down.

"Move!"

Ernie put his hands on the bug deflector. Burly revved the engine. "You have to wait a minute. It won't be long until he goes to the Brown house and we can do it the right way."

"I want it done with. Get off the road. You think Stipe cares how it happens?"

"I do, and if he don't he ought to. My way leaves no evidence. You can't off a man and carry him two hundred yards in broad daylight dripping blood! Besides, there's no poetry to it. There's nothing to give it any class."

"Step aside or I'll throw your body in Brown's house too."

Ernie rushed around to Burly's side window. Burly reached for the shifter.

"You don't want to do that," Ernie said. "I know a million reasons you don't want to do that."

"What?"

"I know where Creighton's hid a million bucks. His life savings, all in gold."

"Bull."

"Think about it. What's he do with all that money he makes? He lives in a lean-to! You can kill me too, if it isn't true."

Burly shook his head. "So why don't you go get it?"

"I need your help. All I know, he's got booby traps all over. He's wily. If you go after Creighton right now, you'll be dead inside of five minutes. I've followed him twenty-four seven for the last two weeks. There's no way you can get the drop on him. He's got eyes in the back of his head. Closest I got was two hundred yards, and that's in the woods. But you wait for him to get inside the basement of that house, those eyes in the back of his head won't matter. He won't stand a chance. When that's done, then we get the money."

Burly frowned and stared down the hill. "You followed him everywhere?"

"I followed the night he got the drop on you after that dog fight, and left you for a black bear to maul."

Burly looked away and spit as if trying to remove a fleck of tobacco from his tongue. "A million dollars, huh? Don't make sense for you to tell me when you could have it all yourself."

"I need your help. Not to get through all those booby traps. What to do with the money, big picture. Think what you and me could do with a million bucks, you being so tight with Stipe. We'll go into business."

Burly grunted and removed his hand from the shifter. "What kind of business?"

"I've given it some thought. I can see from your face you think I'm lying. But that money's real and I'll show you where it is once Creighton can't put a bullet in my back."

"What makes you think I won't?"

"That's a chance I'll take. Think about running your own business, with an operations guy like me handling the paper. Gathering the intelligence. Think of passing men on the street and their eyes light up with fear. Respect. Their voices shake when they talk, and they say 'Mister' if they say anything at all. You wearing a black suit, driving a new Lincoln truck. Tell me that wouldn't make you proud. Let's get real. You'll be bigger than Stipe."

Ernie paused and lifted his hands from Burly's window.

"If I'm wrong, you can go on down the hill and get shot. I'll partner with someone else. But if I'm right, why don't we go back to the lookout? We've got business to talk. We got capital, we can do anything. There's going to be a shortage of top-notch moonshine in a week or two."

"Get in."

~

I sit for two days looking at Fred's grave. Then I'm ready.

Brown used to have a still. I saw it in the basement—little two-gallon can with five, six feet of copper. Operation I have in mind, that's subpar. But there's not a lot of places a man can go for a twenty-gallon cooker.

I slip to the drive, look both ways before crossing. Feel hunted on my own land. Every time I pass where Fred bled in the dirt and grass it's like a fist inside my head and eggbeaters in my belly. The one makes me mad enough to kill; the other makes me want to throw up.

I look from the blood-stained ground up to Brown's house. Bowed porch looks like a dopey smile and the shattered upstairs windows like stoned eyes. I'm reminded everything decays, and that's the way of it. And as soon as I murder every man that watched Fred get chewed, things will be right as rain.

Brown never was a full-time operator. He made soap and he made liquor. Sometimes the one tasted like the other. I study the device he left. A little professional attention and Brown's booze machine'll find its voice.

I glance over tools on the workbench, hanging on the wall, stuffed on shelves. Coffee cans of rusted screws. A carpenter's level. A square. A plumb bob. Trowel. Fishing poles between the joists, tucked above white electric lines. How long's it been since I had leeks and trout?

I carry a hacksaw to the water heater on the opposite corner.

The inch-thick copper out the top is too thick and won't bend. But I already took all the thin, flexible stuff, and the goons hacked it to pieces. I cut close to the water heater until the pipe dangles. Fetch a rickety stool. Saw again, fifteen feet from the water heater, where the pipe hangs below a two-by-six.

With a claw hammer from the bench I pry the U-shaped supports. Carry a long, bowed pipe and the two-gallon boiler from the house. I rest them on the ground out front. Down the road a ways on the Gleason side, a big old rooster plume of dust billows up. Somebody's making good time.

I head back to the basement. Boiler that small, it'll be twice the work unless I get a doubler. I shake a turpentine can and find it empty. I'll drill the sides, slap a couple fixtures. Good thing Stipe didn't burn my toolshed.

There's a motor outside. Door clunks shut. Somebody got a dog to get rid of? That vehicle was coming from town, not the other way.

I think on it.

A long-lost heir come to claim the rust and rot? Or somebody looking to settle a score with Baer Creighton?

Turpentine can in one hand, Smith in the other, I take the steps sideways, each foot slow. I listen. No more sounds. I have electric on my arms and neck. Electric on my nads.

They stay outside. I hear metal tinkle with the timpani sound of a jug of liquid. Jerry cans. Voices mumble.

I climb the steps and stay within the shadows at the top, looking into the kitchen. Through a busted window I see a black Suburban with a shiny white bumper sticker on the front left side.

I bet a bucket a gold it says DEPENDS ON THE DEFINITION OF TREASON.

Burly Worley's Suburban.

Short man crosses in front of the window, with his eyes pointed at the base of the house like he's looking for bugs. He's gone. Says something to another somebody, out of eyeshot.

Glass shatters and metal clangs.

I smell gasoline. They laugh.

"Go ahead. Stand back."

That'd be Burly.

I creep down a stair and ready myself for a kamikaze run. Whole house is a tinderbox.

There's a whoosh and a roar! Wood crackles. Sound rushes around the house; flames shoot past the windows and dance inside.

Burly Worley and some short gidgit is walking back to the vehicle.

Let's think a minute, before all I got time for is raw panic. They won't stay outside forever. Not with smoke headed high and calling attention for miles. They'll scoot.

Black smoke already hangs at the ceiling. Flames flash and glow in each room.

Years and years ago I sat with Brown in this kitchen. He liked to play solitaire while he talked. Telling lies about an eight-point buck he saw eating apples or how he was going under the knife to cut out the cancer. I bet he never foresaw this.

Burly Worley's little sidekick puts me in the mind of a taco dog hopped up on drugs. Each carries a shotgun like he thinks a bird'll flush. I'm the bird. Burly points to the right. Steps to the left, and they split to cover all four sides of the house from opposite corners.

Flames jitterbug through the kitchen. Walls are orange and the ceiling black. Getting right hot. I back down a step as I got nothing needs cauterized just yet, but a draft throws some real heat. I rumble down the stairs and get my mind right in the basement.

Above is pure hell, no way out but through it. If the fire doesn't get me the shotguns stand a chance. There's a door out of the basement, one of them slope-roofed jobs. But Burly and the gidgit would see it pop open, and I'd be in their crossfire.

That electric jolt that upended the hair on my nuts—that wasn't because they came to throw a party. They know I'm here, and they want me a charred corpse. They'll shoot me coming out and toss me back in.

Did one of them torch my house, go to the still site and put a hole in Fred? Did the taco dog leave the child's footprint?

The upstairs roar sucks air out of the basement. See flames between floorboards. Glass shatters. I step half across the basement. Stop, jog back to the stairs. I got that boiler outside.

I don't think good sober. At all.

Two windows let in outside light, but they aren't twelve inches tall, and their bottoms are seven feet up.

I climb in the slope-door cubby. Dank and spider-webby, and the whole joint's getting hot. Smoke even down here, lower and lower. Some point, stuff will start falling through. A cast iron tub on the head would do the trick.

Stone blocks are cool. I press against them and keep my head low.

A rattle sets me back.

Snake!

Where is he? I check my parts and step away. He didn't strike, yet. You'd think I could see his eyes or something. Not exactly easy to see down here, but he's coiled back in the cubby.

There's an old shovel handle with no blade, other side of the basement. Ducking smoke, I run over and grab it. Head back to the snake. He ain't happy, got that tail-rattle snapping. I toss him across the floor and probe with the handle along the steps.

I'm off to the side now; whole house could fall in and it wouldn't hit me. Can't get air from the door—can't open it for fear of two shotguns.

I freeze, all but my heart. Scales and slithering on my leg, where the pant's pulled over the boot. Snake crosses my ankle, give me a shiver up the spine. I got something on my neck feels like a big old freaked-out spider. Every inch of my body tingles and I never knew fear my whole life until now. I'm resolute on that. That rattler's a long somebody, seems like fifteen minutes until the last of him crosses.

I smash some bug was on my neck, wipe my hand on the cement.

"Look'it that!" Voice outside the slope door.

"Shoot it!"

I roll down the cement steps and a shotgun barks. Part of the door blasts inward and I'm looking out a hole. Sunlight sheets in through the smoke, and I see Burly Worley has his shotgun pointed. He grins at the dead snake and don't see me.

I can't breathe. Upstairs is howling. Smoke burns my lungs. I'm low as I can get but the smoke goes to the cement floor. I hold my breath.

They must've seen the still and pipe out front.

I'm ready to come out shooting. Move forward on my belly, Smith up front. Upstairs is all whooshing and roaring. Them boys got to be back ten fifteen feet else they'll get suntans off the house. I blink away the burn in my eyes but it comes right back. Try to breathe with my sleeve over my mouth.

Something upstairs drops. Sounds like the whole place is falling in. Back in the cubby. If there are more snakes in here they're not worried about me. A shaft of light comes through the shotgun hole. The smoke looks heavenly.

That short devil outside shot Fred.

I can't breathe. My eyes are on fire.

I push up on the slope door. Rock solid. I gag out a breath and suck in a new lungful but it's hot and burns like acid.

If I stick my face in the shotgun hole, it's liable to get blown off.

I go flat against the floor and slither with my nose against cement. Spit coming out my eyes, grime in my teeth. That beam of light from the shotgun hole cuts through the smoke. Halts at the center of the cement floor, at a drain hole.

Clear air eddies up through.

I crawl. Blink. Scrape, and I'm there. I stick my mouth on the drain and suck in the sweetest outside air, cool like five feet underground. I pant. The inferno is above me. I'm dead center in the basement, where the whole shebang'll drop in a couple minutes.

I breathe while the clean air lasts.

CHAPTER THIRTY-FOUR

Ernie and Burly stood with their shotguns at the slope doored basement exit. The upper house was flames through and through. If Creighton was alive, he was in the basement, and if he tried to escape, it would be through this door.

"Point there," Burly said. "Don't wave that around all the time. Or put it in the Suburban if you don't know what to do with it. He's dead by now anyway."

Ernie aimed at the basement door. "He's not dead yet. Wait until the whole house falls in, then he's dead."

"Look at the smoke pouring out that hole. He's dead."

"It doesn't hurt to be cautious."

Burly stared a long while across the road at Creighton's woods.

Ernie had watched the idea take hold of Burly as they discussed setting up a stilling operation. The only tense moment came when Ernie said they should keep their ambitions secret.

Stipe would include them in his distribution scheme. His success resulted from exploiting the little guys. But as far as Stipe needed to know, rebuilding Creighton's business would use all their resources. They would keep him uninformed and use their windfall to expand. Develop their own distribution channels. Enter new territories. Buy out existing operators—or take them out the old-fashioned way. Once they'd grown to a position of strength, they'd dictate terms to Stipe.

Burly's caveman brow had crumpled at the thought. "If I'm anything, it's loyal," he said.

"You think Stipe was loyal to the people he shoved aside or outright killed to get where he is now? You can't build something big without being loyal to yourself first. And if that's a problem, we better rethink this partnership."

Burly had frowned. Ernie felt awkward being so brazen. But finding accord on the long-term vision was paramount. They had to want the same end.

Burly's brow did overtime. Ernie fought the urge to hedge. By the time they watched smoke coming from the shotgun blast hole, Burly was on board.

"Two minutes. It's enough smoke that he can't breathe. So we give him two more minutes," Ernie said. "Then we get the gold."

Burly looked at his watch.

~

I gulp one big final lungful of air and I'm ready for battle. Strength's back in my arms and legs and Smith's ready to bark. I lead with my shoulder. Hold my breath and hit that door with all I got. It flies open.

I'm in daylight, looking, spinning, gagging in smoke. It's a furnace up here! Grass on fire!

I run, dive and roll. The ground twists Smith out my hand. I come up on my feet and Burly and his taco dog are gone. The Suburban's gone.

I grab Smith and point. Turn a full circle. A blast of flame lashes out like a fist and it's gone before I can duck. This whole place is going to fall.

Sirens come from down the road, fire trucks leaving a half-mile plume. I beat the flames off my legs. No way I can get across the road to my side before they get here. They'll want water from the crick? Nah, they'll watch this place burn; try and make sure the fields don't catch, or the woods across the road.

I trot back into the orchard and hunker in the brush. I'm fifty yards off and when the wind comes this way it carries the heat.

Need to get my mind around all this.

It wasn't accident, me being inside. Stipe knows I pick apples and whatnot out of Brown's place. Stipe burned my place to the ground. Sicced the law on me. Destroyed my still; went after my customers, and so I couldn't get them back, he burned the Brown place. Maybe me being inside was his good luck, but it seems Stipe wants me out of the picture.

≈

Cory stepped three paces and stopped. The Mauser in his hands was an extension of his body, of his mind.

He had shot three full boxes of ammunition the night before. He'd placed a single cartridge in the chamber. Wedged the barrel between sandbags, like he would experience at the blind. He took aim, and fired. Then he ejected the shell and went through the entire process again. He loaded and fired one shell at a time. He would learn the process and posture. He would learn to be perfect every time.

After every third shot he checked his target and adjusted his sights. His groups had started out scattered. Some didn't hit the target. With sober precision he relearned what he had forgotten. He held his breath steady and fired on an exhalation. He kept his eyes open. He squeezed the trigger slow.

He also reawakened the talent side of the skill. As he became comfortable with the rifle he developed an intuition for how it would fire. He knew beforehand whether a shot would be good or bad. He learned to hold off a bad shot, reacquire his aim, and unfold the process anew.

After three boxes of ammunition, he hit a three-inch group every time. He was lethal.

He disassembled the weapon that night, staying up late to punch the tube and make it shine. He picked carbon from the bolt with a coat hanger hammered flat on one end. He found the device in his father's old Army rifle cleaning kit. He scrubbed the innards with a toothbrush and coated everything that moved with a light layer of oil.

He slept with the Mauser in his bed, under the covers. When he got up, he held the Mauser in one hand while the other aimed his morning whiz into the toilet. He scrambled eggs with the rifle slung over his shoulder. He drove with it across his lap. He understood why soldiers gave their rifles women's names.

Cory couldn't think of a good girl's name.

He wore camouflage and hunting boots, and had a camo net over his face. He approached the rocky lair two hundred yards from Baer Creighton's camp. He stopped and scanned the trees for movement, colors, anything. But the trees were motionless and the silence replete. He stepped forward again and waited. Again and waited. Nothing could break his concentration. He'd learned the first lesson. Remaining in control of every desire, every thought, every action, was the highest high.

Discipline unlocked his unlimited potential.

Cory considered sneaking across the top of the rock for a better vantage. He decided he couldn't afford such a careless risk. Baer was cunning. He would be on his guard, and might detect movement.

Cory halted. Implications…

Baer lived and breathed in the forest. Would he be waiting for Cory, like an animal with a sixth sense for its habitat? In that copse off to the left, decked out in camouflage and hidden behind a fallen log?

In training, Cory had assumed he'd be shooting at an exposed man. If presented with a concealed target, would he be capable of a head shot? What if he could only aim at the top of Creighton's head? If that was all he exposed?

Cory squeezed the Mauser stock.

Would he take the shot?

Standing motionless, Cory evaluated the risk. Facing a skilled adversary and presented with only a head shot, Cory admitted he could miss. His nerves made him a little jittery. It would be a game changer, turning a simple kill shot into a shootout. Disabling his quarry on the first trigger pull was imperative.

Given a less-than-perfect target, Cory would not take the shot. He would wait all day and night if he had to.

He scanned the terrain again. Approaching the rock from the rear, he took three steps at a rightward angle. He waited. Stepped. Waited. He proceeded this way for a half-hour, until he saw movement ahead.

Cory stopped midstride and eased the Mauser stock to his cheek.

Two fire trucks in the drive and six men standing around spitting and jawing. They've hosed the grass but haven't wasted the effort on the house.

I slip across the road and duck in the woods a hundred yards closer to town than I usually do. I trek slow, like I'm stalking deer.

I got a chill on my arms though I'm plenty warm. Realize I've been hearing voices a second or two. I ease behind an oak and peer out.

Ahead is Burly Worley and his friend. Jawing and jabbering all excited.

Burly's got a bucket in his hand and he tips to the right on account the weight.

One bucket.

I pull Smith. Knock out a chunk of dirt wedged in the hammer. I got a lot of wrath inside, a lot of burned-lung, busted-shoulder, fear-in-my-soul anger. I got a dead dog, a burned house, a smashed livelihood.

They won't pass me by fifty yards. Too far for pistol work. I wait a second for a good line of sight.

I let Smith hang at my side but my trigger finger twitches like the tail on a cat. I could leave Burly go. I could give up one bucket of gold. What's that? Fifty pound? Six, seven hundred grand? There's that much more in the tree, twice again.

But that short one killed Fred. I know it.

My heart thuds. They walk toward my burned house. Probably walk right over Fred's grave.

That night I found Fred, I thought on impunity, on men doing as they please to other men. No compass save their own wants and wishes. No victim ever coming back to say you can't do that, so long as I'm around. All this back and forth with Stipe—him fighting Fred, and one of his cronies leaving him for dead. Me shooting Stipe's champion in the eyeball on accident. Stipe burning my house, calling the law on my stilling operation, killing Fred. Landing me in jail. And now burning Brown's house on top of me. All that's him fighting back, saying, "I'll fight dirtier to take what I want than you will to keep it."

Men like that have no law. Society has no hold on them, and it seems like even God turned his back and said it isn't worth the fight. Only thing that ever makes them quit is some sorry chump like me finally meets them at the edge. Says, "No matter how far you go, you'll find me one step farther. And if we both fall off the cliff, then so be it."

I swallow.

So be it.

I skitter across the ground. I'm stooped, my arms out like a hawk gliding low. Rapid as I can. My eyes feel like crystals seeing everything in harsh lines and sharp colors. Fingers tingle.

Burly holds both shotguns in his left hand for balance. I come in from his back right. Thirty yards out, he pauses. I cover ten yards quick. He turns. That short man spins, takes a fighting stance. Burly's eyes flash wide.

Ten yards out I swing Smith. Squeeze off a shot. Burly drops the bucket and the guns. Mouth wide, he slaps his hand to his chest. I'm five yards out and point at the taco dog man. He's stooped to his ankle. I pull the trigger and the shot sets him back a foot, though I don't see where I hit him. He starts to stand and I put another in his chest.

Burly's on his knees, reaching for a shotgun. He falls on top of both, and his buddy collapses across his legs like to keep him in place.

I grab my bucket and take the shotguns too.

CHAPTER THIRTY-FIVE

Cory watched the forest beyond his front sight post. He'd seen motion. Now the autumn colors blended. Nothing stood out.

He stared at the exact place where he'd seen motion. The longer he looked the less certain he was that he'd seen anything. The Mauser grew heavy and he eased it downward.

He could have imagined it.

Movement again.

Cory shifted behind a tree. His hands were sweaty and he exhaled in bursts. He leaned until he could see around the tree into the forest ahead.

A whitetail deer bounded away, flashing its tail high in the air. Two more deer followed. Cory fell against the tree and inhaled deep. He held his breath in his lungs as if it was marijuana smoke. When he released it his nerves had settled.

The deer hadn't seen him—so what had spooked them?

About to step forward, Cory heard a pistol shot. In the quiet of the woods it was abrupt and loud. Cory scanned the trees but couldn't tell where the sound originated. Another shot followed, and another. He guessed the distance to be at least a hundred yards. Cory locked his gaze on a narrow aperture of forest, a slight angle from Baer Creighton's camp.

As abruptly as it started the shooting ended. It had to be Creighton. Warning shots? Cory looked across his shoulder at the openness of the forest and longed for the protection of the cave.

His next steps would reveal the crag's face. Cory hesitated. Everything to this point had been preparation. Now that he was certain his enemy was ahead, moving forward would carry him irretrievably into the execution stage of his operation. The risk grew higher. His performance had to be flawless.

Cory inhaled. Exhaled.

He stepped forward and stopped. He leaned until he saw the rock face. That shooting he'd heard—it could have been anyone. Cory's heart raced and the sweat was cool on his brow. Was Baer in the cavern? Behind the hemlock next to the trail?

Something was out of place.

He surveyed the terrain again. Lifted his leg to step forward. The nagging unknown gave him pause. He planted both feet side by side. He would wait until he knew what was wrong.

Cory studied every contour of the rock face. A rope hung over the edge. He remembered it from before. His gaze drifted to the right. He studied the trail in front of the rock, leaves disturbed by deer as well as man. He squinted at the hemlock to the right of the path, and after a moment he grinned. It was different. The shape was wrong—a branch had fallen across the path.

Cory exhaled.

Relief.

It was good to have been cautious. He did one more visual sweep. He stared in the direction of the recent pistol shots, and stepped forward.

The discovery of the fallen tree branch confirmed Cory's newfound powers. His confidence surged. He stepped five paces, twisted right and searched the forest. He stepped another four. He would avoid the fallen branch and leave no evidence of his passing.

Cory pressed close to the rock wall. He looked to the cave entrance ten feet above. Partly supported by the rock, he lunged for the trail cutting back up the rock face. His boot struck off the edge. Teetering, Cory saw on the trail below a rusted strand of barbed wire that he hadn't noticed before.

Cory swiped at the rope strung from above. He reached it with his fingertips. He bucked out and clutched the rope.

It held a brief moment—enough to restore Cory's balance. Then it went limp in his hand. From above he heard a rumble that reverberated through the air and the rock face he clung to. He looked upward to the sound and a cascade of round rocks dropped upon him. Cory looked to the side and back to the ledge. He raised an arm above his head and stones smashed against his elbow and shoulder. He batted one aside and another glanced his head. His rifle clanged against the rock wall. Another rock struck his shoulder and another his head. Then his forehead, leaving him dazed. He leaned into he wall but still the rocks fell, now striking his shoulders and glancing his back. Finally, when the noise ceased he leaned out and looked skyward. The last crashed into his forehead.

Cory regained awareness mid-fall. He saw the strand of barbed wire and the out-of-place hemlock branch. He twisted, threw his free arm to cushion his landing. He saw pegs hammered into the side of the tree holding the branch in place.

He hit the branch full on. It popped from the tree, triggering a great whooshing sound. Ahead, a bent-over tree snapped from the ground. The barbed wire snapped leaves into the air. The barbs shredded his pants. Wire teeth ripped through the muscle next to his groin. Each metal tooth tore a new path, deeper than the one before it.

Cory gasped. He struck his elbow on a root.

The bowed tree stopped its ascent and the wire ceased ripping his groin.

Cory slipped his hand into his pants. His balls were intact. He exhaled.

He'd fallen into a trap, but he'd survive. He was wet and sticky and bleeding, but he hadn't lost the family jewels. This wasn't a disaster. He rested, gathering his thoughts. Hurt bad. He tried to calm his racing heart. He'd think it through.

He'd stepped into a trap. Where was the next? He glanced above and saw only tree limbs. He felt woozy. His leg was warm, and his groin, and as he rested the blood soaked into his shirt.

He tried to drag himself forward and then rested. Where was he going?

He would wait a moment and get his bearings. But it was growing difficult to think. As his mind succumbed to blackness, he considered the great artery in his thigh that ran close to his groin. He couldn't remember its name.

CHAPTER THIRTY-SIX

Burly left his Suburban parked on my drive with the keys in the ignition. I grab a pair of leather gloves from the shed. Plow the vehicle through a mess of briars down into the wood.

Need supplies.

I stuff a handful of coins in my pocket, leave the bucket of gold in the trunk of the Nova on blocks. The lid doesn't close. No one will look.

Reckon I walk like somebody who feels guilty. But there's no other way when you shot two men and society won't see things your way.

I head for Millany's. By the sun, there's plenty of time. I cut through the woods and avoid the road. Project'll take days, weeks. I have to start while the anger's hot. Before the law shows up asking about that fire, and finds a couple men died of bullet holes.

I take the long way around each field. In town I keep to second streets.

Millany's door says CLOSED. I beat on it. He lives upstairs. "Come on down, you old goat." I rap until a light goes on.

He arrives behind the glass. Shakes his head. Opens the door. "Can't you read? I'm closed."

"I can read. I just got business, and since you ass rape me each time we trade, I figured you'd be game."

"How much business?"

I follow him inside and drop a handful of coins on his counter. Pull two more out the bottom my pocket.

"Nine? Baer, I don't keep that kind of cash in here."

"Let's go the bank."

"What the kind of 'business' you into?"

"Guess you heard they hit my still?"

"It don't take eight grand to build a still, Baer."

"No. No it don't, at that."

He looks at me. "You ain't saying any more than that, are you?"

"Let's go to the bank."

I have eight thousand, three hundred and twenty-five dollars in my pocket. Millany shakes his head. I slap him on the shoulder and leave.

The sign says Big Ted Lombo's restaurant has a brick oven. They serve pizza and red wine. Family-type folks clear out at night and the goons get together. I've not had pizza in a long time.

"Can I help you?"

"I want pizza. Onions and pepperoni."

"Small pizza?"

"Biggest you got. Extra cheese."

"Eighteen bucks."

"Go ahead and cook one up. And I want to talk to Big Ted."

"What for?"

"If telling you would do the trick I wouldn't ask for Big Ted."

The kid looks to a goon posted by an arched door. The goon nods.

"Big Ted's in back."

"Baer, how you doon?"

"You said you got a friend up Merrimon sells cars."

"Yeah—I call him right now. What you looking for?"

"Get him on the phone. You do me a favor and I won't forget it. Tell him to bring the best three-thousand-dollar one-ton truck he's got. Tell him to bring it to you—like it's you that's buying it. You do that for me, Big Ted?"

His smile falters. One eye narrows. He chews the end of his cigar. "Yeah. Dammit, yeah." He lifts his phone and drives his fingers to the keys.

"Guilio, dis what I need. It's Ted. Lissen…"

. . .

Left Big Ted thirty-one C-notes, one for the favor. In an hour I'll have a truck that runs decent. Meantime I need tools. There's a body shop a half-mile east of town. I walk. Cheese in my belly is like a bucket of river mud.

Garage sits between 70 and Old Highway 70, thirty yards behind. Everything between is blacktop, and covered in beat-up Volkswagen buses.

Some wrench-monkey with a pierced lip and three-tone hair looks from under the hood of a Dodge. "Help you?"

"I'm looking Gatchell."

"Who?"

"The owner."

"I own this place."

"What happened to Gatchell?"

"I bought it from Norton."

"Guess it's been a while since I paid attention."

"I do good work. What are you driving?"

"That ain't why I'm here. I'm looking for an acetylene torch and a box of tools. Got cash right now."

"Yeah, well… I use what I got. Sorry, mister."

"You can buy new."

"So can you."

I look at him and he looks at me. Piss on him.

"Mister?"

I turn. "What?"

"Why don't you check Craigslist?"

"Don't know him."

He smiles like we're friends. He knows me, wants to help. Dips his hands in a tub of orange lava at the sink. "I take it you're not connected to the Internet."

"That's mighty astute."

"Why don't you pull that pipe wrench out of your ass? Check this out."

He grins. I grin. He eyes Smith. He whacked my buttons but I don't get any electric or red, and I kind of feel for a smartass trapped as a mechanic. Suspect I'm looking at an honest man.

He steps into an office space, has a computer facing the door. "Come on in. Don't mind the mess. I spend my energy fixing cars, not cleaning up."

I step inside. Check behind the door for the boogeyman, something.

"See?" he says. He taps some buttons and the screen flashes a white page.

"See what?"

He points. "This is Craigslist. This is an ad from someone in Swannanoa with a torch for sale. That's the picture. Two fifty, condition like new. Call the number."

He dials the phone. I take the receiver.

"Yeah. I want that torch you got."

"Two fifty."

"Does it work?"

"Like new."

"Hey, who is this?"

"Frank."

"Buzzard?"

"That's right. Who's this?"

"Baer Creighton."

"Naw. Creighton?"

CHAPTER THIRTY-SEVEN

Joe Stipe wiped sweat from his brow. He leaned on the hood of Burly Worley's Suburban, driven into the weeds and over a steep bank. If not for the tracks through the grass the vehicle would have remained hidden.

Close to the driver-side door a deputy held a flannel shirt to a bloodhound's nose.

A car door slammed. Stipe looked over the slope toward Creighton's driveway. Chief Smylie approached from his car. He strode with a scowl on his face. Stipe spat and looked back to the dog.

The deputy pulled away the flannel shirt and said, "Let's go find 'im!"

The bloodhound bounded away, baying. Stipe wiped the side of his mouth.

Smylie stopped at the edge of the yard. "You mind telling me what the hell's going on?"

Stipe regarded him. "Lots going on, Horace."

"I come home and right off there's a message you've taken over the Gleason police. I don't appreciate that."

"Somebody had to get them off their asses."

"My deputies dream of working a big case, so there wasn't anybody sitting on his ass."

"I needed a man with a dog. I got one."

"All right. That's that. So what's going on? What is this?"

CLAYTON LINDEMUTH

"Burly's truck."

"What's it doing here?"

"Don't know."

"Since I been gone, Brown's house burned. Creighton's place burned. I hear Burly and Ernie Gadwal are missing. And where the hell's Creighton?"

Stipe pushed off from the Suburban's hood and walked downhill in the direction of the baying dog. The deputy had already passed from view. "Come on. Let's see about Burly first."

Stipe had a bad feeling. Burly wouldn't likely drive his truck across Creighton's yard, wreck it halfways in the woods and abandon it. Nor would a crafty weasel like Ernie go into hiding. Even if he'd screwed up, he'd be around trying to turn it into a new advantage.

And Creighton—he'd never gotten around to declaring war like he promised. This looked like it might be a beginning.

Stipe weighed the possibilities. If all three were dead, a host of problems would disappear, and the less he told Smylie the better. Men settle scores all the time. Things tie up neat. But if there were any loose strings, Stipe would have to manage the situation. It wouldn't do to have investigators learn he'd threatened to have Baer killed. Nor would it do to have a police chief concluding he knew enough to bend Stipe to his will.

The situation was on the verge of becoming tenuous.

The easiest way to keep the problem local was to account for each man. Ensure that only men within Stipe's sphere knew anything at all.

Stipe heard Smylie's feet strike dry leaves behind him.

"What's going on with the Brown place? You part of that?"

Stipe turned. "How can a man be part of a lightning strike?"

"We haven't had a storm in a month. What about Creighton? Kind of funny, him not being around."

"How's it funny?" Stipe stopped walking and faced Smylie. "Since when do you care about Creighton? Or anything else, until I tell you to care about it?"

Smylie was silent.

The hound stopped baying and a shout carried through the forest. Stipe headed for it. The up-and-down slippery terrain taxed his lungs. After a few dozen yards Stipe braced his palm to a tree and stooped while his lungs heaved. Smylie went ahead. When Stipe's strength returned he started off again. Minutes later he reached the deputy, Smylie, and the bloodhound.

At their feet were two bodies. Only two.

Blood had solidified and the afternoon sun had brought out black flies. The two men's legs were tangled together.

Neither man held a weapon.

Stipe shook his head. Burly had been a decent man. Followed orders. In the short time he'd been in Stipe's employ he'd demonstrated loyalty. Was a man of high potential. Ernie—he hadn't been trustworthy at all, but he'd had his uses too.

Stipe felt robbed.

The deputy glanced at Smylie, then fixed on Stipe. "Who do you suppose did it?"

"I'd bet it's the man who's missing and we ain't found a body for. My two cents."

Smylie nodded. "That's right. Creighton."

Stipe squatted beside the hound. His knees dropped to the leaves and he scratched between the dog's ears. "You ready to work? I got a big-ass job for you."

The dog wagged his tail.

Stipe said, "Travis, I want you to head over to that tarp by the busted-up still we passed, back by the house. Get this hound after Creighton and don't stop 'til you have a prisoner or a body. I'd prefer the latter."

Travis glanced at Smylie as he turned.

Smylie shook his head. "Hold on a minute."

Travis bent to the hound and leashed him.

"Walk with me a minute, Horace." Stipe rocked to his feet. After a few yards, he looked back. Travis was out of earshot. "You and me need to come to an understanding."

"You're right we do. You can't—"

"I've never gotten on with men who tell me what I can't do. Keep your mouth closed for the next two minutes while I set the table. I got your balls in a vise, and I'm going to squeeze until they pop or you tell me what I need to hear."

"How you figure?"

"This is about that stupid-assed boy of yours."

"What's he got to do with Creighton, or any of this?"

"There's a heap you don't know about what he is involved with. I'm sure you don't want this information making its way to various law enforcement organizations. We're talking Feds. DEA. FBI. He's earned ten years in prison with what I know right now. I ain't even dug. Yet."

Smylie was silent.

"All that comes out, I don't see how you keep your job enforcing Gleason's laws. Not when you can't run your own house."

"He's lazy is all. He's at school right now."

"My money's on him being in Baltimore the same time as you, right under your nose, picking up a truckload of dope."

"You don't know that."

"After the DEA shoves a microscope up your ass, we'll talk about what I know and don't know."

"You're the one that got him into all that."

Stipe lurched into Smylie, grabbed his shoulders, shoved him against a hemlock. "I tried to talk him out of it. I busted him over the head with a two-by-four to get his attention. You know what else he did while you was gone? Kidnapped his kids with a gun! Father needs a gun to get his kids, he ain't a father."

"This has nothing to do with Creighton!"

"You dumbass. It does because I say it does. I own you. I get what I want or I take you down and your boy goes to prison. That simple."

The police chief glared. Shifted from the tree and stepped back from Stipe.

Stipe stared back.

Smylie shook his head. Looked at the ground. Huffed. "All right. What you after?"

Stipe closed with Smylie and draped his arm across his shoulder. "I'm glad you come around. We work this together, we both come out smelling like a rose. Now, you're in charge of your operation. Not me. You'll have to call me with updates so our men don't overlap and waste effort. And I want you to handle this in-house. Deploy every man on tracking Baer Creighton, and when you find him, you turn him over to me."

CHAPTER THIRTY-EIGHT

It's dark. Guess it's late enough to head out.

I let the fire die to a wick of orange and sit on a big rock that doesn't get warm no matter how long I incubate it. Cave at my back, I look downslope. Nothing sounds right but it's my first night here in thirty years. I've been seeing ravens in the trees, shadows moving about like werewolves. Ghosts in my head, already. Burly and his taco dog friend.

Fred is dead. Ruth most likely too.

I muse on Larry and Stipe, and Cory Smylie.

This is my new homestead, time being. Cleaned away all those bones and rotted blankets. Made a bed of spruce for shits and giggles.

But I haven't shit or giggled.

I don't like being in a cave. Plug one hole, you got yourself a grave.

I camped here for weeks with Gunter Stroh back after I quit life insurance. He let me have the front of the cave where it was cold and he slept in back. Told me about a situation called the Weimar Republic. Then he was a Nazi, then he was a new socialist, then he jumped a ship and came here. Then he was an old man who wanted left alone. All he knew was the work he did in the Kraut army. Had a knack for chemistry.

He worked hard. Built a reputation as the finest stiller in the state. I came along when he was afraid all his ways would die with him. I didn't tell anybody but word got out after Gunter died. People said my shine was like his. Soon I couldn't make enough.

Gunter liked to sit nights and sip from different jugs and comment on what made each distinct. With some, you could taste dirt, if you tried. Apples bought from Brown grew in red dirt, and tasted like iron. Whereas you buy from Henderson you're liable to get brandy so clayed up you have to chew it.

He was old as Lincoln's grandmum and walked with a hickory stick. His joints give him trouble until he liquored them up. Sometimes he lost track of years. Right before the end he'd ramble about the art of stillin and call me Heinrich. I'd know he was seeing his earliest days. He talked about how to shave the wood and cook it, and bust out those sugars with acid. Then he'd kind of wake up and his eyes narrowed like he come out of a dream and didn't know what he'd said. That was right before the end.

Truck's parked a half-mile off—I followed a log road until it gave out. No particular trail leads there. I get turned around and have to reorient by the stars and a crick that winds back and forth, more confused than I am.

Finally I'm sitting in the seat of a 1998 F-150 that stinks like they emptied a bottle of new smell on the seats. I twist the ignition and sit with the lights off. Swing through a few radio stations. Listen to the news about a sixteen year old girl, Sophia. Just up and disappeared. Last seen with a copper from Gleason.

I wish I'd turned around this truck in the daylight.

I get out and scout behind me. Rocks and logs and trees. But down a ways is a space between the hemlock. Back inside I put her in reverse. Transmission grinds like somebody pitched a chunk of metal inside a turbine. I jiggle the shifter and she seats.

Back, back. Swing her around. Do-si-do.

I stumbled on an odd place, years back. Take North Fork Road and a turnoff leads to a thirty-acre stretch of strip-mined land. They backfilled the deep dirt over the topsoil. Nothing grows but clumps of switchgrass. Place is always barren and cold. Corroded chunks of industrial metal litter the ground. They left behind a bulldozer, more rust than paint. An International, built in the sixties I reckon. Has a radiator that sits up front and a fuel tank behind the seat.

I got a box of tools and a torch wants to take them home.

These bolts take more WD-40 than I take liquor. I bust them and pull out the fuel tank. It'll hold thirty gallon, by the look. I sever the fuel line and sit the tank in the truck.

Got a boiler.

Now for the work.

Hood comes off with a little elbow grease, but it only covers the top, not the sides or the front. Sides are bolted on with lumps of rust fused to the frame. I chisel them off. Radiator mounts are fixed with half-inch bolts. They're set back where I can't get a hammer, and while I study the radiator I see this won't work at all. If I was making elderberry brandy— but my condenser will have to pull the weight. Man makes this kind of likker, he's got to coax every last drop. This radiator's all gummed up. I'd need ten feet of tube out the backside to catch what steam the radiator let pass. Don't know what I was thinking.

But I got the cooker.

Odds of Stipe appreciating me poking around his garage at two in the morning are nil. But when I shot Achilles, I saw Stipe had a row of oil drums lined on the garage back wall. Since he called the law and they filled my mash barrels with holes, he owes me.

I kill the headlights. Stipe's put up a chain-link fence. I get out and look along the line and see nobody. I guessed Stipe would have added security, but this is just a fence. Whole joint's closed up, lights off. Only sound comes from nothing at all.

In the truck I head for the gate. It's padlocked. My lucky night. I have a torch.

In five minutes I drive in easy like I'm supposed to be here. Head around back. The dog crates are thirty yards off, and I imagine there's some noses pressed against the fence right now. I tap three fifty-five-gallon oil barrels before I find one empty. I hoist it to the truck bed and test the rest. The last in the row is mostly empty. I spill the gritty oil on the dirt and chuck the barrel to the bed of my truck. Two'll do the job.

I'm driving out and the front porch light goes on at the house.

By the time I get the barrels and the dozer fuel tank to the cave, it's light. I head back out.

I could find all the copper I want at Maple's Hardware in Gleason. But by now Maple knows they hit my still. I don't want to answer questions. So I take 70 to Asheville and swing into the Home Depot. It's a big store inside, covers about two hundred thousand square mile. Need a helicopter to get from the lumber to the cinder blocks. Contractors everywhere look as haggard as me. I walk the edge of the aisles until I find plumbing.

I take two packs of fifty-foot copper coils inside a cardboard box. Grab a couple sleeves, solder, flux, a brush. A handful of connecting fixtures and a bunch of associated plumbing. I don't want to come back.

I take two five-gallon metal buckets, empty, and one five-gallon bucket of acetone, full. I spot six-quart packs of battery acid. I'll need ten.

Wait. These people don't have lye.

I pick up thirty pound total from three grocers, and a heavy scrub brush and a straw broom at the last.

Cashier lady handles the lye and looks funny.

"Soap," I say. "Who has time to strain an ash box? Nowadays."

Lady nods with all the polite she can muster.

I drive back to the trail that gets me close to the cave. It takes four trips, filling the duffel with as much as my back can handle. I stow supplies in the cave, acid and lye far apart, and head back down the hill.

I drive out to Stu Caldwell's cabinet shop. "Need a truckload of pine sawdust."

"Pine?"

"Uh-huh."

"I don't keep pine sawdust."

"What if we took a couple boards and run them through your planer there. And I'll take the shavings out that cyclone?"

He looks at the planer, a twenty-inch Delta from 1950. His eyes follow the four-inch vacuum duct to the ceiling. Over to the double cyclone, a vacuum connected to every tool in the shop.

"That's a little strange, Baer."

"What?"

"What you want with all that sawdust?"

He can't see my red. I lie. "Planting tomatoes come spring. Want to get that pH down. You know."

"Uh-huh. A truckload."

"Well, I bet you heard they busted my still?"

He nods. Getting right wary.

"I'm going straight. There's nothing so tasty as a tomato; figure I'll plant a couple acre."

"Tomato… wine?"

I grin.

"Can't you just take the sawdust I already got?"

"What is it?"

"White oak."

"Nah, nah. That'd never do. White oak smells like cat whiz. No one eats tomatoes, smell like that."

"Well, Baer. I'm in the middle of a job here. I can't stop and buzz a truckload of pine into sawdust."

"I'll do it."

"And then I got all this downtime. Why don't you pick up a planer at the Home Depot?"

Now I have a truckload of pine boards, a planer, a shovel, an electric generator, and a ten-gallon can of gasoline. All from the Home Depot. I haul them up to the cave and take a bite out a cold hamburger. I bought a bag of twenty Whoppers to hold me a couple days, but I don't think I'll eat more than one. Not while all these trees have such tasty bark.

Takes an hour with the acetone and scrub brush to get the drums clean and rolled back up the hill from the crick. Another hour to cut a hole in the bottom side of each, and mount a mesh cone inside, and a water spigot on the outside.

I dig a hole, top off the generator, and rest it inside. Stretch a tarp across the ground and sit the planer on a corner. Start the generator, plug in the planer, and pass through boards, taking a sixteenth off each pass.

Shavings pile like snow, then drifts. Pine smells like Ma mopped the floor.

By and by the planer gets hot and I shut it down. While it cools, I build two platforms out of flat rocks from the crick bed twenty feet downhill. Shaped like circles with a gap in the front. I sit a fifty-fiver on each foundation, then gather shavings from the tarp. Fill the first fifty-five gallon drum.

Time I get that done, the planer's cool. Start buzzing boards again.

I fill the second drum and it's dusk. I'm hungry enough to eat bugs off a window, and after a bite of cold Whopper I chuck the burger and the bag with eighteen more. I miss my old still site and wholesome food like cabbage. But this setup isn't permanent. I don't see this operation taking more than a week.

I fill each barrel of pine shavings with crick water and eighteen quarts of battery acid. Mix that mash up good. Cover the barrels with strips of board too thin to run through the planer. Build a small fire inside the cave near my sleep sack. Pile a few logs nearby and settle in the bag. Bones pop as my back settles. I'm about wiped out, but tired feels good because my purpose is vengeance.

Stipe's right on the edge and I'm six inches farther out. That's what I think, heading into sleep. I'm six inches off the cliff.

What the hell...

Big old wet nose on my face, sniffing, grunting.

Fred?

He whines...

Fred!

I try and throw my arms around him and the sleeping bag holds me back. I unzip it from inside and Fred licks my face and eyes and I kiss him back, but he moves too fast to plant one firm. My lips hit his teeth.

"C'mere, you game son of a bitch!"

I get my arms out. The fire's dead and all the woods is silent beneath the husky sound of Fred slopping up my hair. Nylon bag zooshing with each motion. I throw a hug across his chest and pull him easy, and nuzzle into his neck.

"I love ya, Fred, God I love ya!"

He says I love you too, but I ain't Fred.

"Huh?" I press the grime out of my eyes and adjust to the morning light. "Stinky Joe?"

It's the dog that jumped the fight circle that night and dashed off into the woods. He wags his tail, and that shakes his ass, and that shakes his whole body.

"I thought you was Fred."

Stinky Joe grins. It's all good, he says.

"You hungry? You had any food to eat?"

He mumbles something.

It's cold enough for frost. In my skivvies I'm a garden of goose pimples. I grab an eighteen-pack of eggs. Dump a couple cups of dog chow in Fred's bowl—I took it because I'm a sentimental fool—and crack four eggs. Since it's getting cold out I got a block of New York extra sharp in the bag; I crumble some on top.

"You want a soda, something?"

Stinky Joe's got his head canted like he's looking past me. I look out the cave entrance. Grab Smith in one hand and carry Fred's chow bowl in the other. Feet are a couple of ice blocks. I look out on the hillside and nary a thing moves. But there's about fifteen shredded Whopper wrappers spread all downhill.

"I'm glad you liked em."

I head back and crawl in the bag for some heat. "C'mere." I reach to Fred's chow bowl and rest it on the dirt beside my bag. Stinky Joe dives in and finishes in three mouthfuls.

I sit up and Stinky Joe wiggles close. Head low and back high, like a pup that knows I'm the rootinest tootinest dog on the porch. I grab him tight and drag him onto my sleeping bag, and he settles with his head on my lap. I'm about to freeze. I pull the tail end of the bag over my shoulder like a toga, and we sit and talk like old friends.

"Where you been?"

Out in the woods. Nosed my way to a place that seemed safe, from the sound and smell of it. Didn't have anything to eat.

"Oh."

You don't seem too chipper.

"Well, that's on account of Ruth."

Ruth?

"She's dead. Larry killed her."

Stinky Joe pauses, deep in thought. Larry. Well I don't know Ruth but it don't surprise me hearing Larry done her, the way he and his boys did me. I thought he was up to no good.

"Why didn't you find me at the camp and tell me? Maybe I coulda saved her."

I thought on that, but you scared me good. You was drunk.

"Well, uh. Yeah. Hey, listen... my nuts is about to freeze and bust into little pieces. Let me bring you a blanket over, and once I get inside this bag we can keep talking."

Sounds good, Stinky Joe says. He looks ready to shake apart if he doesn't get loved on.

CHAPTER THIRTY-NINE

I lift a half-sheet of plywood from the first mash drum and stand back from a noxious blast. It's been two days slow cooking in chemicals on top of a bed of coals. All that's left is to enjoy the mundane work of vengeance.

Insects that snuck inside float on top—those that haven't dissolved. I dip a stripped oak pole through the foam, into disintegrated pine fibers. Dump in a plastic container of lye. Stir with the oak pole.

The brew fizzes and froths. More acid yet. The reaction eases. I add lye until the fizzing ceases.

Look around the ground. Glance at Stinky Joe.

I dip my finger into the mash. Swirl it around and realize either the acid or the lye could've burned off my finger—but they're balanced.

"That's lucky."

Heading up to the cave, I wipe my finger on my pants. Grab a saucepan, clean it in the creek, and ladle a few inches of mash. I crumble yeast into the pan, stir it with a stick. Watch. The familiar smell rises, and a layer of bubbles foams at the top. I'll give it a few minutes. Meantime I neutralize the second barrel.

I recheck the yeast—still alive, still foaming. Working hard. I dump the mix into the first barrel, add five pounds of yeast, and then test the second.

· · ·

I convert the old International crawler's fuel tank into a boiler and situate it down by the creek. With the torch I fashion a doubler from the empty acetone can. Rig a five-gallon bucket under a two-foot waterfall in the crick. Run the copper coil through the bucket. Tube sticks out halfway down, goes two feet to a flat rock, and that's where I'll have a jug waiting.

Then I twiddle my thumbs and wait on the mash to ferment. Speed it up by keeping a small fire between the barrels.

Each night I carry a ragged washcloth to the stream and use a small pool like a sink. The rough cloth feels good. In spite of the cold I wash—sometimes so hard it's like I want to scrub off my whole life and send it floating downstream. I linger at the stream before heading back to the cave, and then sit by the fire until it wanes. I listen to the trees. Pet Stinky Joe. Rub sleep from my eyes. All the while thinking there's no way to wash away what I am, what I've done, what I'm about to do.

I stay awake late to make sure that little fire between the barrels keeps going. But mostly I stay awake because each night I dream of corpses in trees. Each night I travel deeper on the trail. Close in on morbid terrain. Look in on death.

But each morning when the sun comes up I keep on.

Drop a cinnamon curl to the bottom of each gallon jug. It'll work like the worm at the bottom of a fifth of mescal—give them a goal.

First run, I put a five-gallon bucket at the copper's output end. The sqeezins will come out low-alcohol. It won't be until I run them through a few times, even with the doubler, that they get any potency.

I hold another bucket at the spigot on the first fifty-fiver. Twist the knob and frothy, rank mash rushes out. I pour the mash into the boiler, back and forth until the boiler's three-quarter full.

"What you think of that, Stinky Joe?"

Stinky Joe's mum.

I sit on a log and gaze into the night sky. Prop my chin on my hands, elbows on my knees, and close my eyes. Burning logs pop. Steam spits through the tubes. The crick gurgles. The near-boiling mash rumbles and ticks. My thoughts skirt the bare edge of justice, in a tooth-for-a-tooth way.

The first condensate spurts from the copper. I rock to my feet and kneel at the bucket. Dangerous to be so close... can't touch it. But I can't resist dipping my nose and whiffing the piney product. Smells like Ajax.

I'll tell them it's gin.

CHAPTER FORTY

I don't believe it, but Stinky Joe snores like Fred. Wakes me out of a godawful dream.

I sleep again and wake to Stinky Joe nosing around his bowl. It's dark out the cave front, without a hint of gray. I fix some Alpo, eggs and cheddar. Go back to the sleeping bag. Before I sleep Stinky Joe comes back and licks my face, and that Alpo doesn't smell bad with cheese. I didn't eat last night. Without my usual liquor treatment, my stomach feels like an empty swimming pool. Come dawn I'll eat everything cached in the cave, and then hit the ABC for some store-bought liquor. Yessir.

Can't sleep. Today's the day I've been waiting.

I lay thinking all kind of thoughts. Missing Ruth, thinking it'd be all right if I woke to her licking my face like Stinky Joe. So long as she's not dead.

I lay in the sack until dawn turns the black woods gray. Climb out of the bag, don my clothes. Grab crackers, apple, cheese, take my thirty-thirty and slip into the woods. There's a thicket down by the crick. I sit under a low-hanging hemlock and watch the sun turn everything into color.

That'd be something to wake to. Maybe not Ruth slobbering like Stinky Joe, but a nibble'd be nice. A soft sound with a powder smell. Doesn't take long until a doe comes along with her nose close to the ground. She stops—got my scent—and does this up and down thing with her head. She knows I'm here and her heart's got to be pounding. She steps forward and swings her head like to catch me in a false move.

I'm still.

I watch and she's beautiful. Liquid lines, and I can almost see lashes and mascara. Her ears flick. She leaps, stops.

I shift my weight ever so slight; get the posture; slip off the safety.

She steps away and I ease up the thirty-thirty. Line the sights on the back of her head. She won't feel it.

Her ears twitch. Her tail's high—she's a little puckered, a little tense.

I keep the rifle trained, though my hands tremble and the cold air blurs my eyes. A cool trickle spills down my cheek, one then the other, and the tremor in my hands moves to my arms. She has an innocent position in the grand scheme. One day not long ago she was a fawn with spots, and kind of grew into a world where armed killers like me hide in trees.

I think on Fred, lying there with a hole in his scabbed eye socket, and I close my eyes and can't breathe for the hate and pain. The best deer's got no personality compared to the worst dog. It ought to be easy. I blink five six times and half-hope she'll see, but the doe is motionless. I slide my finger up and down the trigger.

"Ah, hell! Get out of here!"

She starts, then freezes.

Stares.

I wave.

She bolts. Two huge bounds and she's thirty feet gone; another two and she's brown in the thicket.

Don't want to think on that doe. She was meat for a whole mess of dogs. I'll go to the grocery instead. Involves risk, but it isn't like I was going to get away with all this anyhow.

I head back to the still. Park the thirty-thirty against the cave wall. Stinky Joe cocks his head.

"What you looking at?"

Stinky Joe says, I didn't say nothing.

"I'll be back in a couple hours." I scruff his ears.

I walk down the hill with eyes and ears tuned. Crow farts in a beech tree, I'll hear it.

CHAPTER FORTY-ONE

Joe Stipe sat on his porch with a sarsaparilla soda in one hand and a cordless telephone in the other. The delicate scent of diesel exhaust was in the air. He stared across the narrow lawn to the blacktop motorpool. Trucks awaited maintenance. Creighton was out there, somewhere, in the forested hills beyond.

All morning Stipe had a nagging thought that he ought to know where Creighton hid. It was like a word on the tip of his tongue. The Gleason deputies had found no trail. The hound had tracked Creighton from toolshed to still site, back and forth three times. It finally sat down, confused. Stipe's men had no more success. Creighton had disappeared, almost as if he was in the burned Brown house. No dice there. The fire department found no remains.

Stipe had ransacked Creighton's camp and found no hint of where he planned to go.

Anxiety didn't come close to it. On the afternoon before an important dog match, Stipe couldn't account for his enemy.

Stipe had asked Stan to beef up security. He tapped a couple nephews, bulky when they'd played high school football. Got big when they joined the Local. But Stipe knew they wouldn't impede Creighton. He was impervious to ass-beatings.

When Creighton struck it would be for blood. The victor would be the man willing to risk all.

So far Stipe had held back. He could have finished off Creighton that very first night. At that time, he'd intended to pressure him into selling out and working for him. Why destroy a man when you could profit from his labor? Most men could only bend so far, then rather than snap, they'd give up. They'd relent, because at bottom, they valued their lives more than their economic liberty. But not Creighton. He'd die for his still. For his dog. For his niece and the kids. Seemed like Creighton was ready to die for anything that struck his fancy. That wasn't the kind of man to have running loose before an important match.

But for the moment a different problem had become more urgent. Stipe jammed his finger to the telephone keypad and sipped soda while the phone rang.

"Mort, this is Joe, up Gleason."

"Yeah."

"Got a special tonight. Need a favor."

"Halloween special."

"Uh-huh."

"Can't make it. Got the kids and the trick-or-treat."

Stipe exhaled into the phone.

"Like to help," Mort said, "but I'm out of commission."

"You still got Rusty Nails?"

"Accourse."

"I want you to bring him tonight. I got boys coming in from Atlanta, and it's a big deal. Real big deal. Local hoodlum shot Achilles in the cussed eyeball and I need star power. I'll match Rusty Nails easy, and it'll give him another win before you stud him."

"Look, Joe, like I said—"

"Mort, I don't ask a favor twice. You hear me?"

The Atlanta boys had contacted Stipe earlier in the week. They'd mentioned the name of a Georgia man Stipe knew by reputation as the best dog breeder in the state. Stipe was unsure if the two visitors were emissaries for the Georgia man or if they acted on their own. He hoped the former.

Superior genetic lines were difficult to find, but mixing them was the lifeblood of the sport. Breeding was always a balance. You had to exclude inferior animals, but keep the genes diverse enough to keep the line fresh. Tapping champion DNA out of Georgia would pay dividends.

His visitors from Atlanta wouldn't want to meet a redneck fighting labs and rotts. Stipe had decided to fight two of the bait dogs, both female pits, as an opening spectacle. The next few fights were between solid bruisers. But Stipe's Atlanta guests would be looking for true gameness. For that, Stipe needed at least one spellbinder.

Champions were in limited supply. None of Stipe's contacts had been willing to provide his top dog on short notice. The best dogmen took their contests seriously. They owned the best dogs partly because of preparation. A champion dog needed a month walking around with a chain wrapped around his neck. Hours swinging by his jaw from a rope.

None of the dogmen Stipe called took his offer. No amount of return favors secured their interest. He understood their reluctance, based on the surprise timing. But it was almost as if word to avoid Stipe's fights had gotten out. It bothered him, and left no alternative but to flex muscle.

So now he was speaking with Mort, owner of Rusty Nails. The last man on Stipe's list.

Rusty Nails was four-year-old. The sixty-pound red nose had an unbroken string of wins. The dog was so good Stipe had waited to match him against Achilles for the championship. He'd hoped Achilles would improve and Rusty Nails would decline with the delay.

Word had gotten to Stipe through the grapevine that Mort had been grumbling about Stipe delaying the match. Now he needed his adversary's help.

"I've lined up five fights. I need six. I don't like to lean on you, but this is important. For the sacred sport. My boys coming up from Atlanta are big-time. Big dough. You ever want to match a dog in a sanctioned fight in Buncombe County again, you'll give me your word right now. What's it going to be?"

"You play hardball, Stipe."

"I'm backed in a corner. I need you in. So either sell Rusty Nails to me, or bring him down and fight him."

"I'll bring him. But he ain't ready for a real match. You damnwell better take care of him."

"Good. Tonight. I'll put Rusty Nails last, and I'll make sure he looks good as a favor to you."

"Yeah, I really appreciate that."

The phone beeped.

"I got another call, Mort. I'll see you tonight." Stipe pressed the button. He looked up and saw his security man Stan's GMC enter the motorpool drive.

"Stipe here."

"Joe. Dis's Ted."

"Hey, Big Ted, what can I do you for? You coming tonight?"

"Nah. Mebbe. Gotta mind the restaurant. You and Creighton square up yet?"

"Can't find him."

"Yeah. You oughta be lookin' a truck. Guilio—you know Guilio, up on Merrimon—he sold Creighton a '98 F-150."

"What color?"

"Brown."

Stipe raised his voice to overcome the sound of Stan's GMC, idling a dozen feet away. "Thanks, Big Ted. You come tonight and put money on Rusty Nails. That's the safe bet." Stipe drew his finger across his throat and Stan cut the engine.

"Eh, I appreciate that," Big Ted said.

Stipe disconnected the call.

Stan exited the truck, crossed in front of the grill and stood on the steps below Stipe.

Stipe needed to replace Burly. The way things were heating up, he'd have to keep Stan and the other two deployable. Too bad Cory proved such an idiot. Come to think of it, Cory hadn't been around either.

Stipe waited for Stan to speak. For the last few days he'd displayed a lack of imagination. Almost as if he was glad Burly was gone, and finding his killer meant nothing.

"We learned a little more. A little."

Stipe sipped sarsaparilla.

"I visited Larry's girl, Mae."

Stipe leaned. "Yeah?"

"He ain't been around, is what she said. I left Billy to keep an eye on the place until he had to go to work at the plant. To see if Creighton shows up."

"He won't. He's crazy, not stupid. He's holed up."

"Well, I talked to Ruth—you know there was history with Larry and Baer and Ruth? Well, took a while to find her. She's been staying with her father at the home. He's real sick and they was thinking he might keel over—"

"She seen Creighton?"

"Well, she's at her place now and says she ain't seen hide nor hair of him. She spent more time asking questions than answering. She don't know nothing. Then I stopped by to see Eve, since Larry said Baer put the moves on her."

Stipe snorted.

"Yeah, well, she said Baer put the moves on her too."

Stipe laughed out loud. He rocked to his feet and stood at the porch rail. "So you got nothing."

"Not entirely. I started with the bad news, but we got a little good, too. Mechanic outside of Gleason, runs Gatchell's old body shop. He said Creighton tried to buy his welder, same day as Burly went gone. Kid sent Creighton to some guy named Craig Schlitz, like the beer or something."

"Was Creighton driving a brown F-150?"

"That's the other good news. Yeah. How'd you know?"

"Anything else? You've been digging how many days and that's all you got?"

Stan turned partly away. "Well, I turned up one other thing. What do you know about a couple boys poking around Gleason this week? Word is they're asking about you."

"Don't worry about them. What's your plan for Creighton? We're down to the wire and I want him found today. Right now."

Stan removed his ball cap and crumpled the bill in his hands.

Blood flushed Stipe's cheeks. "You fresh out of ideas, that it? Beat the bushes. I don't care if you have to go to Creighton's campsite and start walking circles. You find him, and you put him down!"

Stipe watched Stan's dense, dull, sad face. He'd pushed too hard. But too much was riding on tonight. Sometimes a situation demanded strong leadership.

Stan retreated to the GMC. He climbed inside the cab and started the engine.

How could it be so difficult? Creighton wasn't a man to turn tail. He wanted revenge, and Stipe knew in his bones that Creighton had stayed close enough to get it. He'd bought a truck. Tried to buy tools. He was rebuilding. Creighton thought he would win this war.

A man with the audacity to march into the enemy's stronghold, not once but twice...

Creighton was in the woods somewhere, scheming. Each escalation proved him victorious. Achilles, dead. Burly and Ernie, dead. Cory, missing for days and days. Creighton had even seen through Stipe's longtime associate Pete Bleau. Each time Stipe raised the stakes he found Creighton had already covered and raised. The only thing left was flat-out murder. No time for clever setups or covering tracks. He'd whitewash everything afterward. But you had to know where a man was if you wanted to murder him.

Stipe imagined Creighton sitting under a walnut tree, whittling a stick. Sipping moonshine. Staring blank into the trees, biding his time.

Ernie Gadwal had been certain Creighton would kife what he needed to rebuild from the Brown farm. Stipe had seen it long before Ernie—it was in his mind when he told Smylie to tip off the revenue boys. But any chance of forcing Creighton into a subordinate position died when Ernie went slam off his instructions and killed Creighton's dog.

Ernie. Another dimwit, thought he was smart. Followed Creighton day and night, everywhere, for weeks. Even to a cave up by—

Stipe lurched down the porch steps. Stan's GMC was at the gate.

"Stan! Stan!" Stipe crossed the lot with his hand against his chest. His heart thudded and flopped. "Stan!"

The GMC halted. Stan tumbled out and stood with his eyes revealing confusion.

Stipe looked at his watch. There was time. "Stan! Bring in the boys and tell them to fetch their guns. Now!"

CHAPTER FORTY-TWO

I back out the truck and head into town. It's early and no one knows this truck, but I'm edgy. No way they haven't found Burly Worley and his sidekick.

Back in the day I'd tool along in my Nova nice and easy with the windows down. No radio. Tires crunching dirt, aching to spin. Those days I didn't have a past, just a future. Now I'm old, I have no future so I brood on what's past. Feel like a kid started out with a hundred dollar bill and next I know I'm an old man with empty pockets. How'd I spend a life already?

I go to the Bi Lo so I don't see anybody I know.

I remember that dream.

Sometimes you don't know what triggered the memory. Dreams are all nonsense, but the image smacks me upside the head and I stand numb on the sidewalk.

It's dusk, and the woods are a sketch of black and white, and the trail's emptied to a patch of land different than any other. It's a land of horror. Stepping in means crossing a line. Bodies hang from the trees. Dead people suspended with their backs against the bark. Arms and legs stick straight out. Each tree has fifty people. This tree, that tree, the whole woods beyond the line is dead men and women. The air's tranquil, and though my feet strike crunchy leaves, they land silent.

I step closer to the dead land.

. . .

I shake loose the image. To hell with dreams. I stand at the cooler at the back of the grocery.

"Need ten pound of hamburg."

The man nods. Packs meat in plastic. I'm the grateful hypocrite who didn't slaughter the doe-eyed cow going in that bag.

"You planning some kind of picnic?" he says.

"Yeah."

He drops the wrapped meat to the counter. I grab it. Leave. Buy a jug of Turkey at the ABC.

"The liter?"

"Liters can go to hell. That big jug right there."

"That's one point seven five liters."

"It's a half gallon. By God."

I pay with cash. His eyes go to mine but there's no red.

All these disaffected years—but no one ever surprised me.

"Everything good?" the man says.

"Things is about to get Wild Turkified. That's an improvement."

Ten-pounds of hamburg in the fold of my arm, Wild Turkey in the other. I put the meat on the passenger seat and break the seal on the Turkey. This Kentucky bourbon's smooth as water but you have to drink twice as much.

I'm in the parking lot and two men come out of George's Hot Dogs, other side of the street. They watch me and I gawk a minute back until they mosey toward the corner. They're not from here. Look like law that don't know how to fit in. I don't need another run to the jailhouse so I wait until they turn the corner, then gulp a long snurgle of Turkey.

I drive slow and halfways home a car passes. Inside the cab is the two men from town. My hackles are sky high, but I don't get any juice at all.

No harm comes. Back at the cave I treat Stinky Joe with a handful of hamburg, and dig out that melatonin I bought two weeks ago. I close the meat bag and set the pill bottle beside. Another gurgle of Turkey, and I stretch out on my sleeping bag and close my eyes for a nap.

See if I can steer clear of that land of corpses in the trees.

Stinky Joe growls low and grumbly like he means it. I wake and those dead stiff-legged bodies are still in my eyes. I roll to my side and Stinky

Joe's at the cave entrance, standing taut with his back half shaking. His floppy ears are up and a bad feeling shoots through me. I'm haunted by ghosts and shadows, but living trouble is at my door.

I grab Smith and scoot beside Stinky Joe. "What you see?"

Down there, he says.

I scan the landscape. Block Stinky Joe with my arm and he leans into it. I spot movement fifty yards off—a man flashes a go signal to someone on his right. He bears a rifle. Another man leaves the protection of a giant oak and advances to the next. His rifle barrel sticks out. I keep an eye on both of them and gather my scattered brain.

I got Turkey left in the bottle and two full flask. I slip to the back of the cave and grab the bottle, down it, and grab my thirty-thirty rifle. I pop the lever. Brass in the chamber.

Five jugs with cinnamon line the cave wall, but there's no way out but those goons will know and shoot. They've come for a showdown. I leave the jugs.

Wild Turkey hits the spot and starts pushing back the corpses in trees and the cold mist crossing my mind. The dream slips away but leaves the chill. Stinky Joe's moved to the entrance side. He shakes like he wishes I was there to hold him back.

"I'll show you how to fight, Stinky Joe. Watch this."

Back at the entrance I stay low in the shadows. It's early evening. Downslope is the fire circle, rocks stacked twelve inches high. Got a boulder off to the side where I sit at nights watching the fire. There's trees all down the slope. To the right sits two mash barrels, each half full of slaggy poison mush. I bet one of those barrels would stop a bullet, but not as good as a boulder.

I find the first fellow again, now forty yards away. He looks to his left at a third man. Three, each with a rifle. They're the lugnuts who were in town with Stipe that day. At forty yards I could drop any one of them, but the other two would hole up. The skirmish would come down to which of us brought the most bullets. I got a bunch, that's for sure, and more on my pistol belt, but there's someplace I need to be in a couple hours.

I have but one option: close work.

They'll converge on the cave. If they have any brains they'll send two up and leave one in reserve, covering them. With luck all three will come.

I stretch on the dirt and wriggle until I find a clean view.

All three men stop. The leader has deep thought etched on his face. He

243

stares at the cave entrance, but with the shadows he doesn't know if I'm a rock or a man with a gun trained on him.

Stinky Joe whimpers.

"Shhhh." I turn my head and signal him to slip to the back of the cave.

He steps toward me.

Man down the hill swings his rifle to his eye. I have no choice. I pull the trigger and the cave sounds like the middle of a thunderclap. I cycle a new bullet and take fresh aim. The man stands for a second, then fires his rifle. The bullet zings from the rock overhang. The man staggers and drops.

The fellow on the left hides but the one on the right stays in the open. I move left and grab a new sight picture. He skirts toward a tree. I lead him a couple inches and fire. The bullet catches his shoulder and he spins. I cycle another and pull the stock tight to my shoulder. The third man fires and the bullet zips by close. I fire at the second man again. He goes down.

Dust falls like snow. I look up where the bullet hit and now I got dirt in my eye. The more I blink the scratchier it gets. I wriggle back from the entrance and rub the heel of my hand to my eye. Grind a bit and the water cleans it out. I look deeper in the cave. There's a dark line on the cave floor where Stinky Joe squirted. He's in back trying to nose into my sleeping bag.

Now I have the exact situation I didn't want. A man out front, under cover, liable to see me before I see him. I know which direction to look, but if I do he might drill a bullet in my head.

I wriggle to the back of the cave. Stinky Joe shakes. I scratch his head and it's like giving him permission to come apart. He shivers so deep he forgets his bladder. Fountains up yellow on my sleeping bag.

"This'll be over in two minutes, Stinky Joe."

He's forgot how to use his words. He nods but can't hold my eye.

I pull Smith and check the cylinder. Full. I draw back the hammer. In my left hand is the rifle. I cock it, too. I stand, then squat to test my knees. I twist a couple times and rotate my shoulders. All right—I'm loose here goes.

I run.

Before the cave entrance I fire the rifle. I'm in the light. I hope it made him duck. I point the Smith on the tangent I remember and pull the trigger. Glimpse a man huddled behind a fallen log. I dive to the fire circle and claw behind the sitting boulder. A bullet zings off the rock and a fragment stings my leg.

That log he's behind is rotted pine. Bears have clawed it for grubs. Still behind the boulder, I get on my knees and rest the rifle easy over the top. I pop up my head for a quick look. He's hid. I holster Smith and take up the rifle. Sight on the dead log where I think he is, and fire. I cycle another and fire again at the same spot. I do it again and again and again. Each shot blasts out a bit more log. Finally I'm out of bullets and I can see a hole through the log. It only took twenty seconds. I hope he was dumb enough to stay put.

I leave the rifle and draw Smith.

Walk.

Got a two-handed grip and the hammer's back. I have five bullets to end this mess, then I'll have to reload. I stop and listen. The forest is quiet. Hair stands on the back of my neck. It isn't the electric; my hair stands because these woods are filled with dead mean. We're all dead, one way or the other. I come to the log and Smith leads over the top.

The man is dead.

No dignity at all. Hidden behind a rotted log. He's one of Stipe's lugnuts all right. I got lucky and blasted out half his neck. Blood everywhere. He still has the rifle grip in his hand.

I leave him and find the next body—the first fellow I shot. He fell back with his legs crumpled beneath him. Whether he's in heaven or hell, it can't be comfortable.

The final body belongs to the man I winged then shot a second time. His face snarls. His eyes stare. His arms and legs are straight and stiff. All I'd have to do is tie him to a tree and I'd be in dreamland.

Never been exactly spiritual, but I can't shake that dream. All those bodies. Woods that looked like this. I'm wide awake and feel like I'm still asleep. It's the dream where you know the real horror's about to start. You can't wake. You can't move. You can't scream for help. You lay paralyzed seeing red eyes and feeling the juice.

That's the here and now.

The horror's around the bend.

CHAPTER FORTY-THREE

Dark comes on the woods quick. Even under the big silver moon, distance vanishes and things up close get gray. The night goes from warm to cold. My fingers feel it first. I turtle my hands inside my sleeves.

I parked the truck deep off a side trail on the logging road that leads to Stipe's fight circle. Got all my liquor up close.

A hundred yards off, men stand wood shipping pallets on edge. Pound metal stakes in the ground to hold them. They moved the fight circle left twenty yards. Must be the stink of rotted blood and gut grime gets on their nerves.

Man carries a stepladder inside the circle and hangs a wire jig on a limb. Fetches an orange-glowing lantern and suspends it, then several more. My stomach growls and I ease my flask north about eighteen inches, take a gurgle. I've carted five jugs, trusting the men won't notice the shine's discoloration. Not in the half-light, anyway.

I study the jugs. Remember Fred's eyes, broken open the night I found him.

Headlights cut through the woods, pointed my way. Evening's thick enough they can't see me, but I shrink anyway. This situation has me feeling I have to lay low, and I don't like it a bit. Like I'm wrong exacting revenge on Fred's behalf.

Accourse, it's no good introducing logic in the middle of a tactical situation. I have to keep my bearings. Keep the dreamland at bay.

A line of headlights arrives through the dusk. That'll be Stipe and his perverts. One by one they turn off their headlights and crawl past me in the twilight.

These boys watched Fred get rent.

Ahead is a small meadow where a giant hemlock fell and left a hole clear to the sky. Moonlight pours in and the trucks drive through it. Red, brown, brown, gray, white...

Tailgate is light on the left and a little darker on the right.

Something smoldering in my belly goes aflame.

That's him... that's Cory. That's the very pickup that hauled Fred to this fight circle and then hauled him out. I draw Smith. Aim on the back window, left side. I press the wiggle out of the trigger. Grit my teeth and see Fred with that bullet hole in his eye under a haze of black flies.

But I picked a better way to end all this.

I ease on the trigger and holster Smith.

Man backs a truck close the circle, drops the tailgate and lands a jug on it. Another fellow stands two sawhorses off to the side with a sheet of plywood as a table. More jugs. Moths flap at the lanterns and bats give chase.

I creep closer.

Men drink and laugh. Larry's in the group with Pete Bleau.

Larry. I'm about to kill flesh-and-blood Larry. The one who gave me the electric curse, the one who stole Ruth. Made Ruth lie. And after all these years killed her.

I recognize the other faces but don't see Cory Smylie. I count twelve men and eight trucks. Maybe a couple brothers, a couple father-son, pass-the-sport-through-the-generations kind of instruction. Another reason to nip this right here.

Man grabs a jug, wipes the mouth with his sleeve and drinks. But any man so uptight he has to wipe the mouth on a jug of shine—he's not had enough.

A shadow crosses in front of the moon and things go deep gray except over the fight circle, lit in lanterns.

Larry walks to a truck and opens the driver-side door, leans deep inside. He comes out with a fifth of store-bought liquor and the cloud that crossed the moon cuts loose. Everything's silver again—like the night I found Fred—and that truck, the tailgate cuts a glow on the left side. He's in Cory's truck—but Cory ain't here.

Unless—

I slink as close as I can get without entering the lantern light. Crouch and study with eyes that don't believe a word the picture says.

That's Larry's F-150.

Larry stole Fred.

I fall back. Snap a twig.

No one minds me. They all drink. Every last one finds liquor and gulps. Whoops and war cries cut through the woods. I speculate every animal around has already bugged out, save the ones in crates with no choice.

It was Larry. I can't quite ken it.

A pair of men don't seem so thirsty as the rest; don't tip the jug quite so far, or long. They walk straight, no swagger. Got the faintest smidge of red I ever saw, like a star that disappears the longer you look.

The two circulate. One slaps a regular's back and carries on like they're deep buddies. Conversation ends. The other turns away and the two red-eyes share a look like actors off stage.

Saw these two in town, and again driving away.

I watch it all and struggle to get my mind around the truth that Larry stole Fred.

Stipe finds the center of the group and looks about. He's slow to talk. A man stands beside him jawing and Stipe keeps his eyes to the trees beyond the men. He turns like he knows something's always behind him.

Two jugs of special liquor in each hand, one in my elbow crook, I sneak closer, staying low and hid. Stipe raises his arm toward the two that's separate, and they nod. The revelers whoop. These boys come from Georgia, but this's my show and I'm vouching for 'em—that's what Stipe says.

I keep my eyes on the liquor jugs they have everywhere. Larry's hitting it hard.

"No, he's usually here, but he ain't tonight," Stipe says. "That girl missing from Asheville, I guess. Been gone a week now. Heat's coming down, and word is a cop from Gleason took her."

Scanning faces one more time, there's another man missing. No Sheriff Smylie.

I move closer.

"Let's get this rolling," Stipe says. "First off is Norm and Jeb. You boys gotcher bitches ready? Bring them out."

Men move. They avoid the side of the woods where the previous fights were. They cluster with the trucks and the sawhorse table. I got vantage without getting up a tree. They're already acting drunk, talking bull and back-slapping.

The men hush. Jeb leads his animal with a stick leash into the pit. Every man with money's already studied dog lines like chicken guts on a plate, reveal which animal gets to die.

I carry five jugs. Sneak while I'm in the dark, and closer I get, straighter I stand. I expect every second some lugnut will club me with a ball bat, but something mystical is going on. Stipe has security, but I'm not alone. I know it.

The men stare at the dogs in the circle. Shout at first blood. I ease beside Pastor Jenkins. Land four jugs on the sawhorse table. Move the fifth to my hand. Jenkins eyes the jugs like they're boobs in maple syrup. Finally he looks away.

"Never figured why you come here," Pastor Jenkins says.

"That's a question I'd never guess from you."

"Rough men need a rough sport. And the Lord says to go to the sinners."

"Well, Pastor, you know more than I do."

Jenkins frowns, looks into the crowd. Behind and between men, the silhouette of a fighting dog jumps. Jenkins glances at the jugs. "Stipe got you on liquor duty, I see."

"Yeah. Get your fill of the spirit."

Jenkins's eyes expand. He realizes who he's talking to. He opens his mouth like to shout a warning—but he stops. Lost his will. Lost the power over his mouth. Gets all bug-eyed looking at me, and I unscrew the cap on each of my jugs. Pastor moves his hands to his mouth and his eyes are full of alarm. I grab the jug that was on the table before I came, and rest it under the platform. Tip it over with my boot.

Larry isn't three feet away, but he's not seen me. He's got the focus that only comes with a good drunk. His face is drum skin tight. Ready to shout encouragement to a slave canine gladiator.

Stipes's got tunnel vision. He furrows his brow and looks past me to the trees like he saw the same dream as me. He's lost among corpses and smells and the cold. I'm here but the professed man of God is the only one who can see me. And the Lord's sealed his lips.

I keep my hat low and my mouth zipped. Everything tells me to turn tail. But I stay, and imagine all those bodies suspended from trees, and everything's silent. I see each of these men, the squawking face he wears right now frozen into his death mask. I see them hanging from tree limbs.

I'm the instrument. These boys made a bigger enemy than Baer Creighton. I could gather my jugs and run and they'd still manage to drink them down. Nothing in the world could stop these men from the end they've earned.

Too spooky; too many things coming together and I don't have my wits.

I'll wait in the trees—

"Hey!"

It's Larry. He steps closer but no one pays him any mind.

"You won't learn," he says.

I look him over and he's never looked worse. Rings under his eyes from nights drinking booze and days of cigarettes and coffee. Slumped like he worked a sixteen-hour shift shoveling an elephant stall.

Hate crosses behind his eyes, but no red.

I lift my last jug and show him.

Riled up men watch dogs, shout and call names. Uncanny how nobody knows or cares I'm here. I sense the two men I saw in town have something to do with it. They move like archangels, calm and all-seeing.

Larry growls. Throws his fist.

He's had a couple drinks. I swing the jug and clock his temple. He follows through, off balance, and I shove him. Ride him down. I drop the jug. He's face down on the forest floor and I jab his shoulder, his neck.

I pin one of his arms under my knee but his other's free. He pushes off and topples me. I lunge back and punch his face and glance another off his skull. His brow is crinkled. I'm ready to go round and round, but he's gone from drunk crazy-mad to drunk goofy-sorry. Looks like a ten-year-old boy ready to cry. His arms, holding me back, go weak. I sneak another punch and his teeth cut my knuckles.

The men shout and holler. I look. Every one's got his head turned to the dog circle, where two female pits with no past and no reason to hate have at the fruit of it.

"You stole Fred."

I punch. He takes it. His eyes are wet.

"You killed Ruth..." I pull back my fist.

"Didn't kill Ruth."

His eyes are in the trees, loopy. Blood on his lips and nose, eye sockets. His lungs heave.

I pop him.

"What?"

He spits blood sideways. "Didn't kill Ruth."

I grab his shirt with both fists. We're eye to eye, ten inches apart. He sees I'm about to bust crazy—least he better see it.

Ruth, alive?

"You killed her," I say.

"I should have thirty years ago, when she had your baby. That's when I should have killed her."

"Where's Ruth—you took her! Where is she?"

"Took her to her father's. She got a call while I was there. The nursing home said he was dying."

"Neighbor said you hit her, on the lawn."

"She twisted her ankle. I caught her."

Nothing's right in my head. Nothing makes sense. I'm stuck without words or thoughts to string together. This is about Fred, not Ruth. Larry did some things to her and that's the truth, but that's a separate matter between him and God. I got no standing.

All these years, it's been me that stole her first, and he had the right to steal her back if he could. I don't grudge him that. Now he killed her and that's another story—or he didn't kill her and that's got my head mixed up. But what him and these boys did to Fred and a thousand other dogs is enough to seal their ends, far as I'm concerned. Ruth doesn't have a thing to do with it.

I look up and Pete Bleau gulps from a jug of wood liquor.

I blink. Time sticks. Something flip-flops in me. I've had enough of the killing and the dying. Already I've had enough. It's the corpses in the trees. I'm weary of it.

"No!"

I wriggle off Larry. My legs are weak and my mind's half-blank but I dive into Pete. "Spit! Spit it out!"

He coughs.

"Stick your finger down your throat!"

I put my hand in his mouth and he bites. I pop him quick. He stares. The wood shine's hit him.

Someone takes a jug. Another. Some other has the third. All these men are dead and whether it's God or me doing it I'm sick of it. Sick of Ruth and Stipe and Cory. Sick of seeing deceit in good and bad people alike. I've nowhere to run without seeing bodies in trees, and like in the dream I can't shout, I can't move, I can't wake.

Don't drink that!

Did I even say it? "That's poison!"

Two new dogs wage battle. When did that happen?

I rush to the stinking ugly ground of the former fight circle, scoop a handful of bloody pissy shitty dirt. Tackle Pete Bleau and smack that fist of mud in his mouth. He twists and wrestles and I shove as much of that dirt between his teeth as he'll take.

His eyes are in a pleasant place.

Pete retches. Coughs and gags and vomit busts out on me. Still he smiles. I smell his bile in a stew of cinnamon-flavored wood alcohol. Pete falls flat back. I look up. The other four jugs are each at some man's mouth. There's no way I can get enough mud in these boys to make them yack up that poison.

It's out of my hands.

These little fights with Larry and Pete—it's like the other men see but don't care, or look but don't see. They drink from the jugs and pass them around.

"Smooth!" one says.

"Tastes real good. Real clean," says another.

"Gimme that jug."

The dogs fight. Grunt. Wheeze. Sounds arrive through the hoopla, but every body and thing sounds the same.

Haven't seen those two archangels. Guess they only appear when they want. Angels of death. My jugs circulate from one pair of hands to the next. A man gulps as much as he can stand and there's another grabbing at the jug for his fill. On and on. Wood liquor doesn't take long, and in a handful of minutes they've passed the jugs back and forth and all around. Every man's had enough to blind a whale or drop a horse.

The dogs in the fight circle pull from each other and watch outside the pallets. One sits on his haunches and the other sniffs along the bottom of the cage. Some kind of mystification going on, and the dogs ken it. They're stuck like me, outside the dead men and not making any sense of them.

Off to the edge, the pastor's doubled over, yacking up his guts beside a tree trunk. "Woohoo," he says, and splashes his boots.

A man drops not five feet from me. Don't recognize the back of his head.

Pete Bleau walks with his arms stretched in front and his grin creeps closer and closer to fear. Men wander into the woods. Most groups, every man's aware of the others, and if you watch, they all sway together. One gets closer, the other backs. The whole group breathes together. But now they're each alone and separate. There's no coordination. Each man is stoned in his own world. Lost.

Stipe falls square on his backside. Looks like a mule right after a two-by-four got his attention. He faces me. His bony brow wrinkles like it takes all his concentration.

He knows I tossed him over the ledge. I went one farther. There's no such thing as impunity. He drank justice.

"You!" he says.

"Me."

He smiles at me then his brow contorts. Eyes go buggy.

"Can't see!" Stipe yells. Got a hand raised in the air like some church lady filled with the Ghost. "I'm blind! Can't see!"

Even as he says it, all my jugs dump poison into one man or another. One gurgles into Larry's piehole. Adam's apple bobbing like it's Halloween.

"Blind!" Stipe yells, then laughs. "This for real?"

A man lowers the jug from his mouth and says, "Open your eyes."

He folds over.

Pete Bleau's legs rabbit-shudder. His face twitches. Eyes on nothing.

The dogs peer through the gaps. I keep my eyes on them. Rest of this makes me sick.

These men thought mercy was dropping a half-mauled dog in a field. How many other dog bones did they spread through the woods? How many of these men go home and beat their women, poke their kids? This whole clique's a bunch of heathen and if they have to die so be it, but I'll watch something else.

They hack. Cough.

Wail.

"Oh, Lord!" Pastor Jenkins says. "Lord have mercy!"

I look to the sky for the Lord.

Then I look back at Stipe. He's on his side, throwing up. Each burst weaker than the last, each grunt more pathetic. Clawing the ground and kicking back and forth with his feet in smaller and smaller arcs. He moans and whimpers and I bet none the dogs he killed died like such a wretched coward. Looking at Stipe is a painful thing but I miss Fred so much I can't pull my eyes away until Stipe doesn't shake. He doesn't move at all and his eyes are wide open. I want to bust them, let them run. But the misery all around comes screaming and squealing back into my brain and shakes me loose.

Larry's crawled a few feet from the pit. Half to his truck. I kneel beside him. "You know this's the end, brother. Why'd you go and drink that after I told Pete not to?"

He stops clawing the ground. His eyes are blank and bloody. I pass my hand in front of his face and he doesn't flinch.

"You blind, Larry? That it?"

He smiles.

It's chewed me for so many years I don't know what words to use. So I say, "Why'd you take my daughter from me? Why'd you steal Mae, too?"

He wheezes. Inhales best he can. "I... come home from school... got Ruth back..."

"Easy, now."

"I'm a mule, Baer... Sterile... since you crushed my nuts... that day after school."

I drop back. There's men all around crying to God, except Larry. "Why'd she go with you?"

"I took her. I couldn't have a kid. You took that from me. So I took yours."

His leg goes stiff, straight like a kick. Arm seizes up at his chest. Whole body rocks and shakes, and his crotch goes dark.

I touch his elbow. He yells, but weak. Pure pain.

All these men have to suffer. But I do too.

"Why'd you take Fred? Tell me that, Larry."

His eyes tremble in their sockets. He's close.

I seize his hand. "Why'd you take Fred, brother?"

He whispers, "To hurt you."

I grab Smith.

Close my eyes and exhale deep. Try to get a compass point to lead out all this crazy evil. But the needle spins and spins. I don't know if the right thing is a bullet in his head or one in mine. Larry suffers. Though he has it coming for all he did to me and Fred and Ruth and Mae, I did evil on him, too. All this suffering here—all these men got it someplace else, first, before they dished it on the dogs. The compass needle spins because there's no way out, no way to do right when everybody's compromised.

You can look any direction but the dreamwoods is all around.

Larry groans. He shakes. He's seized up but the death won't come. His face is a frozen mask and his arms and legs are straight. All that's left is for the archangels to throw him into a tree.

I press Smith to Larry's temple.

CHAPTER FORTY-FOUR

He shakes and drools, has his eyes turned back in his head. This is the brother that called our mother a whore, electrocuted me, gave me a life of visions and juice. Stole my girl. Stole my daughter. Stole my dog and fought him, and left him for dead where I scrounged apples every fall the last twenty years. He's tried to murder me deeper than how I'm about to kill him—tried to murder whatever soul I have.

I shake at the thought of pulling the trigger. He'll die without, and it'll be from my hand either way. Blowing his brains into the mud would be a favor but I can't do it.

Larry moans.

I have to end this. I stand Smith perpendicular to Larry's temple.

"Halt!"

I search the darkness.

"Halt, you!"

A man steps from the shadows with a pistol on me. One of the archangels. I pull Smith back, point at the sky, spin it to my holster. I stand. The man steps closer. His buddy's out there, covering him.

"Who're you?"

"Law."

Only a couple men moan. The rest have gone to the dream-land. Bodies contorted with pain, flexed and taut, faces scarred with horror. Men with straight limbs, so many ornaments ready to hang from a tree.

"Higher law?" I say.

"FBI."

The other archangel comes from behind a tree. He dumps his pistol into a holster.

"Good of you to come," I say. "But the work's done."

"You made it quick at that."

"You saw me try and stop it."

"You the one they beat on, a couple weeks ago?"

I nod.

"And before that? Fell out the tree?"

I nod again.

"Why you keep coming back? You ain't part of this group."

"You seen it. They stole my dog and left him blind."

"You did this for a dog?"

"Fred."

One looks at the other. "You're under arrest. I'll want that Smith 'n Wesson."

"I bet."

Larry seizes up stiff, his arms and legs like boards. He shakes and inhales slow like his lungs are a thimble already half full of blood. He lets out the air and it carries a faint moan. He's still.

My brother is dead.

"Think these boys got some bad likker," the lawman says.

"Seems."

"Something I can't understand," he says. He waves to the trucks, the crates. "What were you going to do with all these dogs? Kill them?"

"Got ten pound of hamburg in the woods, with sleep medicine. Thought that would mellow them out until I got them home.

"You planned to take all these dogs?"

"Where's the moral in leaving them to die in wood crates?"

"Where's the moral in killing fifteen men? No trial? No defense?"

I'm tired of yammering but I have to take a shot at making them understand. "All around us is dead men. Look at the lantern glow up in the trees—makes this whole place a cathedral. You got the circle there like an altar. These men come to the last service at the church of death, and the oldest law struck them down. An eye for an eye."

They look at me like I farted a quart of milk. They don't see the dreamland, only murder.

Ah, hell. I'm ready to go.

Except for Stinky Joe. He'll wait all night at the cave. Sometime tomorrow he'll figure he has to fend for himself, and he'll sniff around after something to eat. He'll smell the paper bag that carried the hamburg, and spend a few hours learning I didn't leave it for him. Day after tomorrow he might figure the carton of eggs is fair game, and the cheese, and the bag of Alpo dry. Beyond that, he'll have nothing.

He'll be on his own, looking for a master who won't throw him in a fight ring.

"You boys prepared to shoot me in the back?"

"The back, the front. You're coming with us." He pulls his pistol but his eyes glow red and electric zips through me.

The other is silent.

"You better work on him. He's going to shoot me."

I turn my back and take one step.

"Mister, you walk and I'll fill you with holes."

No he won't. Not him. "These men got what they had coming."

I tramp into the dark. Behind me, dry leaves shuffle. "Freeze! You!"

More rustling leaves. I get electric on my arms. But no bullets.

Ten paces.

Fifteen.

I break left and trot fast, scamper into trees. Raise an arm and rush on.

A pistol fires.

I keep on like a doe I remember, got away and blended in.

Can't help but see these deaths as the work of something beyond me. I stilled the wood liquor rich enough to kill. Had murder in my heart every minute, though I didn't know I'd do it until I done it. Court of law, I'm flat guilty. But when I answer before the Lord, I'll tell him straight up. I wanted to go the other way. Events worked against me, and that's how I mean it was a little beyond me.

But in this world I killed them and it might satisfy Fred to know.

Mae's my baby. Confirmed.

What the hell's a man do with that? Now that I truly know?

Ruth, alive? Yeah, and stuck on me. To hell with her. All this time I lied to myself about her being honest because if I didn't then we were all liars. But there's no starting new and no avoiding the truth. We all lie.

My stomach goes tight and my throat's hot with bile. I choke it back once—the vomit charges again and I puke on a tree. I'm a cold-blooded killer.

Even a killer needs a drink. I rinse my mouth with crick water. It's good and clean, and I drink like I'm empty and never had water. Top it off from my flask of Turkey.

I get in the truck and head back to the old still site for two buckets of gold. Pass my driveway and a car sits in moonlight. Down the road I pull over without hitting the brakes and kill the lights.

I get out, slip my hand to Smith. Tramp toward the burned house, down a gulley and up the other side. There's a rodent, something in the brush, but nothing else.

I've been at the yard at night plenty times, but never since the house burned. Looks like a place to stretch a blanket and stargaze.

Moonlight glints off metal and glass in the drive, but most of the car's in shadows. I circle left along the yard, keep my body against a backdrop of brush. Come straight in when the car lines with the opening to the road and the field beyond.

Figure sits on the hood.

I point Smith. Walk straight.

"Who's there? Baer? That you?"

A woman's voice. Mae?

"Mae?" I tramp fast. Into the clearing. She won't believe but I'm going to tell her I'm her daddy. I come out the shadows and into moonlight.

The car is wrong. It's a chrome boat from the seventies.

No electric, no red.

"Hey, Baer," she says.

Ten feet off, I stop.

"It's me," Ruth says. "The stars are beautiful tonight."

I'm still. Mouth tastes like yack again.

"What you want, Ruth?"

"I—"

Holster Smith. Hands on my hips.

"I—I'm sorry. That's what I want. I'm here to say I'm sorry."

"For Mae?"

"You know—know—about Mae?"

"You carried her ten months."

"Yes. I'm sorry about Mae too. I guess Larry told you everything."

"Didn't have to. You think I didn't see you at the house that time? You got my baby in your arms and standing plain as day saying there was no way we'd ever be together? Saying my baby was his? I could hardly look at you."

"Well, if you knew—"

"What? Why pester you twenty-eight years?"

She nods. "Why?"

"I gave up on everybody else."

She slumps. Her smile is a flower crushed in mud. I don't want to be mean. But I can't take very much of this.

"You were such a wild man."

I turn half away.

"Going fast in your Nova. All souped up. Windows down. You still got that car? Is that it on blocks over there? I saw it with my headlights pulling in and I've been remembering things two hours now."

"You getting by, Ruth? Okay for money?"

"Daddy takes care of me, what the alimony don't."

I got a lump in my throat. "You here? For real?"

"For real," Ruth says. "Looks like you need a place to stay."

I look at the stars because they're there, convenient.

"I thought it might be time…" She pats the car hood. "I thought we'd ride somewhere. Ride all night and all day, until we come someplace pretty and quiet. Like you put in your letter."

I murdered fifteen men. I have no house. No still. I got a daughter and a lot of money. I got my talent.

"Go home, Ruth."

"Home."

"I'm calling quits."

I walk away. I can't ignore the lie and I won't forgive it. All mankind can go to hell. What we deserve.

Way I see it I got two obligations. I'll take care of both and then bust out of Dodge.

"Baer?"

I stop. "Yeah?"

"Write."

I study her a long minute, then head for the truck. Grab an axe from behind the seat. Ruth backs out the drive in her old piece of metal. Her headlights flash off the blade.

Hand at my brow to ward off low branches, I head for the gold tree. They were in it together. Stipe, Larry, Cory Smylie, Pete Bleau—all the time I spent trying to figure who murdered Fred was wasted. They all wanted a piece of what was mine. Stipe wanted my operation. Larry wanted revenge. Pete wanted to be lazy. And Cory Smylie...

Sometimes you don't know exactly why you hate somebody. Can't narrow it down. Maybe Cory had it in for me like that. Maybe it's my simple ways, or looking out for my baby girl, or knocking that pistol to his head. Then Stipe saw he was eager, and gave him money to take a couple shots at me.

If I'm leaving, I better disassemble the mantraps at the Hun site so some kid doesn't wander in and get his guts tore out.

I'm edgy approaching those traps in moonlight. Armed with axe and Smith I trek toward the Hun machine gun nest.

I step easy and slow, around the side, like when the sniper shots were coming at me two weeks ago. I stop and listen. The night is blank, almost no light, almost no sound. I look for red eyes but see none. I hear myself more than anything—the voice in my head says this is the end of the line. You did some pure-ass evil, killing all those men, and you can't blame it on God. He didn't make the wood shine. He just made you.

They call it poetic justice when the bad guy is foiled by his own evil plans. That in mind, I tramp through the dark to my mantraps.

"You out there, Cory?"

I stop. Listen. Keep walking.

Fifty yards out, I creep slow. Axe in my left hand, Smith in my right. I stop, set down the axe, wipe my hand dry on my leg. Resume, each foot-fall gentle as I can on brittle October leaves.

Except for me the woods is silent. There's so much death all around. Bodies in trees. Bodies every place. I hear them calling out, saying they're blind, and in pain. Hear them call out to God. See blind eyes searching. Open hands feeling, reaching for some unknown guide to take them home.

I stalk from tree to tree, pause. Hide. Lurk. Look. C'mon, Cory Smylie, I know you're hiding. I'm hunting you. My heart's about to pound a hole through my chest. My ears hear the seashell whoosh of blood, mingled with a ring that sounds like too much coffee. I raise my pistol hand and wipe sweat from my brow. The Hun nest is twenty feet out; I come from the side.

I hear a faint tap sound—tink, tink, tink.

I'm out in the open. Point Smith this way and that. I know I'm going to see a flash and feel a bolt of pain. I know it. It's God's way of business —he's going to strike me down. Evil is round and I have no impunity.

Tink, tink.

It's with the breeze.

I exhale hard. Need to reach down and find a pair. I tramp ahead. Fire into the Hun cave. Fire again. I head right to it, not on the trail, close under the rocks.

"I'm coming for you, Cory! It's quits this time. It's over tonight!"

I fire again. Stand still below the rock outcrop, looking up for motion. For a glint of silver or the sound of shoe leather. Rustling pant legs. Red eyes. The echoes fade and my ears still ring.

Tink. Tink. Tink.

The breeze turns and I whiff something that recalls the scent of the fight pit. Death.

There's rocks everywhere. I drag my feet. That pungent smell gets strong down among the tree trunks. I ease up on the hemlock where I rigged the branch trigger and the branch doesn't cross the path. I stop. Hair stands on my neck, and I know what I'm about to find.

I holster Smith. Dig a Zippo out my pocket and flick. Kneel. Not five feet off is a black mat of bloody leaves. Furrows dug in the dirt, like from a boot—one. The barbed wire I'd stretched across the trail is gone. The trap is sprung.

I touch the blood. It's dry.

I hold the light a foot off the ground and crawl, yard after yard. Weary of hands and knees, I stand, and continue at a half-stoop. The Zippo flame flickers and whips.

I see a boot.

I come alongside; kneel. His bottoms are black. I bring the lighter to his face. Cory Smylie.

His sunken eyes fix on the sky like he set his gaze on a star. Tried to hang on while the darkness around him swelled and blotted it out. His face is gray-pale; I move the Zippo south and glance at his wounds. Barbed wire ripped out his pants, part of his thigh, part of his groin. All at once a breeze changes direction and I get a lungful of death.

I've had enough. Too much.

I tramp through the dark in footsteps I been setting twenty years. Cross the crick on slippy stones. Duck and weave through scrub. Emerge in a grove of cherry and oak, and it's not a minute until I'm at the rotted tree with two buckets of gold yet in the hollow.

I'm going to swing this blade and cut down this tree.

I'm going to grab the gold and take a bucket to Mae tonight. Tell her

I'm her daddy and I love her but she won't ever see Larry or Cory Smylie again. Tell her to take one coin each to a different dealer in a different town. When she has enough money to ditch Gleason, then keep the rest in gold. Tell her to make sure those kids go to college. And the next man she finds, he better have motor oil under his fingernails and smell like ten hours' sweat. Then she'll know she's got a man.

Come morning I'll take Stinky Joe—

No. His name's Joe from here out.

I'll haul ass west with Joe in my brand new old truck. Keep the windows down and the radio off, and drive until I don't see dead men in the trees.

I swing the axe.

LOOKING AHEAD TO BOOK 2

Sophia Ellen Whitcombe was sixteen. At the age of twelve she'd realized her body was developing faster than her peers at school. Her period had started at nine, long before her mother got around to warning her. If not for the helpful folks on the internet, she probably would have thought she was about to die. Her bust swelled at twelve and grew plump by fifteen. Her hips remained small, but they rounded where they were supposed to, and in the space of five years Sophia metamorphosed from a spindle-legged frog into certified jailbait.

Sophia started her junior year of high school. Her parents had secured her admission into honors classes. Some of her test scores indicated they were not appropriate for her cognitive skills. She struggled. Compromised on sleep. To stay awake during the day, she filled up on colas and iced teas.

She walked home in a haze, dreading her homework. To prove her worth to Yale, she had to maintain perfect grades. Plus take part in a host of worthy extracurricular activities. Theater. Cross country—with boobs. Mock trial team.

Meanwhile, the instant attention from every male got to her. She felt like she was carrying around a plastic bag of a million dollars. Everyone could see, and many would take it by force if given the chance.

She was thankful her father had taught her some skills. But she also wished he hadn't made her fear every shadow. She neared the park on her walk home from school.

The chilly temperature kept people indoors. No one was near.

Sophia didn't notice the police car as it approached her from behind. Not until it was next to her and the driver's window rolled down.

She jumped.

"Sophia? Miss, are you Sophia Whitcombe?"

"Uh, yeah." She looked at the pained face of the police officer inside.

"Miss, I'm sorry to surprise you, but I'm afraid I have very bad news. It's your mother."

"What!"

"I'm afraid there's been an accident. She asked for you. We don't have much time."

"Oh my God!"

"You want to get in the car? I can get you there as fast as possible."

"Where?"

"Miss, we have to hurry. She's in bad shape. We've got to go all the way to Sylva."

Sylva was close to an hour away. Sophia's heart jumped in her throat. Adrenalized terror shot through her. She raced around the back of the car and opened the front passenger door.

"I'm sorry, Sophie. Could you hop in the back? The department has a policy about letting anyone in the front. I'm sorry."

Sophia hesitated. "Yeah, sure." She opened the back door and jumped in. As she closed the door she realized she was in a Gleason police car, not an Asheville or Sylva police car.

"What happened to my mother?"

The policeman pressed the gas, and the acceleration pushed her into the seat. He didn't put on the lights.

"She was in a car accident."

"What was she doing in Sylva?"

"A conference."

"What conference? I know about her conferences. I go to some of them. Did you say a car accident?"

"That's right. I guess she was driving there. I don't know if the conference was in Sylva or someplace else. Knoxville. I don't know. But she's at the Sylva hospital, and they're not going to fly her to Asheville. Said she wouldn't survive the flight. I'm real sorry but she's not supposed to make it."

"Oh my God."

Sophia looked through the window with eyes full of tears. They were already on the highway speeding west.

"Does my father know? Where is he?"

"He's already on the way there. He's the one who called and asked us to pick you up and bring you. He stopped by the school and couldn't find you."

That didn't make any sense. She walked the same route home every day. Her father and mother had reviewed it as part of their safety plan for the household. Her father knew where she was, always. It's why she had a cell phone.

Sophie cleared her mind. The panic receded. The policeman was mistaken. She would call and find out everything was okay. Her mother would be fine.

Sophia dug in her purse and pulled out her phone.

"Don't be stupid," the police officer said.

She looked up. He held a gun up for her to see and, in an instant, Sophia understood. Her mother had not been in an accident. Her father was not speeding to Sylva.

Sophia looked out the window. They passed a car with a female driver. She made eye contact, and the woman looked away before Sophie could think of how to communicate.

"All right. That's all. I want you to push your cell phone through the opening here. Do it now."

Sophie held onto her phone.

"I can stop the car, come back there and beat you senseless before you can place a call."

She pushed the phone through the slot.

"Good girl. Now I want you to lie down across the back of the seat. If you don't do what I tell you, I'm going to pull over up here and knock you out. Understand? You do what I say, you'll get through this all right."

She looked for a door handle. None. Nothing to control the window. She tried to think it through. She tried to calm herself.

"Where are you taking me?"

"I already told you. Sylva."

"Who are you?"

"Police."

"What do you want with me?"

"I want to take some pictures for a scrapbook I keep. After that, I'll take you back home. That's it. I promise."

In the rearview mirror, Sophia saw the nothingness behind his eyes. He didn't want her photograph. She lay across the seat and tried to think of how she was going to survive.

NEXT?

For two free kindle novel downloads, a behind the scenes peek at the next book in the series (no spoilers), along with all the funky one-of-a-kind items at the Baer Creighton Shop...

Enter the following in your browser:

https://baercreighton.com/product/2-the-mundane-work-of-vengeance/

ABOUT THE AUTHOR

Hello! I appreciate you reading my books—more than you can know. If you've read this far, you and I are fellow travelers. I suspect you sense something is not quite right with the world. It's not as good as it's supposed to be. We human beings aren't as good as our ideals. Yet, we prize and want to fight for them.

I do my absolute best to write stories that portray the human situation with brutal transparency, but also I strive to tell stories that are not as bleak as the human condition sometimes seems. There's no limit to the darkness. Light is rare. But it exists, and I hope when you complete one of my novels, you find your values validated.

I'm grateful you're out there. Thank you.

Remember, light wins in the end.

Printed in Great Britain
by Amazon

60094502R00166